A Passionate Hope

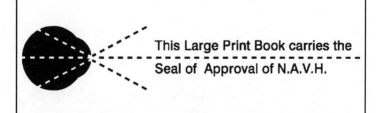

This Large Print Book carries the
Seal of Approval of N.A.V.H.

DAUGHTERS OF THE PROMISED LAND,
BOOK 4

A PASSIONATE HOPE

HANNAH'S STORY

JILL EILEEN SMITH

THORNDIKE PRESS
A part of Gale, a Cengage Company

Farmington Hills, Mich • San Francisco • New York • Waterville, Maine
Meriden, Conn • Mason, Ohio • Chicago

Copyright © 2018 by Jill Eileen Smith.
Scripture quotations are from The Holy Bible, English Standard
Version® (ESV®), copyright© 2001 by Crossway, a publishing ministry of
Good News Publishers. Used by permission. All rights reserved. ESV Text
Edition: 2011
Some Scripture used in this book, whether quoted or paraphrased by
the characters, is from the Holy Bible, New International Version®.
NIV®. Copyright© 1973, 1978, 1984, 2011 by Biblica, Inc.™ Used by
permission of Zondervan. All rights reserved worldwide.
www.zondervan.com
Thorndike Press, a part of Gale, a Cengage Company.

LIBRARY OF CONGRESS CIP DATA ON FILE.
CATALOGUING IN PUBLICATION FOR THIS BOOK
IS AVAILABLE FROM THE LIBRARY OF CONGRESS

ISBN-13: 978-1-4328-5147-7 (hardcover)

Published in 2018 by arrangement with Revell Books,a division of Baker
Publishing Group

Printed in the United States of America
1 2 3 4 5 6 7 22 21 20 19 18

"For this child I prayed . . ."
To Jeff, Chris, and Ryan —
My three sons, children of my heart,
prayed for as Hannah prayed for
Samuel.
Prayed for and loved every day
of your lives.
Always.
This story is for you.

■ ■ ■ ■

PART 1

■ ■ ■ ■

There was a certain man of Ramathaim-zophim of the hill country of Ephraim whose name was Elkanah the son of Jeroham, son of Elihu, son of Tohu, son of Zuph, an Ephrathite. He had two wives. The name of the one was Hannah, and the name of the other, Peninnah. And Peninnah had children, but Hannah had no children.

1 Samuel 1:1–2

PROLOGUE

1141 BC

Hannah walked with her father and brothers and fellow Kohathites from Ramathaim-zophim in the hills of Ephraim, nearly skipping for joy at the chance to accompany them to Shiloh during their week of work. Her friends Meira and Lital had joined her, as they were all at last at an age when they were allowed to participate with the singers at the Tent of Meeting.

"I think I have wanted this my entire life," Hannah said, clasping her hands lest she do something foolish like giggle or twirl in a circle as she'd done when she was small. "The music is always so joyful there."

Meira leaned closer and touched Hannah's arm. "No doubt you will have even more reason to sing once this week is past. That is, if my brother gets his wish." She gave Hannah a conspiratorial grin, and Lital laughed.

"I knew it," Lital said, her smile as wide as Meira's. "I told you that you would not remain at the tabernacle to serve unmarried indefinitely." She gave Hannah a sideways embrace. "You are blessed indeed."

Hannah stopped walking and grasped each friend's hand. "Enough of such talk. We know nothing yet. Elkanah has not even spoken to my father, so you could be completely wrong." Though her heart flipped a little at the thought of Meira's brother making his interest in her known to his family.

"I'm not wrong." Meira's lower lip resembled a pout, and Lital laughed softly again. "Elkanah has waited for you. If he doesn't speak here, you can be sure he will speak soon."

"And I will stay at the tabernacle," Lital said, suddenly sobering. She shrugged at Hannah's empathetic expression. "It is nothing to be distressed over. My father is dead. My mother cannot afford to live if I do not serve in this way, and there has been no man seeking my hand. I am content with it."

Hannah watched her friend, a few years her senior and one who certainly could have married by now if not for her father's untimely death. "Surely you have a relative who would redeem you. I hate to leave you here with no male relative to watch over you."

Lital waved a sturdy hand as if brushing away an insect. "I will be fine."

"But the rumors . . ."

"Are just rumors. What have Hophni and Phinehas done other than take too much meat from the sacrifices? That is wrong, of course, but I don't think they are dangerous." Lital tucked her headscarf closer to her neck. "I look forward to serving the Lord in that place. My father served there." Her gaze held a faraway look. "I think he would be proud."

Hannah patted Lital's arm. "If he could see you now, I *know* he would be proud of you." Meira said the same, and the subject changed as the group drew closer to Shiloh's gates.

"Do you really think Elkanah likes me?" Hannah asked, unable to keep her curiosity in check.

Meira nodded, grinning again. "I think Elkanah is besotted with you. Just wait and see."

Hannah glanced ahead to where Elkanah and his brothers walked among the throng of men. Could he really care for her? Her heart tripped again as she recalled the way he had looked at her at the last feast when

11

she danced with the virgins. She had been ready for marriage then, and Elkanah was twelve years her senior. Why did he wait so long to act?

As they entered Shiloh's gates, she pushed the thoughts aside. She was here to sing, to worship before Adonai, a longing fulfilled at last. She would think about a husband later. Though she knew that in her attempts to banish that thought, she was only fooling herself.

The tabernacle of Shiloh came into view, and Hannah left her friends to join her father and brothers as Meira did hers. Lital remained at Hannah's side.

"Are you sure you want to remain here at week's end?" Hannah looked into the round, tanned face of the girl who had been forced to work too hard since her father's passing, the only child of her mother. "How will your mother get along without you?"

"Ima is strong, Hannah. She urged me to come to earn enough money to help keep us from becoming gleaners in our neighbors' fields. She can manage the house and garden alone." Lital glanced about, her expression curious. Though Lital had come here often with her father, Hannah suspected that without him things seemed new, different. Hannah followed her gaze as they entered the area where the Levites stayed, awed by the lavish houses of the priests.

They had passed the large brown tented tabernacle held upright with poles and the fabric fence surrounding it. The bronze altar with four bronze horns and the bronze bowl filled with water stood before it. More utensils and carts surrounded the area where the priests would slaughter each animal and catch the blood in a bowl.

Hannah closed her eyes, imagining the part she hated most — sacrifice. Sacrifice of the perfect lamb brought the reminder of what God required. Would she ever live up to the law's demands? Sometimes they seemed so impossible, yet at other times she sensed that God was as real to her as her breath. She spoke to him, even in childhood, and always felt a kind of kinship with the Unknowable One — like He saw her and He cared.

A sense of contentment filled her. She glanced at her father, Hyam, who walked slowly ahead of them toward the rooms they would occupy. He turned to face her. "You will room with Lital and Meira between our room and Jeroham's. Take care not to go out at night alone." His brows furrowed. "Not that you need fear, but one can never

13

tell when a wild beast will get past the gates."

"I'll be careful, Abba."

Her father nodded once and motioned the girls toward their room. In the distance, the sound of singing wafted to them, and the scent of the evening sacrifice floated on the breeze.

"Praise the Lord. Praise the Lord, you His servants. Praise the name of the Lord. Let the name of the Lord be praised, both now and forevermore. From the rising of the sun to the place where it sets, the name of the Lord is to be praised. The Lord is exalted over all the nations, His glory above the heavens. Who is like the Lord our God, the One who sits enthroned on high, who stoops down to look on the heavens and the earth? He raises the poor from the dust and lifts the needy from the ash heap. He seats them with princes, with the princes of His people. He settles the childless woman in her home as a happy mother of children. Praise the Lord."

"You have a beautiful voice."

Hannah jumped and turned to find Meira's brother Elkanah watching her. Had she joined in the singing? She shook herself. "I was so caught up . . . I didn't realize . . ."

His smile caused butterflies to take wing inside of her. She touched the clasp of her veil, grateful that she was partially hidden from his perusal.

He glanced around and she did the same. Lital had somehow deserted her during the singing, and she saw that her father and brothers were some distance away, leaving her alone to speak with Elkanah.

"Nevertheless, you sing like an angel." He placed both hands behind his back. "Your father allowed me to speak with you. I hope you do not mind."

"No. No. That is, I do not mind speaking to you. Your sister mentioned you on the walk from town." Hannah felt her hands grow clammy, and she longed to cross her arms over her chest to still a sudden trembling and the fear that she had not said the right thing at all.

He lifted a brow. "Did she? And what did that little mischief maker have to say?"

It was her turn to give him a curious look. "I believe she wanted to warn me about you." Hannah could not hold back a smile.

"I'm beginning to think you are both mischievous." He drew a circle in the dirt with his toe.

"We have been known to consider a prank

or two." Why ever was she talking like this? She sensed that neither one of them was ready to say anything serious.

"Did she also tell you that I have spoken to your father about you?" The sudden turn of the conversation and intensity of his gaze caused a hitch in her breath.

Hannah could not look at him. "She intimated as much."

He stood in silence a moment until she looked up and met his gaze. "I've watched you for several years, Hannah. At past feasts, in town, when you come to worship Adonai, I see in you a kind woman with a love for our God. Exactly the kind of woman I would like for my wife." He ran a hand over his beard, cut in the tradition of the Kohathites.

"Only the 'kind' of woman, or is it me specifically you want?" She held his look, for she realized all of a sudden that she had to know. With their difference in age, he could have married years ago, and her father had hinted that there were others who had approached Jeroham regarding Elkanah.

Is this truly the man You want for me, Lord?

"You. Specifically." He smiled. "If you are willing, I would like to pursue a relationship with you. Your father is willing to allow us to get to know one another. We could simply sign a betrothal, but I realize that you don't know me like you do my sister." He winked and angled his head in the direction his sister had gone. "And I would like to change that."

A wave of shyness crept over Hannah. "I would like to change that too," she said after drawing in a deep breath to steady her heightened nerves.

"Good. Then after our return home, I will call on you." He inclined his head toward her and turned and walked toward her father.

Hannah watched him go, shaken. Elkanah was not at all what she expected. She assumed her father would handle everything and she would have no choice. But here was a man willing to give her time and choice. Both things she valued but had never expected.

1

Six Months Later

Hannah slipped into the tent her mother had set up on the south side of the tabernacle, where the rest of her Kohathite relatives had placed similar enclosures. Though they were from Ephraim, Kohathites stayed to the south rather than the west with the rest of Ephraim's tribe.

"Can I help you with anything, Ima?" Though she was used to Elkanah's visits at their home in Ephraim, Hannah's pulse still quickened with the sense of urgency. He was coming tonight during this Feast of Weeks to celebrate with them! Would this also be the night they would settle the date for their betrothal?

Adva took a sack of grain from a saddlebag on the donkey's back. The beast had pulled a cart filled with their offerings and food to last their entire family during this feast.

"You can grind the grain for the evening

meal." She placed the sack in Hannah's hands and motioned her toward the grindstone at the front of the tent. "There is no time to waste if your Elkanah is joining us this night. The men will be back before the bread is fully baked if we do not start now."

"Yes, Ima." *Soon he will truly be my Elkanah.* But when?

She sank onto the ground and arranged her skirts, poured the grain from the goatskin bag to the stone, and turned the wheel. She worried her lip as she worked, watching as women across their small compound also set about grinding grain. Children ran between the tents, and in the distance a baby cried. If she had a babe so young, she would stay home from such a feast.

She shook herself and gave attention to the grain as she turned the grindstone. As for tonight, she was worrying for nothing, of course. Elkanah and her father would work out the time soon. She had nothing to fear.

Evening shadows fell across the camp and the moon rose high, a round beacon to accompany the stars in guiding the men from the altar to the tents to celebrate the feast. Hannah watched her mother snatch bowls of garden vegetables, leeks, onions, garlic, and cucumbers, and move them from one end of the rugs where Hannah had spread the food to the other end, replacing them with the bread and dipping oil.

"The men will want to break the bread first. And we must have salt." Adva gave Hannah a frantic look. "Where is the salt?"

Hannah had not thought of that. Her father would want bread and salt between himself and Elkanah. It was a sign of continuing friendship, acceptance. "I don't know. I'm sure we packed it." Her mother would not have forgotten such a simple meal staple.

"Look in the bags. If you can't find it, go ask your sisters-in-law. They may have taken it before I could think to do so."

Hannah simply nodded as her mother frantically rushed about the tent, straightening this pillow or that cushion. Was her mother as nervous about the betrothal as she?

She moved to the bags that had been nearly emptied of tools and utensils and food, searching. Finally, from the last bag that had somehow fallen behind the others, Hannah pulled out a small sack of salt.

"It's here." She straightened and handed the sack to her mother.

"Oh, good." Adva placed the salt in a

small bowl and set it near the bread and oil. She rushed to the tent opening and peered into the gathering dusk. Male voices came from a short distance. "They're coming!" She whirled around and hurried to the back of the tent, where she removed her old robe that she used to work in and put on a fresh one. "Go to the tent of your sisters-in-law. You must not be here when he arrives."

Hannah lifted a brow, taken aback by this turn of events. "I am always here when Elkanah comes."

"Tonight is different."

Hannah tilted her head. "What do you know that I don't?" Elkanah had said nothing to her about setting a date, though she had been sorely tempted to press him.

"You will know soon enough. Now go!" Adva pointed to the tent door. "If things go as I think they might, you may speak with Elkanah outside the tent near the door afterward."

"Alone?"

"I will be close enough to listen."

Of course she would. Why should Hannah expect anything different?

"Shall I send one of my sisters-in-law to help you?" she asked.

"Send Malka. Watch her children so she doesn't worry."

Hannah nodded and slipped from the tent. Her mother's nerves were as frayed as an old coat, adding to Hannah's own nervous state. She looked toward the road, where she could see her father leading her brothers and Elkanah in her direction. He carried a clay pot in his hands, no doubt filled with the meat left over from the sacrifice. Her stomach rumbled at the thought of food and the smells of the fresh bread still coming from her parents' tent.

She hurried to the shelter beside theirs and ducked under the flap. "Malka, Ima needs your help." She walked to the corner where Malka had just placed her youngest among the blankets.

She looked at Hannah and smiled. "Watch him carefully. He just ate and is likely to need changing soon." She stood and glanced at her other children. "Be good for Aunt Hannah. Ima will be back soon." To Hannah she said, "There is bread and a little wine waiting for them. Dip the bread in the wine. They will sleep better for me, and I need them to sleep!" She stifled a yawn. "It is unfortunate that Adva could not have allowed you to help tonight. I want nothing more than to rest."

Hannah touched Malka's arm. "I would gladly help her, but she is insistent I not be there for whatever the men plan to discuss."

Malka nodded. "Of course. It was the same way when Dan came to speak to my father. It is the way of things." She touched Hannah's cheek. "You have grown up, my sister. Soon we will be celebrating your wedding feast."

Her smile caused Hannah's heart to flutter. This meal truly was more serious than the ones they had shared in the past. But hadn't she seen it in Elkanah's eyes? Hadn't Meira warned her? Her hands grew moist with the thought of all that could come of this night.

She glanced at the baby, who kicked his feet and cooed. One look around the tent reminded her that she wanted this. She was old enough to enter marriage, and she wanted a family of her own.

Please, Adonai, let this be the night. But also please let things proceed according to Your will.

The end of the meal and time with Elkanah suddenly couldn't come soon enough.

2

Elkanah followed Hyam into his tent, Hannah's brothers trailing behind. The soft light of several oil lamps illumined a medium-sized room spread with colorful rugs and cushions placed along the goat's-hair walls.

"Come, come," Hyam said, motioning Elkanah to sit in the place of honor along the wall farthest from the door.

"Thank you, my lord." Elkanah ducked his head to avoid hitting the center beam and sat cross-legged with his back against a cushion. Hannah's father and brothers quickly joined him, and once Hyam spoke a blessing over the food, he broke the bread and passed it to Elkanah.

Elkanah accepted the bread while Hyam continued to break pieces from the loaf and hand them to his sons. Each man dipped the bread in the oil and salt and ate for a moment in silence.

"So tell me, Elkanah," Hyam said as

Hannah's mother passed various dishes to her husband to offer to those seated, "now that you are thirty, you have had a chance to perform your duties here more than once. What is your opinion of the place?"

Elkanah wiped his mouth with a cloth, weighing his thoughts. Hyam clearly wanted to get into a discussion of the corrupt priesthood. It was the topic on the mind of every Levite. "A few weeks is not much time to give the priesthood a good assessment," he said, gauging his host's reaction. "But I was not impressed with Hophni or Phinehas."

Hyam's head bobbed up and down. "I expected you to feel this way. I knew you would be one to follow the law, unlike our 'distinguished' priests."

"If only we could do something about it. The priesthood belongs in the hands of Eleazar's descendants, not Ithamar's."

Hyam dipped his bread in the oil and then ate it, holding Elkanah's gaze. "You are descended from Eleazar, are you not?"

Elkanah nodded. "Yes, but neither I nor my brothers can march into the tabernacle and declare ourselves priests. Eli has held sway over the holy things since the days of the first Phinehas ended."

Silence followed his remark as Hannah's brothers seemed to contemplate his words.

Had he said too much? He hadn't meant to sound so defensive, but it was true. None in his family were able or called out by God to challenge the current system. It had led to many discussions and debates among his brothers, but they had never found a solution.

"You have been coming to my home to visit my daughter for some time now," Hyam said, jarring Elkanah's thoughts to a completely different focus. He watched the man stroke his beard, eyeing him. "As her father, I have the right to ask — what are your intentions?"

He drew a breath, telling himself that he might as well speak truthfully. "With your permission, my lord, it is my intention to marry Hannah."

Hyam looked at him for a lengthy breath and smiled wide. "You have my permission, on one condition."

Elkanah met his gaze, a sudden kick in his heart. "What condition?"

"You can never divorce her. Even if she proves to be barren, you can never divorce her or send her back to me or to her mother." His intense gaze never left Elkanah's face.

Elkanah felt the heat of embarrassment sweep through him. "I have no reason to ever desire such a thing. I will gladly put my seal on such a promise."

Hyam leaned against the cushion and glanced at Malka. "Go to your tent and send my daughter to join us. We will sign the ketubah once we return from the feast."

"Yes, my lord."

Elkanah felt a sense of relief that the decision was at last made, for he had not known when or how to broach the subject. Strange provision or not, he wanted Hannah. He could never grow weary of her or want to send her away.

Malka moved to the tent door, and Hannah's brothers rose and excused themselves to their tents, leaving Elkanah alone with Hannah's parents.

"You may speak with her under the awning outside the tent." Hyam stood, indicating for Elkanah to do the same.

"Thank you, my lord."

He bid them good night, his heart skipping several beats as he walked outside and waited.

Hannah's hands grew moist as she walked slowly from Malka's tent to her parents'. Elkanah's form came into view in the moonlight as she passed her brothers on their way to join their families. She did not miss their smiles and mild chuckles as they passed. She would take the brunt of their teasing tomorrow, but for tonight, at least, they would allow her this moment.

She reached the spot beneath the awning where Elkanah waited and glanced at the open tent door. No sign of her parents, but she had no doubt they stood near enough to hear.

"You came." Elkanah spoke first. "But of course you would." He seemed as nervous as she, which put her strangely at ease.

"Well, my father did summon me." She smiled, meeting his gaze.

He motioned for her to sit on the ground, for they could not walk away from the tent.

"Let me gather some cushions first." She hurried into the tent, nearly bumping into her mother. "I don't want him to sit in the dirt," she said, snatching the cushions the men had used when eating.

Her mother merely nodded, and Hannah hurried outside again and placed the cushion on the ground for Elkanah. She sat opposite him and clasped her hands in her lap.

"I hope you are at ease?" Suddenly she was nervous again with the knowledge that her parents were listening.

"Quite," he said. He folded his robe beneath him. "I suppose if I'm going to keep my word, I'd better start."

A lump in her throat kept her from speaking. Could he hear the way her heart pounded at the look he gave her?

"I have asked your father for permission to marry you, Hannah. Will you accept me and become my bride?" He looked almost uncertain, which seemed strange since her father had likely already made the arrangements.

"Yes, of course. I would be most happy to become your bride." Hannah smiled, and he reached for her hand.

"We will have the betrothal when we return and set the date for the wedding." He touched her chin and gazed into her eyes. "Which I hope is very soon," he said softly.

She smiled shyly. "As do I."

Hannah's mother appeared at the tent's opening. "I think it is best for you to come in now."

Hannah stood, thinking the time much too short. But by all accounts she was now spoken for and would soon legally belong to Elkanah. Her heart beat in a new joyous rhythm at that thought.

3

Hannah walked with her mother and sisters-in-law the next morning to the tabernacle, where they stood in a long line waiting their turn to pray. The women who served at the door to the tabernacle moved about the courtyard, some refilling the bronze basin with fresh water, others joining the singers as she had once done at the side of the tented building, lifting tambourines and their voices in worship to Adonai. Still others assisted the Levites as they prepared for cleansing or made sure their garments were straight and true before they entered the Tent of Meeting to attend to their duties there.

Hannah watched them, reminded of her earlier fascination with their work. "I wonder if we will find Lital in this crowd," she said to her mother. She strained to see above the heads of the women in front of her but could not make out the distinct faces of the singers.

"It is highly doubtful, though perhaps your father can look for her before we leave. She is likely visiting her mother somewhere among Ephraim's tribe, for I did not see her with the Kohathites."

Hannah glanced about once more, catching sight of the high priest Eli sitting beside the tabernacle door while his sons inspected the sacrifices and burned them on the altar behind her. Eli was old, but not so old that he could not perform his priestly tasks. Why then did he just sit and watch his sons?

The line moved forward and Hannah slipped closer to her mother, listening to the music of the singers. She closed her eyes, caught up in the sound.

"We're almost there," her mother whispered, touching her arm. "Save your prayers for the proper place."

Hannah gave her mother a curious look but said nothing. Was there a proper place to pray? Did her mother never long to walk in the fields when the new spring flowers were in bloom and just thank Adonai for His goodness? Must prayer be kept only for mealtimes and feast days and Sabbaths or directly in front of the tabernacle?

She looked ahead and to her left. A small group of women, arms full with baskets of bread left from the wave offerings, walked toward some outbuildings that housed such gifts meant for the priests and Levites.

"It is our turn." Her mother interrupted her musings again.

Hannah stepped forward behind her sisters-in-law and knelt before the tent's door. The noise of hurried feet and rushing servants, the song of the singers, and the low thrum of male and female voices made prayer suddenly foreign and strange. She opened one eye to see her mother prostrated before the tent, speaking aloud.

How could she pray in such chaos? Her head began to throb, and no words would come to her mind, but she remained bowed in the position of prayer, doing exactly what Elkanah had once said he found false among worshipers. She pretended to pray, though as she attempted to shut out the sounds, a few words finally came to her silent heart.

Oh Adonai, forgive me. I cannot speak aloud to You among so many people. I . . . Nothing feels as it should . . . Forgive me.

When at last her mother stood, Hannah rose, relieved. She looked about her as they made their way toward the fenced opening, past the altar, away from the joyous singers and serving women. Her mother touched her elbow, guiding her away as a group of elders with a guilt offering came before Hophni, who slit the throat of a bull. His brother Phinehas caught the blood in a bowl and walked to the altar to sprinkle it there.

Outwardly, they seemed to be doing everything they were supposed to do as priests. But as she caught Phinehas glancing with open interest at one of the passing serving girls while he was supposed to be placing the blood on the altar in sincere reverence, she turned away, repulsed. What was he doing? She knew the priests ruined many a sacrifice, but had she seen lust in his gaze? She shivered, praying it was not so.

"I saw you at the tabernacle today. I don't think you noticed me, though." Elkanah had come to share the evening meal with them again, and this time, given their new promise of betrothal, Hannah's parents allowed them to walk among the tents that bordered theirs.

"I saw some elders there with a guilt offering. Were you with them?" She certainly would have recognized him, and though he was not yet an elder, perhaps he had joined them when she was not looking.

"I was actually speaking to my cousin off

to the side of the tent near the buildings
that Hophni and Phinehas built for their
families. I had some questions for my next
turn serving here." He glanced at her. "You
seemed troubled."

She looked at her feet, careful of each
step, then stopped to face him. "Everything
felt strange here today, not like it was when
I came months ago with my father."

"Everything is strange. Serving here can
be wonderful when the priests are not
around, but it is hard to avoid them."

She knew that now, especially after the
way Phinehas had looked at one of the serving women. But he wouldn't actually *touch*
one of them, would he? "I don't like them,"
she whispered.

"Nor do I," he admitted. He dug his toe
into the dirt, then looked at her. "Worse, I
would like to do things to them that make
me guilty of sin in my heart." He paused.

She waited, watching him.

"One of my cousins was recently
forced . . . by Hophni. Now she is ruined,
and there was nothing my uncle could do
about it."

Hannah gasped. "How is that possible?
They are the priests! Can't Eli do something?"

Elkanah shook his head. "Until recently it

was only the sacrifices they desecrated. Now their lusts have driven them to worse practices."

Hannah linked her arm through his, suddenly feeling the need for his nearness. "I saw one of the priests look unseemly at a serving woman today."

Elkanah stopped to look into her eyes. "Obviously, this is not the first time."

"But surely there is something the Levites can do." She heard the desperation in her voice.

He frowned and rubbed the back of his neck. "The priests threaten to withhold the forgiveness of God from our people, Hannah. The Levites are helpless against them."

"They cannot do that! They are not God!"

"No, but they stand in God's place and represent Him, so they think they can do as they please." He lowered his voice. "They are playing a dangerous game."

She nodded. "Did your uncle confront Hophni?"

Elkanah nodded. "My father, my uncle, their brothers — they all came together, but Hophni just laughed in their faces. He told them that he would do as he pleased with the serving women, and if they even tried to stop them — Phinehas does it too — then they would refuse to accept every future

36

sacrifice brought by our families and prevent us from fulfilling our Kohathite duties."

Hannah covered her mouth with both hands. "How can they threaten such a thing? Moses passed down those duties to us. We are Levites. Only Levites can care for the tabernacle."

Elkanah leaned closer. "You and I know that. Truth is, everyone knows that, but everyone is also afraid of the priests." His look held anguish. "Who among us wants to feel as though he can never sacrifice to the Lord as He requires? Would we build our own altars and avoid the feast days? Would we not be guilty before the Lord for such neglect of His tabernacle?"

Hannah met his gaze, drawn to the fire in his eyes. "But is there nothing the Levites can do? Appeal to Eli? Appoint new priests? Surely the actions of these two cannot please the Lord." She glanced beyond him a moment before searching his gaze.

"It's not a simple or easy thing to do," he said. "I have never seen it done or heard of such a thing in Israel, except for the time when God struck down Aaron's sons and when Eleazar's son Phinehas had no able-bodied male to take the priesthood. It fell to Ithamar's line then and has been that way since."

"The priesthood was better during the civil war with Benjamin?" Hannah knew Israel's history well enough to know this good Phinehas had lived during that terrible time. But his descendants had not been able to continue his good work. Perhaps the evil of that time had affected the priesthood then too.

"I don't know that they were better. That Phinehas was a good priest. But times have not improved. And the leaders have become more corrupt. We haven't had a godly judge in many years."

He shook himself. "I did not want our short time together to hold talk of evil in the land again. Forgive me."

She smiled. "It is all right." She looked beyond him again. "I used to long for this place. But the crowds, the noise . . . I must confess I could not even pray, though that is what I had come to do."

His smile showed white between his dark beard and mustache. "I admit, I find it easier to pray in solitude. Did not Moses say that our God is near to us whenever we pray to Him? I think He hears our prayers no matter where we pray them. I don't think our God is hindered by where we are."

"Another thing on which we can agree." She started walking again and he fell into step with her.

He squeezed her hand ever so gently, then released it and slowly led her back to her parents' tent. How grateful she was for him in that moment. He would not be like Hophni or Phinehas. He would love only her and be a caring, protective husband.

4

Hannah lifted the last of their provisions into the cart for the return home, her heart as anxious as her thoughts. She looked about at the disarray of the camp, a semi-organized mix of women putting things to rights, leaving the area as they'd found it until the next feast. Men grabbed the reins of their pack animals to head west, back to the hills of Ephraim.

Hannah nodded to her father that the cart was ready and drew up alongside her mother. Meira hurried to join her and pulled her aside.

"I want to hear everything that happened, since it seems my brother spent the entire feast with your family instead of ours." She winked and smiled at Hannah's embarrassment.

Hannah glanced beyond her friend — and future sister-in-law — to see Meira's mother Galia hobbling toward them. "I'll tell you later, when we are on the road." She motioned in Galia's direction.

"Oh, don't worry about Ima," Meira said, leaning closer to Hannah's ear. "She's come to talk to your mother, and you know they will discuss Elkanah." She pulled Hannah ahead of the mothers and sisters-in-law, following the men and pack animals and skipping children. "Now tell me everything."

Hannah laughed. "There is not that much to tell. Except . . ." She searched the crowd, spotting Elkanah with his brothers, then looked into Meira's anxious gaze. "He asked me to become his wife!"

Meira squealed. "I knew it! Elkanah is so private with his words that no matter what I said, he would not tell me."

Hannah dug her toe into the dirt, hiding her embarrassment. "Then I suppose I should not have told you either until the betrothal." She looked at her friend. "You will not tell anyone?"

Meira linked her arm through Hannah's. "Of course not! I'm just so happy that we will be related!" She pulled her arm free. "Although once I am wed, we will not see each other often."

"I'm sure there will be time for visits." How much would change with her own marriage? To leave her father and mother

41

and cleave to her husband, to be part of his family . . . The whole thing was exciting and yet caused a hint of fear.

"It is a little hard to imagine, isn't it?" Meira suddenly sobered. "I mean, everything is going to change."

Hannah nodded, her gaze shifting to the men walking ahead of them. Did Elkanah think of her now? Or were they back to discussing the corruption of the priesthood? Did men talk of love or only about political and religious machinations?

"Oh, we were quite impressed with him." Hannah's mother's voice carried to her from behind, interrupting her musings.

The running feet of children caused Hannah and Meira to turn. Peninnah, the young daughter of her mother's friend, stopped with her friends when they saw Hannah and Meira. Hannah turned to see Yafa, Peninnah's mother, join Galia and Adva.

"What are you talking about?" Peninnah asked, looking at Meira.

"Nothing that would interest you," Meira said, showing her obvious annoyance with the child.

Peninnah scowled, sadly a too typical expression in one so young. She turned to her companions. "Probably because it's about boys." She laughed, the tone sarcastic.

42

Her friends laughed with her, and they walked off, but not before Peninnah tossed another comment behind her. "Well, I'm not too young to talk about those things. I already know who I want to marry when I grow up." She stalked off, and Hannah and Meira exchanged surprised glances.

"She's terribly sure of herself," Meira said.

"Yes. And too young to know anything of such importance," Hannah agreed. "When I was her age, I had no such certainty." She kicked a stone in the path.

"She's a child," Meira said. "Children often say foolish things."

Hannah glanced behind her at her mother, deep in conversation with Galia and Yafa. Yafa was not a woman Hannah knew well, but her mother had uttered plenty of complaints about her over the years, despite their friendship. Peninnah was her only child, and her husband doted on the girl. Everyone said the child was spoiled and that her parents ought not to give in to her ways so often.

"She will find marriage difficult unless she marries a man who puts up with her attitudes. I fear even at thirteen she is already ruined." Hannah glanced again at her friend. "At least that's what my mother says. I hardly know the girl."

"Well, I know her." Meira also glanced behind and ushered Hannah forward out of earshot of the older women. "Yafa has been close to my mother for years, and she brings Peninnah with her wherever she goes. When they visit, Peninnah is always getting in my way." She lowered her voice to a whisper. "I know it is not nice to say such things of a child, but I am always relieved when she leaves!"

Hannah touched Meira's shoulder. "Well, at least she is too young to be part of your betrothal or be among the bridal virgins."

Meira gave Hannah a look.

"No." Hannah's eyes widened. "Your mother would allow it?"

Meira shrugged. "My mother and Yafa are friends. I had no say in the matter, even though Peninnah should be two years older before she is allowed such a privilege. It was not worth fighting about, though if she makes a nuisance of herself at my wedding, I will find a way to send her off, even if I have to beg every one of my brothers to lock her in a room somewhere!"

Hannah laughed, but quickly stopped when she saw Meira's serious expression. "Perhaps I can keep her from being too disruptive," she said.

"Well, I was hoping you would attend

me." Meira smiled. "I would appreciate you keeping an eye on the girl. Maybe do something to help her feel important. I think she acts worse than she is. At least I hope so."

"I hope so too." Hannah tucked a strand of hair beneath her scarf. "Did you see Lital while we were there? I wanted to look for her, but once Elkanah stated his intentions, it slipped my mind."

Meira tsked. "Well, I should hope my brother, *your future husband,* would take precedence over a friend we never see anymore."

Hannah pondered that a moment, wondering how well Lital actually fared after the things Elkanah had revealed. After the way she had seen Phinehas lust with a look . . . "I do worry about her. She has no one to watch out for her."

"She's pretty strong, though. And fast. We used to race each other when we were young and she always won." Meira looked into Hannah's face. "You're truly worried, aren't you?"

"It would be nice if we could talk to Rinat to see how her daughter fares." Hannah glanced behind her but saw no sign of Lital's mother. She released a sigh. "I will ask my father to check on her the next time he serves."

"A wise idea. Now let's talk about something else." Meira put her hands on her hips. "Did Elkanah say how many children he wants?"

Hannah blushed briefly and waved off her friend's comment. "Has Amachai told you the same?" She had learned to deflect unwanted questions from her brothers, who were masters at avoiding any attempts at probing into their personal affairs.

Meira hid a slight smile. "Amachai wants a big family." She glanced Hannah's way. "Elkanah does too."

Though they had not spoken of it, the thought pleased her. *Oh Adonai, let me give him everything he desires, and may he do the same for me.*

"Of course, every Hebrew man wants sons, and every good Hebrew woman wants children. A houseful. The more the better, I say." She looked Hannah up and down. "You will have no trouble giving Elkanah more children than he can count."

Meira's girlish giggle lifted Hannah's spirit.

The sun had risen just above the horizon, licking the dew from the grasses, and began to warm her from head to toe. But the heat from the sun could not match the warmth

46

of excitement and fear and embarrassment she felt at what awaited her when they arrived home. Soon she would be a woman betrothed.

The walk home had taken two days, but the women did not bother with the tents the last night. The sky was clear and so bright that they all decided to sleep in a circle under the stars. Hannah yawned, recalling her inability to rest that night and almost every night since. There was so much to do and so little time to complete it!

She tossed the covers aside, though dawn had yet to crest the ridge. Her father had gone far beyond the normal provisions for her in his dealings with Elkanah's family. "He will never be able to divorce you, my daughter, even if you never bear him a son," he had said.

Even if Elkanah thought he needed a son and took another wife to get it, she would not be sent home to her father. Did her father fear she would be treated as his sister had been, cast off for displeasing her husband? The thought and the fear it brought haunted her more than it should. Of course she would have sons. Hadn't it been her longing for most of her life? Was not God good? He would not deny her heart's one desire, would He?

She took a lamp from the niche in the wall and went to the sitting room to take up her weaving. She still had so many things she wanted to make to take with her, and the more she had ready by the betrothal tomorrow, the better. Especially if Elkanah requested a quick marriage.

Even one son would be enough, Adonai. Please let me conceive quickly to put everyone's mind at ease.

Why was she praying such prayers? It was her father's provision in the contract that had conjured such fears. She shook herself. Her father was simply looking out for her welfare, doing his best to protect her.

Oh Adonai, please help me not to be so foolish as to doubt You. Surely You will grant Elkanah sons.

The God she knew — the One she walked with in the gardens and among the wheat fields, or sought in prayer near the large oak trees or at times like this when she was alone — heard her. She knew He did. She had always felt close to Him. Talking with Him was as easy as speaking to a friend.

Except when she feared. Sometimes she feared He would ask too much of her. It was then she felt distant, as though He had become a stranger to her. How did a woman

48

give Adonai Tzva'ot, the Lord of Hosts, control of everything she longed for? Everything she held dear?

She picked up the shuttle and began to work the weft by the light of the lamp. How weary she was! But tomorrow Elkanah would come with his father and mother and brothers and sisters-in-law and Meira to celebrate the betrothal, and she must finish this shawl to drape over her robe. She had only a little left to add before she could stitch the symbol of the Kohathites onto the edges.

Elkanah would be pleased to see it, wouldn't he? More than that, she wanted to be her best for him.

Please, Adonai, let him not find me wanting.

"Hannah?"

Her mother's whisper caught her off guard. The shuttle slipped from her hand and hung by the thread it was attached to.

Her mother moved closer. "What on earth are you doing up at this hour? Have you slept at all since we returned?" She knelt at Hannah's side and touched her knee.

Hannah shook her head. "A little. I'm so anxious that all goes well, Ima. And I wanted to finish the scarf, and there are so many things going through my mind. What if his mother does not like me?"

Adva held up a hand and pressed a finger to Hannah's lips. "Galia will love you. And if she gives you trouble, you just tell me. You have nothing to fear, my girl. Everyone loves you."

"Everyone in my family."

"Everyone in the whole village. You burden yourself over so many little things. Let go of these fears, Hannah. You will make more trouble for yourself and your marriage if you cling to them." Her mother took her hand, lifted her up, and held her close for a brief moment. "Now, come. Back to bed with you, and I won't hear another word about it. I will finish the scarf if it comes to that. You take the morning to refresh yourself — rest, go for those walks you love, sing, play with the animals, help your father. But no more worries — understood?"

Hannah stared at her mother. Adva was the one who always fretted, and now she was telling Hannah to take time off and relax right before her biggest day? Perhaps it was her mother who was delusional from lack of sleep. Hannah would rest for now, but she would not play the day away. She would be a bride ready and waiting by tomorrow evening. She would not give her new mother-in-law or sisters-in-law cause to fault her in anything.

5

Night came too soon. Hannah's heart beat fast and she had to tell her breathing to slow as her sisters-in-law Ariel and Malka placed kohl over her eyelids and helped her dress.

"Stop moving," Ariel said, taking a step back from Hannah. "I don't want to get black *under* your eyes. You'll look like an Egyptian!"

Hannah held still. She wasn't used to wearing anything except the occasional ochre rubbed into her cheeks. But Ariel had made some kohl the day before and insisted that a little just above her eyes would make her even prettier than everyone claimed.

"I shouldn't be nervous." Hannah clamped her hands together, trying to keep from fidgeting.

"Of course you are nervous. All brides feel the same. But this is not your wedding night, so the only reason to be anxious is because you are meeting his whole family at one time. But do not worry, Meira will be there, and your mother and Galia are already friends." Malka bent to tie the sandals to her feet. "I am sure they already love you."

"I hope so." Hannah had her doubts about Galia, partly because Meira had confided that her mother had tried to get Elkanah to wed more than once during the time he had waited for Hannah, but she held her tongue as both sisters-in-law finished their work.

"There," Ariel said, smiling. "You look wonderful."

Hannah turned for Malka's inspection. Her mother entered the room at that moment. She gasped, hands to her mouth. "Oh, my girl." Tears filled her eyes as she came forward and grasped Hannah's cold fingers. "How beautiful you are."

Hannah offered her a trembling smile, but she could not speak.

"Are you ready? Elkanah's family is coming down the street even now." Her mother tugged gently on her hand, and Hannah allowed herself to be led into the sitting room, which her mother had transformed into a whitewashed wonder. Low tables spread with sweet treats and sweating skins of wine sat waiting. Hannah took the seat piled with the thickest cushion in the center of the

52

room, while her nieces and nephews ran squealing around her.

Hannah's sisters-in-law came to shoo the children to a side room as the voices of Elkanah's family drew nearer. Torches blazed in the courtyard, and her father and brothers greeted Elkanah, his father, and his brothers, while her mother welcomed the women in his family.

"Come, come." She could hear her father's voice above the others, but then the chatter of men and women drowned it out.

At last the crowd quieted and Elkanah's family entered the house. Her father led the way to a side table where a parchment, the ketubah, was spread out awaiting their seals. Her mother had heated the clay in a small dish. After a few moments of silence while the men read the words of the agreement, both fathers pressed their seals into the clay and affixed them to the parchment. Hannah watched as her father rolled the parchment into a scroll and both fathers affixed one more seal to secure the document.

Elkanah took the document and came and knelt at her feet. Hannah's heartbeat quickened as he placed the ketubah in her hands. Their fingers briefly touched in the exchange. She met his gaze, noted the longing in his look. But this was not the time for them. Not yet.

"Have we agreed upon a date for the wedding?" Galia asked once the formality of the document sealing and gifting had taken place.

"I think a year is sufficient time," her mother said, stepping closer to Hannah's side. "We will need the time to prepare all the things Hannah will take with her."

Galia's eyes narrowed the slightest bit. Elkanah stood, but his gaze never left Hannah's. If he could have his way, would he wait as long as her mother suggested?

"A year is too long," Galia said, glancing first at her husband, then at Elkanah. "Our son has waited a long time for your daughter to grow to the proper age. We tried —" She stopped and shook her head. "A year is too long."

"Ima, please." Elkanah's tone held a pleading note, and Hannah sensed Galia had embarrassed him.

"You know I'm right," Galia said, crossing both arms. "I want to hold your children on my knees before I grow too old to enjoy the pleasure."

Hannah flushed hot at such bold words and looked at the parchment she still held in her hands. Meira had intimated Elkanah's patient waiting. How could she possibly allow her mother to force on him another year?

"Ten months then," she heard Adva saying, drawing her back to this motherly bartering.

Galia frowned, still appearing unconvinced. "Eight months, not a moment more. Six would be better, but we will agree to eight. It will be a perfect time between festivals."

Adva crossed her arms, her lips set in a thin line. Hannah looked to Elkanah for some sense of what he wanted. If she could be ready in three months, would that not please her mother-in-law? Dare she speak her thoughts? This was a ritual dance between the mothers. It was not her place to interfere.

And yet, Elkanah's dark eyes probed hers in that moment, and she felt as though he had touched her.

"Three months would be doable." Had she actually spoken? She clamped a hand over her mouth. "Forgive me, Ima. The decision is not mine. And of course, there are so many things still to make." She had not even started on the bed linens or extra pillows or material for coming children.

"Six months is much too soon. We can manage eight," Adva said. She and Galia scrutinized each other until at last Galia nodded.

"Agreed."

The women closed the gap between them and kissed each other's cheeks.

Hannah breathed a deep sigh of relief. Elkanah took a step closer and offered his hand. She took it and let him help her to her feet. She tucked the ketubah into her robe and allowed him to walk her into the courtyard while their families laughed and ate and talked inside the house.

"Tell me my mother did not embarrass you in there." Elkanah did not release her hand, and the longer he held it, the more it felt right, like they were made to fit together.

Hannah laughed softly, a musical sound of relief to his ears. "Your mother was just playing her part. She wants what's best for you." She looked up at him, and moonlight splayed over her face. Torches lit the corners of the courtyard, and some of the children had snuck outside to sit on the stone benches and eat the sweet treats.

"My mother thinks she knows what is best for me," he whispered, chagrined. How much should he reveal to this new bride about the struggles he had had with his family over his choice of wife? Or the strife that

56

sometimes arose between his mother and father, his brothers and sisters-in-law? He tilted his head and gave her a curious look.

"What is it?" She pulled him away from the children toward the farthest edge of the court. "Something troubles you. Tell me."

"You can already read my thoughts?"

"It is not hard to notice the expression of an anxious man. I can see it in your furrowed brow." She smiled, and he knew he could deny her nothing.

He cupped her cheek, tracing a line along her jaw. "You must understand something, Hannah . . . about my family."

She tilted her head to better look at him.

"My parents' household is not always congenial. My mother and father have been known to raise strong wills against the other, and my brothers and their wives, except for Tahath, do the same." He paused at the astonished look on her face. "But you need not fear that from me. I will not fight with you. And if my mother becomes too difficult for you, I will find a way to move us apart from them." He squeezed her fingers. "You must trust me in this."

She nodded. "I trust you." She studied their interlocked hands. A shy look crept into her eyes.

He turned toward the door of the house.

The children had slipped inside again, leaving them blissfully, momentarily alone.

"I know we are supposed to wait, but legally this is not wrong." He bent low and brushed his lips against hers, a gentle kiss. "I love you, Hannah." He kissed her again, the slightest touch, lest he awaken desires they could not fulfill for eight months, legally married or not.

He pulled back and heard her breath release as though surprised by his actions. But then a slow smile spread over her beautiful face. "I think three months would have been better."

"I wish we could have convinced your mother."

"As do I."

"But it is done now."

"Yes." She touched his arm. "But I fear love has awakened and will beat in harmony with you until that day." She moved her hand to touch her middle, the seat of her emotions.

He placed his hand over hers, careful not to touch more than her fingers. "Until then, I will count the days." He longed to kiss her again, but his sister-in-law burst from the house, chasing after her son, the moment lost.

Hannah pulled back and chuckled softly

at the boy's antics. Elkanah placed a hand on her back and leaned close. "Someday we will be faced with similar high-spirited children. I look forward to the day they are like olive branches around our table."

She looked at him and rewarded him again with a wide smile, which by her expression was meant only for him. He glanced heavenward and offered Adonai a prayer of thanks. God had granted his heart's desire and given him the woman of his dreams.

6

Three Months Later

Hannah walked with Meira along the river's path, where trees lined the embankment and dry brush crunched beneath their sandals. Meira's wedding to Amachai was only days away, and Hannah had worked long hours to complete some of the linens and garments she would need for her own wedding five months hence.

"Are you nervous?" Hannah asked as Meira bent to pick up a stone and toss it into the river. They had been shooed from their homes by their mothers, who told both girls they needed a few hours of rest. Hannah had resisted, but relented for Meira's sake.

"A little." She released a long-held sigh. "Yes." She looked at Hannah. "That is, I'm excited and anxious. One moment I'm constantly looking at the sun's movement across the sky, and the next I'm thinking I will never be ready on time."

"Which is exactly why you needed this break." Hannah touched her friend's arm. "In a few days you will look back on all of the frantic work and wonder why you worried at all."

Meira gave Hannah a sidelong glance. "*You're* telling *me* to not worry? What about you! Tell me you haven't felt the same since the day of your betrothal."

Hannah released a deep breath. "You are right. I am nervous and fearful of the future, while at the same time I can't wait for it to begin!" She smiled. "We are both pathetic, are we not?"

Meira nodded and returned the smile. "I suppose all brides feel the same." They continued their walk, drawing closer to the river's edge. "I love the way the water rushes over the rocks here. It makes a person respect the river and yet gives us a sense of excitement at such power. I mean, can you imagine trying to stop the water from moving? If I put my hand in it or dip my foot, the water will simply move through or around it. The river won't halt for me, for anyone."

Hannah stopped as they reached the bank and looked out. "It is both beautiful and terrifying," she said, watching as the rocks caused the water to turn white where the protrusions slightly broke the surface. "This is definitely not a good spot for bathing or washing."

Meira laughed. "Good point. But I do love it here." She sank onto the grass and pulled her knees to her chest. "I could sit and watch this for hours."

"And get nothing at all done that needs doing." Hannah sat beside her, her mind whirling with the number of things waiting for her back home. Still, she attempted to relax, for Meira seemed to need her here. "Of course, a break is good when one is working too hard."

Meira didn't respond right away, and Hannah looked out at the water, trying to quiet her own anxiety. She breathed in the scent of the river, the trees, and slowly let peace settle over her.

"We won't get to do this once I am wed," Meira said, her tone somber. She turned to face Hannah. "Amachai's home is half a day's walk from my father's house. We won't be close enough to get away to enjoy a day like this."

A sense of loss swept over Hannah, but she brightened a moment later, unwilling to ruin this moment with her dearest friend. "And yet we will be sisters, so there will surely be times our families will gather together. Perhaps we can find a new place to escape the chaos and noise of the household."

"Perhaps." Meira took Hannah's hand, squeezed, and released it. "You are a good friend, Hannah. I'm glad Elkanah chose you and that you agreed. You won't regret it, I promise."

"I don't expect to regret anything." Hannah clasped both hands around her tucked knees. "But I suppose we should start heading back. I don't think they wanted us to stay away the entire day."

Meira nodded but did not rise. "One more moment." She gazed again at the winding river, and Hannah could not help but imagine the stories of old, of how God stopped the Jordan so that Israel could move across on dry land. Such impossibility! And yet, did they not believe in the God of miracles?

Meira stood at last and helped Hannah to her feet. "I'm ready." She smiled. "And not quite so nervous."

"Good. Because your wedding is coming, like it or not." Hannah glanced up at the trees towering over them, then fell into step with Meira.

"Let's go back the other way," Meira said,

turning. "If we go a little farther this way, we can circle around away from the water and see how the fields are growing."

Hannah lifted a brow. "You just want to avoid going home."

Meira's smile held a conspiratorial glint. "Perhaps."

Hannah shook her head but followed her friend just the same. They moved toward a copse of trees not far from the river's edge, kicking dry leaves and pebbles as they walked. The extra time it would take to circle around caused Hannah to want to push Meira along, but she forced her anxious thoughts in check. This was Meira's time. She still had five months before she needed to fret. The thought troubled her.

Oh Adonai, I fear so easily.

Meira kicked at a fallen leaf-covered log at the edge of the small forest and stopped abruptly. Hannah looked at her friend's wide eyes, seeing fear replace the peace they had just enjoyed.

"What is that?" Meira's voice had dropped to a mere whisper. She looked at Hannah.

Hannah backed away. Strange creatures lived among the trees. What if they had come upon one that could do them harm? "We should go," she whispered back.

64

Meira stared, her obvious terror not abating.

"What are you waiting for?" Hannah hissed. "It could be sleeping and awaken and attack us." She stood frozen to the spot, watching helplessly as Meira crept closer and knelt.

"It's not a log," Meira said softly. She brushed leaves aside to discover a bunched-up cloak.

Hannah found the ability to move. "Who would bury a cloak in the woods?" She felt suddenly braver and came to kneel at Meira's side.

Meira touched the cloak and slowly lifted it from beneath the brush. It was a woman's cloak by the design and size of it. She turned it over and slowly stood, holding it to the sunlight. Hannah stood as well, half afraid to touch it but too curious to leave it.

"It looks familiar," Hannah said, trying to remember where she had seen it or one like it before. Most women in Israel wore a similar simple design.

Meira gasped. "It's caked in blood!" The wide-eyed look returned and she held it higher. "That looks like blood, doesn't it?"

Hannah's heart pounded and she glanced quickly around them. Had some woman been attacked by an animal? Did animals bury things they had killed? "We should go."

"Yes." Meira didn't move. "But maybe we should look around first. What if some woman is lying hurt nearby? I would want someone to look for me."

"But no one is missing from our tribe. We would have heard of it." Hannah's heart beat faster, if that were possible, and she couldn't stop the trembling that made her knees grow weak. "Maybe we should go get our fathers and brothers to help."

Meira seemed to ponder that thought, then shook her head. "First a quick look, then if we find nothing, we will go back and just show the cloak to the women. Maybe someone will recognize it."

Hannah did not agree at all, her mind telling her to run as far away from here as she could get, but she could not desert her friend, stubborn though she was. "A quick look," she finally said.

Meira turned to enter the trees, and Hannah followed, searching the ground. The crunch of leaves sounded like drums in her ears, and the river's waters raced downstream to the pace of her anxiously beating heart.

They walked slowly, searching, until Hannah finally said again, "We really should go back."

But a putrid scent and Meira's screech stopped them both. "Look!" She pointed to a mound a short distance ahead of them.

Hannah squinted, trying to make out what it was, knowing in her heart it was not living. Meira stepped closer, Hannah on her heels. Both girls fell to their knees beside the body of a woman.

"Oh!" Hannah covered her mouth as bile rose in her throat. Decomposition and the buzz of insects filled the air around them, making them both instinctively move back.

They looked at each other. "It's hard to tell for certain, but I would wager that it's Lital." Hannah spoke softly, tears clogging her throat. She swallowed several times. "That's why the cloak looked familiar. She wore one like it all the time."

Meira nodded. "We need to get our fathers." She backed away. "Someone needs to examine and bury her. There is a reason her cloak was coated in blood."

"I thought she was in Shiloh." Hannah stared at her friend's body, recognizing the shape of her mouth and noticing the way she was placed with her arms folded over her chest, as though she were merely sleeping. "However did she get here?"

Meira shook her head. "Why was her cloak removed? Was she killed? Why wasn't

67

she properly buried?"

Hannah met Meira's gaze, and the horror she was feeling showed on her friend's face. "Let's get out of here," Hannah said at last, tugging Meira's arm.

Meira obediently followed, and Hannah's pace increased until they were through the trees.

Meira still held Lital's cloak in her arms. "Rinat will be devastated."

Hannah looked down at the cloak, her throat raw from the exertion of holding back a river of tears. They both glanced once more at the small forest, then took off running toward home.

7

Hannah raced toward her father's pottery shop while Meira ran to the fields to find her father, Jeroham. Before the sun reached its midpoint, the men of the town had gathered at Jeroham's home and moved in the direction Hannah and Meira had told them.

Hannah sank onto a cushion beside Meira as their mothers and sisters-in-law discussed how to tell Rinat once the body was confirmed to be her daughter.

"She will be bereft of everything," Adva said, wringing her hands while Galia paced the sitting room. "Whatever will she do?"

"Is there no family left to take her in? I know Lital was working as a cook for the Levites and serving as a singer to help her mother this past year, but how could she have gotten from Shiloh to here and end up in the forest?" Galia stopped her pacing long enough to look at Hannah and Meira.

"You're sure it was Lital?"

"As sure as we can be, Ima," Meira said, fidgeting with the belt of her robe. "It was dark and we didn't want to touch her."

"No, of course not," Adva said. "You girls did the right thing." She stood and paced the opposite direction as Galia. Meira's and Hannah's sisters-in-law had taken the children to the fields behind the house.

"The rest of the women in town will need to know," Galia said, halting her frantic movements and sinking onto one of the cushions.

"Surely not before the men identify her and we tell Rinat," Adva said.

"Of course not."

But Hannah wondered if Galia would keep quiet until then. The woman seemed itching to tell the entire town, while Hannah simply wanted to sink into the cushions — or better yet, her bed — and hide beneath the covers for days.

Oh Lital. What happened to you?

Commotion in the courtyard brought her thoughts up short, and she jumped up with the rest of the women. Her father and father-in-law entered the house together with Elkanah not far behind. She could hear the sound of men's voices in the courtyard.

"Well?" Galia asked, staring Jeroham

down. "Was it Lital?"

Jeroham nodded, but Hyam spoke. "We all agreed that it has to be Lital. All of us have seen her working at the tabernacle and been served meals at her hand."

"Was she . . . murdered?" Hannah could not get her voice to work above a whisper. Her heart thudded with the weight of grief until she wondered if it would continue beating.

"I don't think so," her father said. "There was no sign of forced injury, although . . ." He paused, his gaze glancing off hers to her mother's. "It is possible she gave birth to a child. We will need a woman to examine her to know for certain."

"So she died in childbirth?" Hannah's mother looked at Hyam, aghast. "Lital did not have a husband."

"Not that we know of." Her father rubbed a hand over his beard. "We will have to investigate that to be sure. We need to speak to her mother."

"Lital worked at the tabernacle only a year, Abba. She could not have married and borne a child in such a short time. And if she bore a child, where is it?" Hannah stood and came toward her father, allowing him to hold her close. She caught the look in Elkanah's eyes. Fear and anger mingled in his gaze.

Hyam patted Hannah's back. "We will investigate what happened. Though I'm not sure we will find any satisfactory answers." He released Hannah and faced Jeroham. "We need to summon Rinat. Then we need to bury Lital in a proper grave."

"My sons have already begun work on the bier." He glanced at Elkanah. "Will you go to get Rinat, my son?"

Elkanah nodded. "Though perhaps it would be best if my mother and Hannah's mother accompanied me?"

Both women hurried closer to Elkanah. Hannah felt the sting of not being included, but a moment later she realized a sense of relief to be left here where she didn't have to face Lital's mother just yet.

"We must hurry," Galia said, taking Elkanah's arm and ushering him through the door, as if she'd been waiting for permission to do exactly what she'd been longing to do for hours.

Elkanah met Hannah's gaze after he stepped over the threshold. Clearly finding Lital's body had shaken him as much as it had shaken her. She knew none of the Levites would rest until they had answers. And no woman would feel safe until then.

Elkanah led the women from Rinat's home to his father's house, heart pounding. They approached the courtyard in somber silence, and his mother led the poor widow to the bier, which now rested on the courtyard wall. The body was partially wrapped, waiting for Rinat to confirm their suspicions. He glanced toward the house and saw Hannah emerge, her brow lifted in the curious look she often gave. He nodded once and Hannah moved to the court to join the other women, Meira close behind.

"Is this your daughter, Rinat?" Hyam asked as he lifted the cloth from the girl's face.

Rinat crumpled and fell into a heap on the ground before the bier. Loud wails came from her lips, and she rocked back and forth, her whole body swaying with the obvious signs of one who grieved. "No! No! No! Adonai Tzva'ot, why?" She gulped back a huge sob. "Lital! My Lital!"

Elkanah watched, helpless, as the women surrounded Lital's mother. Soon the entire household erupted in the weeping and wailing one expected when a soul slipped into Sheol.

Oh Adonai, how can she bear this?

What if Hannah had worked at the tabernacle? Would something like this have happened to her? But no. They had no proof that anyone from Shiloh was responsible for Lital's death.

But someone was responsible for her pregnancy, for Rinat had confirmed that her daughter was with child at the last feast. Why had she told no one else?

"I should have made her come home." Rinat's soft cry pierced his consciousness. "I should have insisted, no matter what the priests promised."

Elkanah glanced at his father and Hyam. His father-in-law stepped closer to the circle of weeping women and knelt in front of Rinat. "What did the priests promise?" If anyone could find the truth, Hannah's father was the man.

"They said they would care for her and her child, that she would be safer living among the Levites at Shiloh, and that their wives would look after her." Rinat sniffed against a flood of tears. "That way she could still work and support me."

Weeping followed the remark, and Hyam stood and walked toward the men. "We need to bury the body before the sun sets." He glanced at the women.

Elkanah's heart ached with the pain so evident in the widow's gaze. To lose a child. Was anything worse for a woman already a widow? He shook his head, unwilling to even imagine it. Everyone died, but not like this. Something was very wrong.

Elkanah walked over and pulled Hannah aside. "Can you ask her if Lital told her the father's name?" he whispered. Trying to ask a woman such a question made his knees quake. *What a coward you are, Elkanah, that you would put such a thing on your wife.* But he waited for her answer just the same.

Hannah nodded and moved closer to Rinat. She touched the older woman's arm. "Did Lital tell you . . . that is, do you know who fathered her child? Perhaps if we know, we can find out what happened to the child."

Elkanah leaned in, trying to hear the woman's soft-spoken words.

Rinat met Hannah's gaze and lifted her chin, a hint of defiance in her eyes. "My Lital . . . she was afraid when I saw her. She would only say that one of the priests had been with her."

"Hophni and Phinehas?" Hannah asked.

"One of them, yes." Rinat attempted to stand, and Galia and Adva helped hold her upright. They walked toward the bier. "We must bury her," Rinat said, suddenly sounding stronger than Elkanah could have thought possible.

His brothers lifted the bier, and the small group made its way to the cave where Rinat had buried her husband only a few years earlier. Elkanah walked with Hannah behind the others.

"What does this mean?" Hannah whispered. "You said Hophni ruined one of your cousins not so long ago. Is any woman safe to serve at the tabernacle anymore?"

Elkanah stroked his beard, feeling as though he had aged ten years in the past few hours. "It sounds as though desecrating the sacrifices was not enough for the priests. But to defile the serving women too? How far has it gone? Was Lital the only one? And what happened to her child?" His voice dropped in pitch, though the sounds of weeping drowned out their conversation.

"Can you or one of our fathers find out? Rinat would be so comforted if she could raise Lital's child." Hannah's look held such hope. "That is, assuming he or she lived."

"I will talk to my father — and yours. If there was a living child, surely we can find it."

"But there was no other body found with Lital. If the child died, they might have thrown it in the river." He saw the shudder work through Hannah and put one arm around her in comfort.

"What I want to know is why they brought her body and dumped it in the woods. If you and Meira hadn't happened to walk that direction, we might never have found her." Elkanah stopped with the rest of the group at the cave's entrance.

"Meira wanted to go a different direction. If we had gone home the way we had come, we would have missed her." Hannah met his gaze. "Perhaps Adonai was directing our steps."

He nodded. "Undoubtedly. But I don't like what it all implies. Perhaps God is showing us that things are much worse than we thought. The problem is, what can we possibly do about it?"

"Can't the Levites approach Eli?" she whispered, but his response was interrupted by his father's words of condolence and the final goodbyes and prayers for Rinat as they laid her only child to rest.

Elkanah pondered Hannah's question long after the group moved back to his father's house and later dispersed to their homes. If only he could give her an answer that would satisfy and fix the mess that was their priesthood. But he had no answers, and he knew in his heart that no one but God could fix this.

8

Three Months Later

Meira sidled up beside Hannah as the whole town traveled to Shiloh for the Day of Atonement and the Feast of Tabernacles. The crowd held a subdued tone, in part because the Day of Atonement was a solemn moment of confession and reflection. But Hannah also knew that the minds of the men of her Kohathite clan were on what to do about Israel's corrupt priests. And every woman walked with a little less confidence along the dusty road, not feeling quite as safe as she once did.

"I wonder what they are discussing," Meira whispered. She had been married nearly three months, but Amachai had joined the men who walked ahead, so she took the moment to talk to Hannah. The two young women glanced in the direction of their mothers, who were talking with Yafa. "I wonder why Rinat has not joined them."

"Maybe she still will." Hannah had seen the widow talking to other townswomen earlier in their walk. "I wish they could have found Lital's child for her. Perhaps the child died with her." Hannah looked beyond Meira and caught the frown lines evident along her mother's brow. "My mother worries that the same thing has happened to other serving women, but no one has been able to prove such accusations."

"My mother-in-law speaks of it often as well. I think every Levite in town has decided no daughter of theirs will ever serve in that place again." Meira glanced ahead to where the men walked. "Of course, as Amachai's wife, I don't have to be part of that anymore. And we are surely safe at the feasts with our men to protect us."

Hannah nodded. "Yes, at least we are safe at the festivals." Though even now she wondered. History told tales of virgins captured by Benjamites in a plot other tribes had devised to give wives and children to the devastated tribe, which had been almost lost to civil war. Had Shiloh ever been a truly safe place?

The thought brought the memory of her father's soft words coming through the walls as she lay in her bed.

"It's not safe there anymore, Adva. Hophni

and Phinehas have gone too far. It wasn't enough for them to defile the sacrifices, now they have to defile the women who serve Adonai Tzva'ot as well?"

Hannah shivered. She hated feeling this way — unsafe in her own land. And what if she ever ended up like Rinat? If something happened to Elkanah and their only child . . . The very thought of having no family to love and care for and to care for her when she was old was terrifying. One she considered too often for a young woman, as her mother often reminded her.

"You are eighteen, my Hannah. You are betrothed to a wonderful man. You have nothing to fear. God will take care of you, of all of us."

But that was before Lital's death — this horror that had stunned the town. Did God really care for them? He hadn't protected her friend.

"Why didn't God protect Lital in this very place where He put His name?" Hannah looked at Meira, searching her friend's face, longing for reassurance, comfort, something. "And why not let the child live and be found? Why should Rinat have to lose all?"

"What child?" Yafa's daughter Peninnah and some of the younger girls crowded

81

closer, unnoticed until now by Hannah and Meira. Hannah's stomach tightened with that sick feeling she got when she'd said something she shouldn't or spoken too loudly, allowing others to hear. The news of the child had been kept from most of the town, and here she was, frightening children.

"It is nothing," Meira said quickly. "Hannah and I were just talking."

"About that woman who died?" Peninnah's dark eyes grew round. "My ima talks about her a lot. My abba says the girl deserved what she got."

Hannah stared at the child, a girl too young to be listening to such talk. Too young to have such opinions.

"No one deserves to die," Hannah said, looking from one child to another. "Now why don't you all run off and play. We will be at Shiloh and have to set up camp, so enjoy the leisure while you have it." She shooed them away, and silence fell between her and Meira.

"Peninnah's parents shouldn't talk like that in front of her," Meira said at last.

"I'm sure if she really knew what happened, it would frighten her as much as it does us." She shoved a small branch aside with her toe as they walked.

"Amachai and his brothers talk of it often. It's even worse when my brothers join us." Meira lifted her hands in a helpless gesture. "Honestly, it is growing difficult to listen to talk of the priests' corruption and the evil spreading through the land. It is not as if they can do anything about it, though they have offered plenty of suggestions. No one dares go against the priests. If a foreign country were trying to invade us, we could join forces and oppose them, but we are corrupt from within our own tribes and leaders. How are we supposed to battle that?"

Hannah adjusted the scarf at her neck. "Men want to fix things," she said after a lengthy pause. "And I think our Levite men have wanted to fix the priesthood for a long time, even if they don't think they can."

Meira sighed. "Let's talk about something else. Like your wedding!"

Hannah laughed lightly. "It is coming so quickly! We will barely return from the festival and have only two months to finish everything." She glanced in her mother's direction and saw that Rinat had now joined them. Tears streamed down the widow's cheeks, and Hannah felt a kick in her gut that she had talked of joyful things in the midst of the woman's continuing sorrow. She motioned Meira to look their way.

"I wonder if anyone will talk of anything good at the feast," Hannah whispered. "I feel guilty talking of happier things."

"Well, my wedding came only days after Lital's burial. We can't help the sadness, but life does move on." Meira touched Hannah's shoulder. "You deserve some happiness too, you know."

"I know. But it's hard to think that way." Hannah glanced ahead toward Shiloh. What had once brought joy now simply brought dread.

Later that evening after the camp had been set up and most people had settled, Elkanah walked with Hannah not far from her father's tent.

"Only a few more months and we will not need to be near the watchful eye of your father," Elkanah said, taking her hand. He lifted it to his lips and kissed the back of it. "I long for the day I can call you my wife in the fullest way." His smile warmed her, and she returned it.

"I too long for that day, but with all that has happened, there is much sorrow in the camp."

He nodded and glanced beyond her. "There is no denying that."

A sigh lifted her chest. "In all honesty, Elkanah, I am having a hard time trusting God right now in the face of what has happened. I do not understand how the God I worship could allow a widow to be so bereft. Or why He allows the priests to act as they do without consequence." She searched his face. "Do you know?"

He slowly shook his head. "You ask hard questions, my love. Who can truly know the mind of God? He tells us to pray, He commands our obedience, but His ways are not our ways. How can one created understand the One who made him?"

"And yet didn't He make us so that we could know Him?" She played with a strand of her hair, then took a quick glance at the stars.

"Yes. That is, I believe that was His intent. But sin changed all of that, at least on our end, for now we cannot see Him as Adam and Eve once did." He raked a hand along the back of his neck and looked heavenward as well. "We see the stars, but they are too far away for us to know what they look like. Are they as big as the sun? Or are they larger still? Why are they fixed in the same place? And if God created so many lights in the sky, what is man that He should care for us too?" He looked back at her. "I find myself struggling to understand Him as well, but I do not think He will abide evil forever. The priests will not get away with their actions any more than Aaron's two sons did."

"But God struck them down immediately. He didn't allow their sin to continue to hurt His people." She caught sight of the Bear and Orion and Pleiades and the constellations of the south. How big God was to create such things. Did He only concern Himself with the larger universe? Yet Israel's history proved that was not true. He cared about individual people. "I wish I could know Him better."

He stopped, turning to face her. "You are devoted to our God, Hannah. He may not reveal His ways to us now, but I daresay one day we will understand." He tilted his head as though to get a better look at her.

"I cannot fathom His ways, but He is my hope. I cling to His laws, though sometimes they do not make sense to me." She hesitated. "But I will admit to you, I fear Him. And I don't always trust Him as we are commanded to do." She released a deep breath.

"What causes your struggle, beloved?" He touched her cheek, traced a line along her jaw for a brief moment, then let his hand drop to his side.

She reached for his hand and squeezed. "Rinat's loss. Loss of any kind. Why do some people live long lives with a houseful of loved ones while others are widowed or orphaned with no one to care for them? Why does God withhold good when it is in His power to give it?" She waved a hand over the area, encompassing the camp and the many people called by God to be His own. "This is my struggle, Elkanah. And my fear. I fear being like Rinat."

His gaze softened, and a slight smile tipped the corners of his mouth. "Your struggles are those of each one of us, Hannah. Even I, as a Kohathite who spends time near the holiest of places, cannot even begin to say I know the ways of our God. But you will never need to fear being alone." He leaned closer, his lips hovering over hers. And though they should have waited, he kissed her as the law allowed, and he didn't raise his head until he'd left her breathless.

9

Hannah awoke with a start, feeling strangely out of place. She rolled onto her side and bumped into Elkanah's back. How long did it take a new bride to adjust to her surroundings?

Light filtered through the window in their small room, and the sound of footsteps could be heard outside the closed curtained door.

"Are you all right, my love?" Elkanah pulled her against his chest and kissed her forehead.

She shook her head and blinked several times.

"You've been waking with a start for weeks since our wedding. Is something wrong?" He stroked the side of her face, and she allowed herself to rest against him. But the sounds of the household waking and a child crying down the hallway caused her to sit up and pull the sheet to her neck.

She looked at the curtained door, then back at Elkanah. "I feel . . ." She paused. She had no right to complain at the room they'd been given in his father's bursting house. Elkanah was not the firstborn — he did not have the rights of a double portion of anything, and since they'd agreed on only eight months to wed, his father had claimed there was no time to add another building to the circle of stone houses surrounding the courtyard. She was forced to share his small room that he alone had used all his life.

A child peeked around the curtain, one of Elkanah's nephews. The boy was only three but was used to rousing his uncle and coming and going into the room as he pleased. Hannah stiffened when she saw him. The boy turned around and ran down the hall.

Elkanah pulled her back into his arms, leaning close to her ear. "This arrangement, it distresses you."

She could not deny it. "If we had a door that latched . . ."

"I will see to it today," he said. "And truly this room is too small for us. I will speak to my father again about expanding off the back of the house or in the small space left around the court. If only there was space left on the roof."

The houses were clustered together with space for the animals in the outer court. Some of the families lived above them in rooms on the rooftops, but with so many brothers, all of the spaces were taken.

"We can make do with your room. If there is a door." She smiled at him, wanting with everything in her to make him glad, grateful that he had married her. The wedding tent with its privacy and an entire week to be alone had been such bliss compared to this living with his family. But she did not say so.

He kissed her and rose quickly to dress for the day. She followed suit to help his mother and sisters-in-law prepare the morning meal. He stopped at the threshold and touched the flimsy curtain. "You have my word. By tonight this will be a door with a firm latch."

"Thank you." She kissed his cheek and hurried past him.

Sounds of the household now fully awake greeted her as she stepped into the area where the women prepared the food. She released an anxious breath and smiled. "Good morning," she said, looking at her mother-in-law. Four of her six sisters-in-law were already at work grinding grain and stirring porridge over a fire. How she wished Meira was among them, but a bride joined her husband's family, as she was now bound to Elkanah's.

Galia frowned, looking Hannah up and down. "Your wedding week is over, and unless you are waking up with the morning illness of pregnancy, I suggest arriving a little sooner."

"Forgive me." Hannah's stomach twisted as it always did when Galia seemed displeased, even if that displeasure was not aimed at her. This was the first sign that her new-bride status was over. She looked quickly about the area to see what still needed to be done. But Alona and Batel were working two grindstones, and Dana and Kelila were making flatbread and stirring the quick wheat porridge over a large clay kettle. Varda and Orah were shooing the children away or caring for young babies.

Panic nearly swept over her that she had missed the important tasks, until she saw the dates and raisins and apricots resting on a board on the courtyard wall. She could make her mother's best topping for the porridge. Surely that would please Galia.

She moved quietly to the side to work, chopping the fruit and heating it over the fire, stirring in some honeycomb at the last.

"What are you doing?" Galia came from behind, her tone hard.

Hannah startled, nearly spilling the contents of the pot she'd been stirring. "Forgive me," she said again. "I thought to make my mother's topping for the porridge. I saw the dates and raisins and apricots, and the recipe is so simple . . ." Her words trailed off at the glower on her mother-in-law's face.

"Did you ask me? How do you know I did not have other plans for those things?" Galia put both hands on her hips and shook her head, then whirled about and stormed off, leaving the courtyard.

Dana stepped closer to Hannah and glanced into the pot. "That smells wonderful. The porridge is almost done and I'm sure it will taste delicious." She glanced toward the place Galia had been and lowered her voice to a whisper. "Don't listen to her. Well, listen to her — I don't mean we shouldn't try to please her, but the truth is . . ." She glanced toward the door once more. "You can't please her. Nothing you do will ever be right. So don't let it concern you." She smiled, then moved back to the kettles with the porridge. She had spoken too softly for even the other women to hear, and Hannah wondered if Dana would be the only one brave enough to show her kindness. Up until now, Hannah had not felt truly welcomed by anyone in her new home.

She bit her lip, fighting the urge to give in to tears. She was a grown, married woman after all. There were obligations that came with living in the home of her father-in-law, and she simply must get used to that fact.

But as the day continued, the atmosphere around her mother-in-law did not improve.

Elkanah left the field where his brothers tended their flocks to hunt for a tree he could chop into boards to make a stout door. His brother Tahath had offered to help, but his father could not spare any of the others. Refused to spare them was more the truth of it. It had taken half the morning to convince his father such a door was necessary.

How much had Hannah suffered in silence in the few weeks they had shared his room? Everything they said and did could be heard through the curtain, especially if someone was passing by or purposely chose to listen. He fisted his hands, frustrated with the whole situation. His room was much too small for the two of them. And what if a child were to soon come along? The house was bursting with too many people as it stood, and each new marriage had only made things worse.

"This looks like a good tree," Tahath said, stopping at a medium-sized oak. "Once we cut it down, we will have to cut and smooth the pieces and tie them together. I hope you don't think we can get this done in one day."

Elkanah glanced at his brother, then assessed the tree. "We can if we both work hard."

"Father expects me back in a few hours. I'm afraid most of the work will be up to you."

"Then I will work until dark." He grabbed his axe and swung at the base, landing a clean blow. Anger fueled his strength, and the tree fell faster than he had imagined.

"Perhaps you will finish today." Tahath patted Elkanah's shoulder. "What's eating at you, brother? Already weary of your new bride?" He laughed, but Elkanah did not join in.

"The problem is not Hannah and you know it. It's this household. It's Mother and Father and the way they treat her. It's a room that's too small with no privacy for a newlywed couple, and a young bride who has to deal with seven women who are all older than she is and look at her as though she knows nothing."

Tahath picked up his axe and began to shave the bark from the tree. "I won't argue with you there. But you've always known what they are like. And the house is too crowded. Why Father wants to keep it smaller than it needs to be makes no sense."

"Has anyone else besides me spoken to him about this? For all the good my requests have done, I'm ready to move out and build a place of my own." Elkanah stopped, surprising himself at the vehemence of his words. He had not even given this arrangement a chance. There was no need to rush off and change everything yet. Perhaps when the first babe came along.

"Amminadab tried talking to him about it before your wedding. Of course, he has the double portion, so for him there is no problem. He has plenty of room." Tahath scowled as he continued to work. "I personally think that Mother has been keeping Father from acting on your behalf. I don't think she ever got over your refusal to marry sooner — and someone of her choosing."

"Well, it was not her place to choose for me. She pushed beyond the mere polite suggestion." Elkanah grabbed a handful of sand and began to smooth the wood Tahath had cut. He would still need to cut leather straps to hold the wood together and make a strong latch, but his anger toward the situation continued to feed the speed of his work.

"You and I know that," Tahath said. "But our mother is rarely pleased unless she gets her way. You've known that your whole life, so it shouldn't surprise you."

Elkanah looked up at this brother, closest to him in age. They had always seen life from a similar perspective, something he could not say about his four other brothers. But then the others were not deep thinkers like Tahath. How often had they sat with the sheep under the stars and talked of God? Tahath shared Elkanah's curiosity about their Creator, as Hannah did.

"It doesn't surprise me, but it angers me," Elkanah admitted. "Hannah has been the girl I longed for since she danced one time at the feast in Shiloh. I watched the look of awe in her eyes, and I saw the way she worshiped Adonai. Any other woman Ima thought right for me never impressed me the same way."

"It sounds like you made the right choice. Give it time, brother. Hannah will fit in eventually and Mother will accept her — grudgingly, perhaps, but she will have no choice. She can't make you divorce Hannah, so she might as well learn to live with her." Tahath handed a long cutting of the log to Elkanah.

"Let's hope she agrees with you." Elkanah rubbed more sand over the wood, wondering if even a door would be enough to separate Hannah from so much antagonism in his father's household.

10

Hannah stood in the courtyard later that evening, watching the road. Elkanah had not arrived in time for the family meal, but sometimes the men stayed with the flocks. She knew this. Yet he had given no indication that this was his plan, so was his promise to make a door keeping him away so late?

Her shoulders ached with the tension as she worked the spindle and distaff in the growing dusk. She had never watched anything being made out of wood, but he would have to cut a tree to get the wood in the first place. She should have told him to take his time, that there was no rush. They had survived the curtain these past weeks — a few more days would not matter.

She peered again at the road, straining to see him coming her way. Footsteps behind her made her turn. Galia stood in the entryway, her eyes narrowed, her gaze moving from Hannah to the road.

"He has not come yet?"

Hannah shook her head. "Not yet."

"Humph." Galia stepped through the door and entered the courtyard. She took a seat on a bench opposite Hannah, closer to the courtyard gate. "Tahath said Elkanah was determined to finish making a door for his room. Ridiculous idea. The curtain is perfectly fine, some of my best weaving, and how does he think he's going to attach wood to the stone frame?" She looked at Hannah. "You put him up to this."

Hannah's stomach roiled, and she feared she would be sick against the accusation. Was this what her life was going to be like from now on? Would there be no living with this woman?

Oh Adonai, she's right. It's my fault. What if something has happened to him?

Fear crawled up her spine, a reminder of how she and every other woman in town had felt when they found Lital's body in the woods. They weren't safe. Not like they used to be. Though there had always been the threat of bandits and wild animals, this new fear for safety had remained at the fringes of her heart.

For months, during her wedding preparation and Meira's wedding celebration, she had been able to push the uneasiness aside. But now, as she sat alone with Elkanah's mother, it came to its ugly head. Whatever would she do if Elkanah died? Even if he were hurt, she would be to blame.

"We discussed a door," she said once her voice grew steady again. "I'm sure he will be here soon."

"You know nothing of the kind." Galia crossed her arms over her chest and stared at the road. Did she plan to sit with Hannah the entire night until Elkanah arrived?

Hannah couldn't leave now. She had intended to sit in the court until dawn if she had to. But to stay in Galia's presence . . . A sudden longing to run away, to run home to her mother and father, rushed through her.

"Are we working out here in the dark?" Dana carried a lantern and lit one of the torches that stood along the perimeter of the court, and Hannah released a relieved sigh.

"We are waiting for Elkanah," Galia said, her tone still curt.

"Oh, that. There is nothing to worry about. Tahath told me that Amminadab and Korah were helping him bring the door home. It was heavier than the two could carry, and you know Amminadab. Stronger than some of the oxen I've seen." Dana laughed, obviously trying to lighten the mood. She was married to Tahath, Elkanah's closest brother. No wonder Hannah felt such kinship with her.

Dana sat between Galia and Hannah. "They should be along shortly," she continued when no one else spoke. "I'm sure they are fine."

Galia muttered something Hannah could not hear, but when her gaze was on the road, Hannah exchanged a look with Dana. "Thank you," she mouthed.

Dana simply nodded and smiled and took up her own spindle and distaff. She worked with Hannah in relative silence except for an occasional grunt from Galia.

The moon rose higher until at last the women saw movement on the road ahead. Elkanah's father and brothers emerged from the house and headed down the road to meet the men. When Hannah at last heard the sound of Elkanah's voice, she wanted to sing, but instead she quietly set her spindle aside and rose quickly. Galia jumped up and ran ahead of her through the gate and down the road. Before Hannah could reach the bend in the road, Galia stood at Elkanah's side, plying him with questions, ignoring the heavy load he and his brothers carried.

Hannah caught his words as she walked closer to the group. "Mother, I am fine. You had no need to worry or fuss. It just took longer than I expected to make the leather straps for the latch."

"Enough, woman," Jeroham barked. "Stand back and let us get this into the house. We won't sleep until Elkanah hangs this thing, so step aside."

Hannah moved to the edge of the road, though Galia moved barely at all, receiving another scowling bark from Jeroham. Hannah sighed and turned to walk back toward the house. She would melt into the wall if she must until the door was in place and she could hide behind it with her husband. What she wouldn't give to move away from these women. Except for Dana, she would miss none of them.

Hannah touched the edge of the door as she passed through their room on her way to the fields. A month had passed since Galia's impassioned objection to Elkanah's door, but at last the woman seemed to have accepted the change. Though Hannah still struggled to accept Elkanah's household.

She stopped in the cooking rooms, deserted now since the morning meal had passed, picked up a basket from a shelf, and filled it with some leftover bread from the morning's baking, a round of soft goat cheese, and some choice dates recently picked. She would check the garden behind the house on her way to meet Elkanah to see if the cucumbers were ripe enough. Someday soon she would make a cucumber sauce for him to dip his bread in . . . if his mother would allow it.

She glanced about the large room filled with shelves and cooking utensils and even a large oven that vented to the outside for them to bake their bread. Elkanah's father had definitely amassed a good living. Surely he could grant more of it to his sons.

At the sound of footsteps, she snatched up the basket and hurried through the back door. She did not wish to face Galia and have her come up with some reason to stop Hannah from spending the day in the fields. Perhaps it would be better to wait until next time to visit the garden.

She slipped around a corner of the house and half ran toward the path Elkanah had taken earlier that day. Guilt filled her that she was abandoning her work, but it had been Elkanah's idea for her to join him, and she did bring her spindle and distaff.

She tucked the scarf tighter about her neck against the wind and continued her hurried walk, looking this way and that. When at last she could see the house in the distance and the fields just up ahead, she slowed her pace and released a long-held breath.

Elkanah stood and walked toward her, glancing behind him at the sheep eating among the grasses. She picked up her pace and ran into his arms.

"Well, this is a greeting I could get used to." He swung her around, basket and all.

She laughed. "And coming to see you is something I could get used to."

He set her on her feet and kissed her soundly, then took her face in his hands. "Do you know how much I love you?" He brushed his thumbs across her eyebrows down to her cheeks, then kissed her again.

"You have a nice way of showing it." She smiled up at him, wishing this moment could last forever.

He turned and walked her toward the sheep and the place where he had settled beneath a terebinth tree. "The others have split the flock and taken some of them elsewhere to graze. And three of my brothers are with my father, checking the olive groves."

Hannah smiled again, a feeling of ease settling over her. "The grape harvest and olive ingathering are two of my favorite harvests. I hope your mother will allow me to help," she said, watching his expression. "At my father's house, pressing the olives was always a time of celebration and joy."

"If my mother gives you any difficulty, you must tell me. I will speak with her. But," he said, gently taking her chin in his hand, "you also must try to ignore her slights."

"I try." Hannah sighed, sorry she had mentioned Galia at all. She did not want to ruin this moment. "Dana is teaching me not to let her words wound me. I think your sister-in-law may become a good friend."

He touched her arm. "I am glad. I have hoped that at least one of the women would befriend you." He glanced at the basket she held and rubbed his middle, which rumbled at that very moment. "Did you bring me something good?"

She chuckled at his hopeful, almost child-like expression, feeling a release of the tension that had built up for weeks. "I have bread and some cheese I made last week, and some of the dates we picked a few days ago. I would have brought more . . ."

"This is plenty." He lifted the cloth she had placed over the food and picked up the bread, broke it, and shared it with her.

"I wish I could come out here with you

always." She looked at him, courting a smile, hoping he did not think her ungrateful. "It is easier to pray and worship Adonai here than in a noisy household." She spoke truth, for she truly did miss walking in the fields behind her father's house, but felt a hint of guilt that she had used worship to cover her desire to complain.

"I too find it easier to pray here than I do even at the tabernacle when it is my turn to serve," he said, apparently unaware of her wistfulness. He reached for her hand. "And you may join me in the fields whenever you feel the need." He took the goat cheese, pulling off a small hunk and popping it into his mouth.

"You may find I am here every day." She touched his cheek, feeling the softness of his beard. "But of course, that would not be possible."

"No, I suppose it would not." He took her hand again and looked out over the sheep, silent for a moment. She knew he was mentally counting to make sure they were all there.

"Let us pray things improve at home and in Shiloh," she said.

"I have to take my turn there next month." He looked at her. "Do you want to come with me?"

She held his gaze, wide-eyed. "You can do that? But what would I do? And would it be safe?"

"It would be safe. I would check on you often, and when I cannot be near, you will stay with Hophni's wife. At night you would be with me."

She searched his gaze, memories of Lital flashing through her thoughts. "And Hophni's wife can be trusted?" How skeptical she sounded.

He nodded. "Raziela and Irit both detest their husbands' indiscretions. I have no fear for you if you are in either of their homes."

Relief filled her, and she threw her arms about his neck. "Yes, yes! I would love to go with you!" To be alone with her husband without fear of censure . . . What could be better?

He pulled her down beside him in the grasses, both of them gazing at the heavens. "In a month then. We will be together without strife."

Hannah simply leaned her head against his chest and sighed. This was a good day.

11

Elkanah held the reins of the donkey and walked beside Hannah as they made their way to Shiloh the following month. Several male cousins followed behind them, all of them of the Kohathite clan, taking their turn to serve at the tabernacle. Uneasiness crept through him that Hannah was the only woman among them, and more than once he had jerked awake in the night with the horrible thought that he would not be able to keep her safe from Hophni or Phinehas. Was he a complete fool to have suggested she come?

But his mother had been positively difficult with Hannah during their entire three months of marriage, and he was growing restless as to how to help the situation.

"Are you sorry to have me along, since your cousins did not bring their wives? Will they think it strange?" She stepped closer to him as she walked, having refused to ride the donkey, which carried their supplies.

"Of course not." He glanced at her. "My cousins may tease us for being newly wed, but that is the nature of men. They know the way it can be in our household, and most of them have small children who cannot come." He leaned in and kissed her nose. "Whereas we are still free to enjoy each other before you are too busy with our own children to be bothered with me."

"I look forward to that day," she said, touching his cheek. "But I could never grow tired of or bothered with you." She released a sigh and kicked a stone out of the path as they walked, and he wondered what thoughts went through her mind. "I truly want to help you," she said. "I want to be safe, but is the only way to do that to stay with the priests' wives? Surely the priests do not bother all of the serving women."

They had discussed her options and the duties she could perform during their month of preparation for the trip, but he had discarded most of them. He stroked his beard a moment, thinking.

"I don't suppose I can help you with your duties?" Her tone was hopeful, but by the look on her face, she knew the answer.

He shook his head. "But don't fear. I will make certain that Eli knows why you are there, and I am certain Raziela will appreciate your help with her four sons and infant daughter."

Hannah's hand moved to her middle, and he wondered for the briefest moment if she could already be expecting their first child. They'd been married long enough . . . but dare he ask her?

Her look held acceptance. "It is enough to be with you. I will be happy with whatever you decide," she said, taking his free hand. "If you would like me to lead the donkey for a while, I could give you a break."

He met her gaze. "It's fine. The donkey is not so stubborn, thankfully. He follows with the slightest tug of the reins."

She reached into the sack strapped to her side. "Then, if you don't mind, I will spin as we walk."

He always wondered how a woman could walk and work at the same time. Spinning always made him dizzy and took greater skill than he possessed. Give him an outdoor task or the carefully detailed duties of the tabernacle and he could handle it fine. Shearing the sheep he could do. Even combing the wool was something his mother had tasked him with when he was a young boy. But he could never get the spindle and distaff to work together. He chuckled. His mother had given up in frustration, which was fine with him, as it was considered woman's work, after all.

"What's so funny?"

He hadn't realized his thoughts had caused him to laugh outright. "I was just recalling the time as a boy that my mother tried to teach me to spin." He grinned. "Some tasks were just not made for my clumsy hands."

She looked at him sideways, a twinkle in her eye. "I'm fairly certain that a man who can handle the articles of silver and gold in the tabernacle and take such care with the sheep could learn something as simple as spinning." She laughed with him. "Unless that boy was trying to get away from his mother and out into the fields. Now, that I could understand."

How he loved the sound of her laughter. He could not wait for the day when she carried his child. How they would celebrate!

He glanced at her again. Was it possible? Already? But he looked away as heat flushed his face. It was not his place to ask her. When the time came, she would tell him. Until then, he would wait.

Hannah's heart skipped a beat as they approached Shiloh's gates. The city was set in a valley with mountains in the distance. Priestly and Levitical families from the sons of Aaron, along with other Shilonites and temple servants, lived and worked in the area surrounding the tabernacle, which took the center focus of not only the town but also the valley. A wide swath of empty land circled the tented tabernacle, the place where the Israelites camped every time they came to one of the prescribed feasts of the Lord.

They started down the hill toward the buildings where the Kohathites and other Levites lived when they came to serve, but Hannah stopped midway, her gaze taking it all in.

Elkanah halted the donkey and came up beside her. She could feel his gaze on her, and she smiled into his dark eyes. "Without the crowds with us, it is even more beautiful." A sigh escaped, and she let the spindle wind to a stop.

Elkanah gave her a curious look. "Even from a distance you see Adonai." Wonder filled his voice.

"Is it not grace that He called Israel to be His people and gave us the exact instructions to build this structure? Even from here it shines like gold in sunlight." She tucked the spindle and distaff into her leather sack and started walking again.

He fell into step with her. "I wish the beauty of the place carried to the people within its walls."

The reminder made her pause to look at him once more. She searched his furrowed brow, his concerned gaze. "Despite your assurances, you are worried, aren't you?"

Elkanah stroked his beard. "It is a husband's job to worry."

"I thought that job belonged to a mother."

His expression changed and a smile touched the corners of his mouth. "Fair enough. But sometimes a husband worries too. It is my job to protect you no matter where we are." He took her hand. "You will always be safe with me, beloved."

"There was never any doubt," she said.

They continued on and reached the housing for the Levites. Elkanah settled the donkey into the nearby stables, then found an open room for them to stay. Hannah set the things they had brought on a shelf and spread their pallets on the dirt floor.

"Come," Elkanah said once she had finished. He took her hand and led her across the compound. They entered the tent where the Levites took their meals.

She let her gaze take in the place. "Lital cooked here," she said softly, glancing his way. "Perhaps if I worked here, I could learn something from the women about her."

"No." His abrupt comment did not surprise her, despite its slight sting. She should have known he would be against her trying to find answers that the men had already attempted to discover. To continue asking, especially as a woman, could cause consequences, even dangerous ones.

She released a sigh and settled beside him to eat a light meal, then walked outside with him again as the sun began to set beyond the hills. The priests' homes with their gold-plated doorposts shone in the fading light.

"This is where Hophni lives." Elkanah spoke without inflection. "Phinehas lives next door." He pointed to the other elaborate home. "But your father would have pointed them out when you were here with him."

She nodded. "Yes. I remember how impressed I was."

"The priests are giving the evening sacrifice now, but Raziela will be here with their children. I will introduce you. You will like her better than Irit."

He knocked on the door before Hannah could ask why. She leaned close to his side without actually touching him. Her pulse quickened with the thought of meeting these women whom she had only seen from a distance in her youth, women who knew the rumors about their husbands and yet lived with the situation. They could not possibly approve.

The door opened and a servant ushered them into the waiting area. "We are here to see Raziela," Elkanah said. "I want her to meet my wife. She is here with me during my week of service."

The servant nodded and called a young boy, who appeared as though he'd been standing nearby. The boy bent with a water basin and washed their feet. Elkanah and Hannah waited in silence until at last they were ushered into a large sitting room. A woman dressed in fine robes and jeweled sandals strode like a queen into the room, a babe on her hip. The image seemed so out of place. Shouldn't a woman so wealthy have a servant caring for her child?

"Raziela, thank you for meeting with us." Elkanah nodded in her direction as though addressing someone of royal status, and for a moment Hannah wondered if he would bend his knee.

"Of course, Elkanah. You know you and your family are always welcome in our home." She smiled, and Hannah thought her one of the prettiest women she had ever seen. Why on earth would her husband be unfaithful to her?

"I want you to meet my wife, Hannah." He put his arm around her and pulled her closer to him, something he never did in public. "She came with me to serve you and perhaps serve some in the tabernacle while I am on duty there. She is also of Kohathite blood and could assist in certain responsibilities, but I thought perhaps she would enjoy spending time with you and your children first."

A wide smile spread over Raziela's face. "How very thoughtful of you!" She looked at Hannah, kindness twinkling in her dark eyes. She glanced at her daughter, who was swinging her head this way and that and bouncing on Raziela's hip. "I would love some help with this one." She smiled into her daughter's eyes. "She is a handful for everyone. The boys were easy in comparison to this little one."

Hannah felt an instant kinship with this woman, a desire to get to know her better. "I would be most happy to help you." She looked at Elkanah and squeezed his arm, then met Raziela's gaze. "When do we get started?"

12

Hannah woke early the following morning to help Elkanah dress in his Levitical garb. Together they went to the tents where the workers were fed, then to Raziela's house. The servant greeted Hannah, and Elkanah paused only a moment to take a glance about the house, then turned and promised to return for her before the evening meal.

Hannah watched him leave, her nerves on edge. She looked about the large sitting room, listening to the sounds of servants hustling here and there while she waited for Raziela. At last the woman appeared, this time without her daughter on her hip.

"Hannah, how good of you to come." She looked less elegant in her dress this morning, which put Hannah more at ease.

"It is my pleasure. I hope I can be of service to you." Hannah smiled as Raziela took a seat near her.

"Yes, with the children when they awaken.

The baby still keeps me up nights, so I let all of them sleep later than I should." Raziela stifled a yawn and released a deep sigh. "Besides seeing Hophni off to tend to the morning sacrifices, I have Eli to help as well. Ever since Eli's wife passed away, we often have him over for meals." She glanced at Hannah. "Irit and I take turns."

Hannah nodded, not sure what to say. "It must be hard for him to have lost his wife." She had heard rumors a few years ago, but not much was told of Eli's wife.

"Hila was a kind woman," Raziela said, her eyes taking on a distant expression. "But she doted too much on her sons." Her tone turned slightly irritated. "If she had insisted on more discipline, encouraged Eli not to look the other way . . ." She paused and glanced about her, then lowered her voice. "The truth is, it is not safe here for most women. Hila helped keep some of them safe, but . . . she couldn't help them all, and Eli did little more than tell his sons they should behave better. Hila did not push him to say more."

"Did Hila really have much influence over them? It would seem that Eli would be most responsible." Hannah studied her host, hoping the question was not beyond the bounds of propriety.

Raziela simply nodded her understanding without censure and waited as a servant brought them silver cups of herbal tea and small date cakes. She motioned for Hannah to eat, while she lifted the cup to her lips and drank. "You probably wonder the same thing about Irit and me." She looked at Hannah over the rim of her cup. "Why don't *we* exert influence to stop our husbands from sleeping with the women who serve at the tabernacle? Tell me you aren't thinking this."

"I wasn't thinking it exactly." Hannah set the cup aside and folded her hands in her lap. "I know what it is like to live in a household where you have no control. I rather doubt your husbands give you any choice in the matter." She drew in a breath and searched Raziela's gaze. "Tell me . . . are you in danger?" Were Hophni and Phinehas abusing their wives?

Raziela did not speak for a lengthy moment. "As long as we say nothing and give them what they ask when they ask for it, they treat us well." She looked beyond Hannah. "They lavish us with gifts and give us children, and we are well protected behind these walls."

Hannah glanced at the elaborate carvings on some of the walls and the intricate stonework that had gone into building this house. "Your home is beautiful." A moment later she had a sudden, horrifying thought. "Are you ever allowed to leave these rooms?" She studied Raziela, surprising herself at her boldness.

Raziela's gaze clouded. She touched a date cake but did not eat it. A child screamed from the back of the house, making both women jump.

Raziela settled back into the seat. "A servant will tend to him." Obviously she knew her children and her staff well. "We are allowed to leave to go to market with a servant — sometimes. But you have guessed correctly in that it is rare that we can leave these houses our husbands have built for us. If we did, we might come upon them with the other women or discover something they do not wish us to know. We hear the rumors from the servants, but there is nothing we can do. If we try . . . if we say anything or were to leave and walk about Shiloh without permission . . ." She did not finish the sentence, but Hannah could guess what would happen if she disobeyed her corrupt husband.

Raziela released a sigh. "I have said too much, and I barely know you."

"Your words are safe with me. You need

120

not fear." Hannah stood as Raziela did.

"Thank you," Raziela said. "I do not usually trust anyone with the truth unless they work for me. But you are a guest and a willing helper, so let us go and see what can be done today to fill the hours for both of us."

Hannah followed her down a hallway that led to the sleeping rooms and the place where a Levite tutored her boys. "If you are up to it," Raziela said, "I am working on a new weaving project to hang from the wall in our oldest son's room. I would enjoy working with someone to take turns with the warp and weft."

Hannah smiled. Weaving was something she enjoyed, though she had never thought to use such work on a wall hanging. She was used to weaving coats and tunics and rugs — practical items. But Raziela was used to more gold than Hannah could imagine. The wealthy lived in palaces that needed decorating. How much better it would be if that gold could be put to use to feed the poor or help the orphan or widow. But she would never say so.

Instead she took her place at Raziela's side and began the work.

The sun set over Shiloh in blazing colors, brilliant beauty after a tiring day. Elkanah took Hannah's hand and walked along the perimeter of the tabernacle's tented fence. Their week of service had gone so quickly, with only two days left.

"We'll be heading home soon," he said.

"Yes." Her tone held hesitance, and he sensed she dreaded the return to his father's house. "It's been a nice break from the normal routine."

He nodded. He did enjoy serving here. But he would not miss running into Hophni and Phinehas and seeing the smirks they gave him or hearing the comments about Hannah he would not repeat to her.

"Beautiful wife you have there, Kohathite. Seems like a man would leave such a woman behind to wait for him rather than expose her to so much debauchery." Phinehas had laughed long and hard at his own statement, and it was all Elkanah could do to keep from putting both hands about the man's thick throat and knocking some sense into a body bulging with meat from stolen sacrifices. But Hophni was standing near, and strong as he was, Elkanah was in no mood to take on both men.

"My wife has seen no debauchery in Hophni's home, I assure you. Nor in yours when you are not there." He met Phinehas's scowl with one of his own. "If you think this tabernacle is a place for debauchery, as you call it, then you do not deserve to be priest."

He'd turned then and stomped off before Phinehas could reply. While Phinehas might threaten to stop him from coming or threaten his sacrifices on feast days, Elkanah had had enough. He didn't care what they did. Besides, God would surely protect him.

"Your thoughts are deep tonight." Hannah's words interrupted his concerns, things he could not even share with her. There was no sense in troubling her with a situation that was not likely to come to pass.

"This place always gives me cause to worry," he said, squeezing her hand. "Phinehas and Hophni just get more vile every time I see them. If only Eli would stand up to them."

"Perhaps it is not as easy as it seems." She looked at him as the sun faded in the distance. The moon rose brighter and stars began to dot the heavens.

"Tell me what you mean." He faced her where they stood on the west side of the tabernacle. They still had to circle the tent to reach the housing for the Levites.

"It's just something Raziela said that first day. When Eli's wife was alive, Raziela said she doted too much on her sons, and even then Eli looked the other way when they started taking other women to their beds. He is so passive, and Hila did nothing to convince him to do something harsh, like go to his brother's family and offer the priesthood over to them."

"It's the least he could have done. He should have removed Hophni and Phinehas long ago. Those men were never fit to serve the Lord." Elkanah turned and started walking them toward their quarters. "I'm sorry. I did not mean for our last few nights here in the shadow of God's tabernacle to focus on them. But this place, despite my devotion to obey the Lord, always brings to mind the evil that goes on here, and I wish we could stop it." He paused. "I may have caused a problem with Phinehas today."

He halted his agitated walk. He hadn't planned to tell her, and now he was opening his mouth.

"What is it?" She cupped his face with her soft hand.

He sighed. "He made a worthless comment about me bringing you here, and I told him he didn't deserve to be priest."

Hannah gasped. "Oh Elkanah. Has it ever come to that before?"

He saw the lines form along her brow, the

worry in her eyes. "No. But I walked off before he could threaten me. If he even remembers our conversation the next time we have a sacrifice, I will deal with him then. But I suspect all of their threats are just showing off their own self-importance. They don't have the courage to refuse a man's sacrifice. Besides, it would mean less meat for them."

"But you are worried." She took both of his hands in hers and held tight.

He nodded. "Perhaps a little. But God will protect us. And Phinehas knew I spoke the truth. I wanted to choke the man for what he said. But at least I kept my hands at my sides."

"That's a good thing."

He laughed at her slight smile, then ran a hand over his beard. "I truly hope I haven't ruined things for us."

She shook her head. "I am sure you have not. I will speak to Irit of it tomorrow. Their wives may not have much sway over their husbands, but I have come to discover that they have their ways. If I make her or Raziela aware of the situation, I think they will find a way to make their men forget the whole thing." She bent forward and kissed his cheek. "Do not worry, my love. Phinehas does not deserve to be priest. I am

125

certain God will deal with him and Hophni. Speaking the truth was not wrong. Perhaps you are one of the only people with the courage to do so."

He looked at her for a lengthy moment, love for her surging within him. "How was I ever so blessed to have married you?"

She smiled, and he pulled her into his arms. "This place troubles me, yes, but I have far more worries that trouble me right now, my love." She kissed his cheek and he kissed the top of her head.

"Surely not," he said, his tone falsely aghast.

She nodded and looked up, wide-eyed. "Have you not realized it? In two days we return to your mother."

He pulled her closer. "You are right. That is a longer-standing worry, though at least it is far from evil."

"No, not evil. Just . . . trying." Hannah linked her hand with his as they headed to their quarters, and Elkanah turned over in his mind again how he could make their circumstances different.

13

One Year Later

Hannah walked with Dana toward the river, baskets of laundry atop their heads. How was it possible that she and Elkanah had been married well over a year and yet still she felt no stirring in her womb? She glanced at her sister-in-law, whose children were back at the house, watched over by the other women while Hannah and Dana had volunteered to head to the river.

"You're terribly quiet today," Dana said as the sound of the flowing water drew near. Trees stood along the shore and the grasses grew tallest before the slow decline toward the river's edge. The water moved at a gentler pace here, the perfect place to scrub the linens and let the water rinse the soap away.

Hannah glanced at the surroundings, taking in the scent of the nearby fir and oak trees mingling with that of the fresh water just over the ridge. "I'm enjoying the morning, I suppose. We so rarely get this chance to be away from the household and behold the beauty God has made."

Dana paused in her step and met Hannah's gaze. "This is true. And I know how much you love time to worship. You put the rest of us to shame." She said the words lightly, but Hannah felt the slightest sting.

"I'm sorry. I do not wish to make you feel less devoted than you all must think me to be. I just find it easier to pray away from the noise of the household." She almost revealed that she prayed for a child, but it seemed so obvious that she held her tongue.

"It is harder for you than it was for the rest of us. But I think Galia does not help things." Dana touched Hannah's arm, then turned to walk down the embankment toward the river. "These clothes will not wash themselves."

They knelt in the grass and took tunics and undergarments and even a few robes from the baskets, especially those of the children, who tended to drop food in their laps. Hannah took up the homemade soap and hyssop branch and scrubbed each one.

"I can wash the personal items," Dana said as Hannah scrubbed a small tunic, trying to hide the tears that streamed down her face. How she longed for such a tunic to belong to her own child! And the baby wraps and swaddling clothes. Her sister-in-law Kelila had borne another child during the year that Hannah waited.

"Thank you," Hannah managed, handing her the linens. The cool water would wash the blood away . . . along with her dreams. Every month it was the same. She knew Elkanah had to wonder what was taking so long, but he never asked.

"Are you worried?" Dana held the linens in the water, allowing the chilly liquid to soften the fabric.

Hannah met her friend's gaze. "I should be, shouldn't I? I mean, yes, I am, for Galia will not let me forget my duty. I feel her standing over my shoulder each month, adding to the feeling of failure I already have."

Dana nodded, then focused on the linens she was washing. At last she met Hannah's gaze once more. "I've asked Tahath to speak to his father and Elkanah. I think you need to move away."

Hannah felt as though something had pierced her insides, her thoughts whirling with the suggestion. She swallowed hard, fighting emotions of both hurt and relief. "You want me to leave?" Surely Dana did not think such things.

"Of course not! I don't want you to go anywhere but where you are, but I think that living with Galia is too hard for you. I wondered when you first married Elkanah — remember, he is twelve years older than you are." Dana pointed a finger at Hannah as if she were a child.

"I am well aware of how young I am compared to all of you." She didn't mean to sound harsh, but sometimes being the youngest woman felt awkward. It was as though no one took her seriously.

"I didn't mean it that way." Dana smiled. "How sensitive you can be sometimes! Now, don't get offended by my suggestion. I only thought that if our father-in-law would agree to let Elkanah and Tahath have a piece of property near the end of the barley field, they could build homes for us and we could both be away from the chaos. Even Jeroham realizes that the house is too small for the many babies that keep coming." She put a hand to her mouth. "Forgive me. You know I didn't mean anything against you. Your time will come. Perhaps it would come much sooner if you had more peace."

Dana grabbed the hyssop and put her full weight into scrubbing the linens as if chasing away the devil himself. Hannah laughed at the scowl she wore in her determined efforts.

"I think your idea is wonderful," Hannah said, laying one of the tunics on the branches to dry. "To live near each other but away from the others — at least *some* distance away — would be . . . well, wonderful!"

"Wonderful indeed." Dana smiled again. "I wish I could think of a better word, but that sums it up. Now we just have to convince our husbands to convince their father."

"Galia will not be pleased."

Dana nodded, her expression suddenly sober. "It won't be easy to convince anyone."

"No. It won't."

"But I think we should try. Agreed?"

Hannah smiled. "Definitely."

Elkanah walked the length of the barley field that bordered the far edge of his father's land. Three months had passed in negotiation with his father and brothers, but in the end he and Tahath had convinced Jeroham that his household needed to expand, and more houses some distance from the first were simply an extension of his home with a few fields in between.

Elkanah dug his staff into the soft earth, releasing a deep sigh. The land, a gift from a grateful Ephraimite, was larger than any Levite should expect, but it had been in the family for decades now and Elkanah knew his father's wealth was not to be taken for granted. The parcel he had requested was adequate for both his household, with room to grow, and Tahath's bulging home. The thought of his brother's success in this brought the sting of failure to his heart.

Dana had already birthed three sons and recently announced they were expecting another child, while he continued to wait and watch but was too timid to ask what every man wanted to know. *Does your womb grow life?* But he could not broach the subject. Instead, he endured his mother's quiet suggestions that his wife was barren, words that often came back to haunt him at night, especially when Hannah did not know that he heard her weeping.

"You know it is within your right to take another wife if your first wife is barren." Galia folded her arms and lifted her chin in that proud way she had. "I realize, of course, that Hannah's father made it impossible for you to send her away, but that doesn't stop you from adding another."

He stared at her, wondering why she

continually wanted to meddle in his business. "I have a wife, Mother, and I am not going to discuss this with you."

"You have a barren wife, my son."

"You do not know that."

At his scowl she had simply raised a brow and given him a look that made him feel like a child again. He had turned and walked away then, and he increased his pace now. He and Tahath would begin building soon, and the quicker the better. Hannah's problem was more likely his family's treatment of her, of them, than barrenness. He'd heard of women who could finally conceive once they were in quieter settings.

He could travel with her, visit Mount Moriah or some of the other landscapes in Israel's history. Moriah. Where Abraham had offered Isaac, who became a man of patient waiting. A man who prayed for his wife when her inability to conceive had gone on too long.

Had *he* prayed for Hannah? He stopped midstride and stroked his chin. The scent of ripening wheat wafted to him, and the sun had reached the midpoint in the sky. He glanced heavenward, shading his eyes.

Adonai, won't You please bless my Hannah with a son? You know how much we desire a child, Lord. Is there a sacrifice I can give, something I can do, to convince You to bless my beloved?

He paused, listening for some response — a whisper, a sense of peace. Nothing. Had God heard? Were such prayers only heard at the tabernacle?

A sudden feeling of fear hit him square in the gut. Had his words to Phinehas caused this? Corrupt or not, the man was a priest, and men and women were to respect priests. Even Levites needed to honor their leaders, whether or not they deserved such honor.

Should I offer a sacrifice? An apology to Phinehas?

He recoiled at the very idea, for he knew no apology was truly needed. He had spoken the truth. It might have been better if he had taken another Kohathite with him as witness, but as it stood, he knew his words had not been wrong. They had done no good, for there had been no change in the practice of either priest, but they were as true today as the day he had spoken them.

Perhaps a sacrifice was in order. The next time they went up to Shiloh for a feast, he would offer a special sacrifice in case of any unknown sin that might be keeping Hannah from bearing. Surely then God would listen and answer their prayers. Though he had never prayed so specifically for her until this

134

moment, he was fairly certain her walks alone behind the house at night were for that very purpose.

He continued moving, examining the area where they would build the stone houses. He stopped near the river, listening to the sound of the water meandering here, rushing over rocks there, on its way to the sea. Laughter caught his attention, and he glimpsed some women on the opposite bank, one older and one much younger.

"Peninnah, don't get so close to the edge. You know better," the older woman scolded. "You are almost a woman. Stop acting like a child."

Elkanah gripped his staff, not wanting to be noticed. He recognized Yafa and her spoiled daughter, who was by no means a woman yet. He shook his head. His mother was a friend of the irritable woman, and Elkanah had no use for women's gossip or manipulative ways. That daughter would make some man's life miserable someday.

He stepped slowly back and slipped behind the cover of bushes to make his way to the place where their house was to be built, considering just how to design the house to make it most pleasing to Hannah. He glanced heavenward, a sense of gratitude filling him.

Thank You, Adonai, for my Hannah. I would rather live with her barren all of my days than share my life with anyone my mother would have picked for me.

The words surprised him, for he definitely wanted sons. But he realized that it was Hannah who made his life meaningful. And despite his mother's good intentions, he would rather live with peace and no children than contention and a houseful of sons.

14

Six Months Later

"I hope you know what you are doing." Galia stood watching, arms crossed over her chest, as Elkanah and Hannah filled a cart with their few belongings. Dana and Tahath had already gone on ahead of them with no reprimand or comment from Galia. Why did her mother-in-law always make things so difficult?

"We aren't going very far, Ima," Elkanah said, using the more endearing word. "I'm sure you will find reasons to visit now and then." He gave his mother a smile, then looked Hannah's way.

"Of course you will be welcome," Hannah said. She smiled but knew her lips were taut. She turned to the cart and fussed with the bedding, though she had already folded and refolded it twice. "I think we are ready," she said, keeping her voice low.

Elkanah moved from the cart to hug his

mother, then waited as Hannah quickly did the same. He moved to take the donkey's reins, and Hannah hurried to catch up to him. They said nothing until the house was well behind them and his mother out of earshot.

"I can't believe we are actually getting to move!" The exuberance in her heart brought a true smile to her lips. "And to our own home."

He laughed, but a moment later he sobered. "I am sorry it took six months. Between tending the sheep and the crops and dragging the rocks from the river and the fields, it took far longer than I'd hoped."

She took his hand and kicked a stone in the path. "It matters little now, my love. We are at last going to be truly alone. Even occasional family visits cannot change that fact."

He ran a hand through his hair and held her gaze. "Except for the fact that Yafa lives across the river and is almost as annoying as my mother can be at times. I hope you do not have to endure too many visits from her on her way to see my mother."

"Or mine," Hannah said, chuckling. "Remember, they are all friends — when they are getting along."

"Well, Yafa has to get a handle on that

138

daughter of hers. She's going to make a miserable wife — like her mother — if they don't stop spoiling her." Elkanah patted the donkey's head. "In building the house, Tahath and I often heard the girl calling foolish things to us across the river."

Hannah pondered that Elkanah had taken so long to tell her this. She recalled when Peninnah had acted far too opinionated for a child of thirteen. "She is about fifteen or sixteen by now, is she not?"

Elkanah shrugged. "I didn't ask. You would know these things better than I. She is a child."

"She is much closer to being a woman — in fact, she is probably already considering marriage."

"Which is why I hope whoever marries her is ready for a spoiled wife." He smiled. "I am so glad you are nothing like that."

She blushed under the compliment. "Well, I will continue to try not to act like a child." She returned his smile.

"As for my mother . . ." He paused.

"Yes?"

"I know she annoys you."

"I can't imagine how you ever came to that conclusion."

They both laughed, but Elkanah soon sobered again. "We all know it is true. But I

139

don't honestly think my mother realizes how she acts, and truly, she doesn't mean to be unkind. I saw a very giving side of her in the years of my youth. I think she's just feeling less useful and is afraid of not being needed." He searched her face, his expression earnest, as though trying to convince her to believe the exact opposite of what she had experienced in the past two years. "Try not to think too ill of her?"

Hannah drew in a breath. She lifted a brow, giving him a curious look. "She has not been very kind to me since we wed, beloved. Forgive me if it's hard to find reasons to see her that way."

"But you can understand fear, yes?"

Why was he pushing so hard now that they were moving away from his mother?

She nodded. "Yes. I can understand fear."

"That's where her caustic tongue comes from, Hannah. She fears so many things. She fears I will never have a son. She fears growing old. Think about how she must have felt to give Meira away and replace her with daughters-in-law. Her sons don't show her the time or attention Meira used to. They simply don't have time with all the work of the household."

Hannah felt a sudden longing for her own mother and father. She hadn't seen them in weeks, months even. It wasn't a daughter's place to go home to her father's house once she married. Did Ima miss her as terribly as she missed them?

"I imagine being a mother is a hard thing from either perspective. Having a child and then having to give it up someday . . ." How could she possibly do such a thing? She touched her middle, where a babe should lie, and sighed. She could never do it. If God ever saw fit to give her a child, she would keep it close, boy or girl, all her days.

But of course, society's demands and the nature of growing up would not allow her to do as she thought now. She glanced at Elkanah, whose eyes had returned to the road. By God's grace, she would do what she must. She wanted to be a mother who stayed close to all of her children. Surely God understood that desire. Surely if she prayed, God would honor that request.

Hannah walked with Dana a few weeks later to the market in Ramathaim-zophim's town square. How good it felt to slip away from the daily routine and finally have the authority to bargain for or purchase her own items. She had worked hard weaving cloth in her spare time, and today she hoped and prayed to get a good price for it.

The streets were already filled with women and children, though she and Dana had hurried to arrive shortly after the sun had risen. Everyone loved it when caravans came from exotic places to ply their wares. The scent of camel dung and sweaty men mingled with that of the spices they carried from afar. Children squealed and ran in and around the merchants' booths, and Hannah kept her gaze trained on Dana's two youngest boys. The oldest had gone with Tahath to the fields, and Dana held the youngest, a girl, in her arms.

"Boys, do not wander ahead of us," Dana said, shifting the baby's weight to the other shoulder. "I should have tied her to my back." A sigh escaped, and one look into Dana's eyes revealed her weariness.

"Would you like me to hold her for a while?" The words carried a sudden wistful longing Hannah had not expected to feel. After all, she helped Dana with the children often. At Dana's willing nod, she smiled.

"Here, let me take my scarf and tie it so she can rest against you until she wants to eat again."

"I can use my scarf." Hannah blinked away the emotion that threatened, wishing for an intense moment that she could be the one to nurse the child. She pulled the scarf from her head, twisting it to fit into a type of sling. Dana placed the baby in the folds of the material and helped Hannah tie her securely in front of her.

The scent of baby skin wafted to her. *Oh Adonai, why do You withhold this blessing from me?*

She cuddled the child with one arm and carried the weaving basket in the other hand while Dana took hold of her sons. They should have taken the children to Galia, but neither one of them had the energy to make the extra trip.

The sounds of the market grew louder, the sights and smells filling their senses. Warm yeasty breads and pastries were piled in baskets spread out on tables in one booth. Pottery lined the floor of another. Several weavers' booths filled the area, along with the fishmongers at the far end and people selling fruits and vegetables and date wine in some of the other stands.

Merchants from the caravan pulled out jewels and perfumes and all manner of oils and lotions for smoothing the skin. "Do they think we live in kings' palaces?" Hannah asked, leaning close to Dana, who stood glancing over the variety of lavender oils and the heady frankincense.

"They are probably on their way north

and east to places that have kingdoms. Perhaps they hope they can sell some of them along the way."

"Perhaps." Hannah touched a sample of the lavender oil and held it to her nose.

"It is lovely, is it not?" The merchant noticed them and hurried over, arms flailing. "And such quality! You will not find anything as nice anywhere in Judah or Israel."

"I'm afraid a lowly Levite cannot afford such things," Hannah said before Dana could reply. She motioned Dana to follow and headed toward the closest weaver. "I'm sorry. I would love to have bought some of that oil, but I'm not sure what Elkanah would say." She gave Dana an apologetic look. "I need to see if I can sell these cloths."

The baby started fussing at that moment, so they took time to switch her to Dana's arms and covered her with the scarf so Dana could feed her as she walked about with the boys close beside her. At least the boys were obedient, unlike some of the cousins they no longer lived with.

Hannah left Dana at the edge of the tent and ducked her head into the weaver's booth. She pulled one of the pieces from her basket and showed it to the merchant, an older, semi-toothless woman.

"Uh-hum," the woman said, her smile revealing a wide gap. "Are there more?"

Hannah nodded. "I have four lengths done and one I'm still working on at home."

The woman ran her fingers over the smooth cloth, turned it over, held it to the light, and finally proclaimed it good. "I will pay you in trade if you will take it, as I do not deal in gold."

Hannah drew her lips taut, disappointed. She took the piece back and tucked it into the basket. "Perhaps I will see what the other merchants can offer." She had no need to trade cloth for cloth!

"My husband owns the pottery booth. My niece runs the vegetable booth. My sister sells many baked goods. And the oils you were admiring next door come from my cousin. When I said I deal in trade, I meant many things, my dear."

Hannah held the woman's gaze, her thoughts churning. She couldn't possibly trade for the lavender oil, but a piece of pottery or some of the special pastries for tonight's meal might be nice. But gold would help Elkanah with bigger purchases, such as adding on to their home or buying more sheep.

She shook her head. "Let me think about it." She hurried off before the woman could argue with her, though she did hear her huff and mutter as she left the tent. She glanced at Dana. "She only deals in trade."

"Ah, I see. Most of the merchants have taken to doing that as gold and silver are much harder to come by." How was it that Dana knew so much? Of course, she had been in the family far longer.

Hannah turned about and stepped back into the tent. She did like the woman, after all, and maybe they could strike a bargain.

"So you're back already."

"I have a question."

"Then ask it."

"Do you also deal in sheep and animals and other larger items?"

The woman looked her up and down. "I have a brother who owns many animals and is sometimes willing to part with a few. But their cost is far more than four pieces of cloth."

"What would it take to purchase an unblemished lamb?" She could simply ask Elkanah for one, but if she purchased it herself, maybe God would finally answer her prayers.

The woman held her gaze, unflinching. "You want this for something personal."

Hannah nodded but said nothing.

"Bring me a man's robe, and you can have

your lamb."

Hannah smiled. She could do that.

"In the meantime, are you going to sell me those four pieces or not?"

Hannah laughed as she picked out her items in trade. When she arrived at home and unpacked them, she found the woman had included a small sample of the lavender oil as well. This relationship was going to work out well.

15

Shavuot, the Feast of Weeks, had Elkanah's and Tahath's households in an uproar of ordered chaos. Elkanah dressed quickly and headed to the small stable he had added in the year since their move away from his parents' home, while Dana's children burst through the back door to the cooking room, where Hannah stood packing food for the trip.

"Are you ready, Aunt Hannah?" Adam, Dana's oldest, said. "Ima is asking if you can come and help her."

Hannah had been wise to pack their extra clothing and other necessary items the night before, for she sensed Dana would need an extra pair of hands this morning. Her heart soared with a sense of gladness, grateful that she had long ago finished the robe for the merchant and secured the unblemished lamb to take with them. Elkanah had given her a curious look when she told him of her plan but had not said anything to stop her, and he had helped her to care for the lamb since. He allowed her to keep it more as a pet rather than risk damaging or injuring it with the rest of the flock. The animal's nearness caused her heart to beat with anticipation and sorrow, for she had come to care for it, never expecting how much its loss would mean.

Please, Adonai, look on me with favor. How often had she prayed thus?

She forced her mind to the present, tucked the last of the dates and almonds into a sack, and handed them to the boy. "Take these to Uncle Elkanah to put in the donkey's sack. I will come and help your mother."

Adam rushed off to do her bidding, and Oved, Dana's middle son, led Hannah out the back door toward their home up the hill overlooking the river. She grabbed a handful of her skirt and lifted it so she could half run, half walk up the incline, trying to keep up with the boy. She arrived nearly breathless and followed him into the house.

"Aunt Hannah is here, Ima! I got her for you, just like you said to!" The child's shouts rang through the house and brought Dana from another room, baby girl in tow.

"Oved, don't shout in the house. How

many times have I told you to use a quiet voice when we are inside?" Dana sighed and blew a loose strand of hair from her eyes. "Thank you for coming." She met Hannah's gaze. "As usual, I am way behind, and we all need to leave soon or we won't make it to join the others on the road."

"What can I do?" Hannah glanced about the cooking room, and before Dana could answer, she grabbed empty goatskin sacks and began filling them with nuts from pottery urns sitting along one wall.

"Thank you. Yes. We need enough food gathered. If you will do that, I will finish stuffing their tunics in sacks, and we can get the utensils and load the cart."

"I will have this done in a few moments and be back to help you."

Dana nodded and turned toward the hall, her shoulders sagging. It was obvious that she was exhausted. Perhaps Tahath could find a maid to help her. Or Hannah could spend less time weaving and come to visit and help more often. Guilt nudged her that she had been so focused on her own needs that she had not taken Dana's into account. At least when they all lived under Galia's roof, there were many hands to help watch the children, cook the food, launder the clothes, clean the house, tend to the garden,

150

and even help their husbands with the harvests.

And there was always the need for spinning and weaving and either trading their work for pottery or going to her father or another merchant to purchase more when something broke. Hannah should have realized that moving Dana away from the larger family with so many children was not something she should have to handle alone.

She turned back to the food and finished tying the last of the goatskins, grabbed the three-pronged griddle and a few cooking utensils, and carried them out to Tahath's cart.

"Are we almost ready?" he asked her.

She nodded. "I'm going in to help Dana finish the rest." She rushed back inside but stopped short in the doorway of the children's room. Dana sat on the bed changing her daughter, tears streaming down her face.

Hannah approached and knelt at her side. "Whatever is wrong?" Had something happened? Was Tahath angry with her? Hannah could not imagine Elkanah's brother taking out his anger on his wife.

"I'm so tired," she said, her voice barely more than a whisper. "I can't get enough sleep because Lihi is always hungry. I never have food ready on time, and the boys are

151

becoming more unruly. They need to go off with their father, but Tahath says they are too young." She looked at Hannah. "I should never have moved. When we lived together, we had help."

"I will help you more. I've been selfishly working on weaving to earn money or items in trade, when all along you needed me. Forgive me." She touched Dana's arm. "When I finally have a family, perhaps our husbands can find us maids to help."

Dana laughed, a good-natured sound. "I will gladly help you in return when that time comes, but I doubt very much that our husbands will be able to afford maids."

Hannah shrugged. "Perhaps not." Dana was probably right. But there was some comfort in knowing that if Elkanah could not afford a maid, then he could not afford another wife, something she had begun to fear he might consider since a year had passed in this quiet place and still she had not conceived.

She shook her worrisome thoughts aside. "Have we gathered all we need?"

"Just grab that last basket" — Dana pointed to the far corner of the room — "and take it to Tahath. Then we can gather up the children and go."

Hannah nodded. *Gather up the children.*

How she wished those words could be her own.

Elkanah stood to the side of the bronze altar and watched as Hannah led the perfect lamb she had purchased to the priest, weeping as she went. She had wanted to do this on her own, bearing the full weight of her feeling of guilt for her apparent barrenness. But a part of him couldn't deny the kick in his gut that he should do more, should pray more for her, as Isaac had done for Rebekah. Had Isaac offered a sacrifice of his own? Had Rebekah?

The records of these details of their ancestors were lost to history, and no one was alive to ask. Still, shouldn't a husband take some responsibility in the pain his wife carried?

"The only way you will know if the problem lies solely with her is if you take another wife," his mother had said on the road to the feast.

He had walked away without a word in response, but he could not deny that her comments often haunted him. Three years of marriage and still no sign of a child. *Must I wait as my ancestors waited, Lord?*

The line ahead of Hannah shortened, and as Hophni approached with the blade and

Phinehas carried the bronze bowl, Elkanah moved ahead, spurred by a sense of duty and guilt of his own. In a moment he was at her side, just in time to cover her hands with his as Hophni slit the lamb's throat.

"May the Lord grant what you require of Him," Hophni said, but Phinehas interrupted by tipping the bowl so part of the blood poured onto the ground.

"What are you doing?" Hophni demanded, looking squarely at his brother. "You have to pour the blood on the altar."

Phinehas shrugged, but the look he gave Elkanah held a smirk. "That's right. I'm sorry, brother. I suppose this sacrifice is ruined now." He dumped the rest of the blood on the ground.

Hophni stared after Phinehas's retreating back as he went to the basins to wash off the blood. He looked at Elkanah, who could barely hold his anger in check. The look of horror and despair on Hannah's face heated his belly with fire. But he could not react or lash out at these men. Not here. Not now.

"I'm sorry, Elkanah," Hophni said. "It appears your sacrifice cannot be accepted." He seemed genuinely sorry, but Elkanah did not trust the gleam in his eyes.

"Offer it anyway. The blood has been shed, there can still be forgiveness." Elkanah stepped closer to the priest, his hand still clinging to Hannah's.

"I don't know . . ." He glanced back at his brother.

"I will take the matter to your father if you do not." Elkanah clenched one fist lest he lose control and grab the priest by the threads of his ephod.

Hophni laughed outright. "My father will do nothing." He glanced at the lamb, lying now in its pool of blood. "But I will say he hates to see a good animal go to waste." He looked up, meeting Elkanah's gaze. "All right. I will offer it after I take the portions for the priests."

"Burn the fat first. You know the law."

"And I'm choosing to do this my way. Either that or we toss the carcass to the carrion birds." Hophni's smile was calculating.

Hannah leaned against him as though she might faint.

"Just offer the sacrifice," Elkanah said at last, fearing Hannah would be sick on top of this awful travesty.

"I thought you'd see it my way." Hophni picked up the lamb and carried it off to the side, where he cut up the parts, took what was meant for the Lord, and had the serving women carry them off to his own house. The less desirable pieces he lifted in his hands and tossed on the fire. Smoke rose, but it did not have the sweet aroma of the fat burning off, nor did Elkanah have the knowledge that the blood, now slick on the ground, had been accepted.

Oh Adonai, what have I done? I should have known. Didn't I know Phinehas holds a grudge?

This was his fault, and even when he put his arm around Hannah as she wept, he felt no comfort in his prayer, because he knew there was no undoing his own foolish need to protect her. He should have allowed her to make the sacrifice alone.

Please answer her prayer regardless of the priests' cruelty. Surely a corrupt priest's curse would not carry weight with the Almighty against the righteous. *Please, Adonai.*

But if God was listening, Elkanah could not hear Him past the anger brewing inside him.

16

Four Years Later

Hannah bent over her personal linens and scrubbed them in the river, a ritual that had grown so common she wondered that there were still tears left within her. And yet the tears fell like rain, dripping into the river and slipping downstream, along with every last vestige of hope. She had come when Dana was busy with the evening's baking, promising her that she would wash the clothes from Dana's household as well. Dana's large household. Would the woman ever stop bearing? Three sons and one daughter had grown to four sons and two daughters in the years since Hannah's failed sacrifice.

Elkanah had offered other lambs from his own flocks, but the priests could not be trusted. He'd even offered to build a personal altar, but that felt like idolatry to her. Their forefathers who built altars hadn't had the tabernacle or the priesthood or even the law, and Hannah could not bear to go against what she knew was right.

She brushed more tears away, taking time to wipe her face with a piece of linen. Seven years. She had been married seven years with no sign of a child. And Galia's suggestions that Elkanah take another wife had only increased. On their last visit, Galia had not even bothered to wait until Hannah had left the room, as she usually did.

"You both know that Elkanah needs sons." Galia's words seemed aimed at Hannah, and she could not look away from the pleading in her mother-in-law's eyes. "And the only way for that to happen is to let him take another wife."

"Mother, this is not your decision," Elkanah said, taking Hannah's arm and ushering her toward the door.

"Yafa's daughter Peninnah is the perfect age and would make a fine wife for you. And with Yafa recently widowed, you would be doing her a favor."

"I'm not marrying Peninnah, Mother. And you are upsetting Hannah." Elkanah gave his mother a stern look, even glanced at his father long enough to make the man speak up.

"Elkanah is right, Galia. You need to stop

meddling," Jeroham said.

"And you need to start!" Galia raised both arms and flailed them like she was swiping at flying birds or insects, but it was just her way of making a scene. "You need to speak to your son and talk sense into him. Adonai knows, blessed be He, that I have no say in anything. Elkanah listens to Hannah, and *she* certainly isn't helping him make a wise decision."

The memory of the conversation brought another onslaught of silent tears. Hannah draped a tunic over tree branches, then collapsed to her knees, longing to bury her face in the dirt and stones at the water's edge. If only she could make the Almighty see her pain, convince Him to act on her behalf, *remember* her as He had Rachel of long ago.

She should never have married.

Oh Adonai, I do not want to share him with another woman. She groaned inwardly as she rose, grabbed another tunic, and let her gaze travel the distance across the river and up the hill. Peninnah's house was not visible with the trees blocking the view, but she knew it was close. How often had she seen the woman — one who could have already married — and her mother sharing this task that Hannah should be sharing with Dana even now?

159

Peninnah had grown into a comely girl. Five years Hannah's junior and seventeen years younger than Elkanah. Now at twenty-one, she had plenty of years to bear ahead of her if she married soon.

"But I'm not so old that I cannot still bear!" She jumped at the sound of her own voice, surprised she had spoken aloud. She was only twenty-six. Why did everyone think she was without hope?

Oh Adonai, please! Did God hear a woman's anguished cries? If He did, she had seen no miracles, no answers in all the years she had asked for them. And she had lost the hope that He was even listening.

I don't understand You, Adonai. I have loved You and prayed to You and tried to obey You all of my life. I was an obedient daughter, and even when Galia speaks unkindly to me, I have tried to honor her as You command. What possible reason could You have for withholding a child from me, from Elkanah?

Was the fault truly just hers? As Galia had continually pointed out, the only way to know was to let Elkanah take another wife.

Her stomach knotted and a feeling of nausea rose within her. She pushed hard against her middle, praying she would not be sick. She glanced again in the direction of Peninnah's home, thinking perhaps if she

160

talked to the girl, she might find her more acceptable. And it would be helpful to Yafa to find a husband for her daughter. A man who could care for her also since her husband's passing the year before.

But every time she even considered the thought of the sharp-tongued, opinionated Peninnah, whose words had been too harsh for one so young — and worse, the thought of sharing Elkanah with her, with anyone — it was too much. She did not want to know that the blame of barrenness lay squarely with her. She did not want to know the truth that she already felt clawing its way to a place of acceptance in her heart.

I wish I had never been born.

She looked again at the river. What purpose did her life hold if not to bear children? What worth did she have if she could not do this one simple thing?

She scrubbed harder on one of the spots on a child's robe and shoved the thoughts and feelings deeper inside her. She couldn't lie down in the river or jump off a high cliff or wander the hills until a wild animal found her and took her life. And she couldn't refuse Elkanah's need for a son forever.

Oh Adonai, what am I supposed to do?

Elkanah sat on the hillside not far from the

161

home he shared with Hannah, keeping a sharp eye on the sheep. Tahath had taken a hundred of them to another pasture, and for a time Elkanah missed his company. His brother's chatter helped him to think about anything and nothing and was especially good at blocking the one overriding thought that he could not shake from his mind.

Now, sitting alone with the sheep grazing in the distance, he could think of nothing but the dilemma he faced. Seven years was a long time to wait for a child, wasn't it? His mother claimed it was. But even the prophet Samson had not been born in the early years of his parents' marriage. Perhaps God had a reason for withholding this blessing from Hannah, from him.

His mind whirled, recalling all of the drama his ancestors had faced when they added another wife. Hagar had given Sarah trouble. Of course Leah was Rachel's bane for years. Could he not be like Isaac and just patiently wait?

Is there something wrong with waiting, Lord?

He looked up at the sound of someone whistling, heading his direction. His father. The closer Jeroham drew, the more distinct and familiar the whistle. What now?

He stood to greet the man and gave him a steady look. "Has something happened?"

His father rarely left the fields to check up on his sons, so there must be a greater reason.

Jeroham settled among the grasses and motioned for Elkanah to do the same. "Sit, Elkanah. Is there something wrong with a father wanting to talk with his son?"

Elkanah raised a brow. "Of course not. But my father rarely does so."

Jeroham chuckled. "Then I suppose it's time he did."

A sense of foreboding rose within him, and Elkanah had the wild urge to get up and run. But he couldn't exactly leave the sheep or his father. He wasn't a child, after all.

"Well then," he said after a lengthy moment, "tell me what you came to say."

Jeroham glanced at Elkanah but couldn't hold his gaze. He stared out toward the sheep instead. "I want you to know from the start that if you are against this, I won't fight you. Your mother has it in her head that you need to hurry up and have children, whereas I can't imagine why she's so worried. It's not like we don't have a houseful of grandchildren to keep her busy. Except for Tahath's children, of course."

"Of course." It had been a source of contention between all of them when Elkanah convinced Tahath to move with him. There was no sense in revisiting that sensitive topic.

"But I can't say your mother's ideas are completely without merit, my son. She has been known to be right at times, and when it comes to women's issues, she seems to have a sense about these things." The awkwardness his father must have felt was evident in his halted speech and the way he kept twisting his hands in the belt of his robe.

"From the beginning God gave one man to one woman, and every story I have heard of my ancestors breaking that initial plan ended in frustration." Elkanah ran a hand through his beard, then along the back of his neck, almost causing his turban to turn askew. "I love Hannah, Father. I don't want to marry anyone else."

"Your mother seems to feel an obligation of some kind to Yafa." Jeroham held Elkanah's gaze this time. "You know they've been friends all of their lives, nearly sisters, and when Yafa lost Assir, your mother promised to do what she could to help her."

"Then let her help. But my mother's promise does not include me." The old anger simmered near the surface. "There are many men in the town, and Peninnah deserves to marry a man who will make her his only wife."

"Your mother tells me that Peninnah wants you — even if she has to be a second wife to you."

Elkanah stared, dumbstruck by this news. "Peninnah is a child. She has been spoiled her entire life and has no idea what it means to share a husband. She doesn't even know me, so why would she say she wants me?"

Jeroham shrugged. "It is what your mother tells me. What do I know of it? I only know that it would make your mother happy." He lifted his hands in entreaty.

"While making me miserable and Hannah impossibly sad. Do you not see how hard it is for Hannah right now? Every time we visit, Mother manages to toss a barb her way and make her feel like she has failed the entire family because she is barren." Elkanah paused, clenching and unclenching his fists. "What does my mother's happiness have to do with this, Father? Peninnah would not be living under her roof. I cannot afford to build the girl her own house, and I am certainly not going to bring her into the home I built for Hannah."

"I will see to it that you have the materials you need to build Peninnah a home of her own."

The words felt like a knife to his gut. "So you are taking my mother's side when you told me it was my decision? Why are you doing this? Why is no one willing to let me wait? I am not so old that I will never bear children. If Hannah still cannot bear after we've been married twenty years, then perhaps God will give us an answer as He did for Isaac." Elkanah stood and paced the ground between his father and an ancient oak tree.

"Peninnah will be too old in thirteen more years. She needs to wed now."

"Then tell Yafa to find her another husband."

"She wants you."

Elkanah stopped, the reminder another kick to his gut. "I don't care. I don't want her."

"Apparently Peninnah assumes that you will treat her as you do Hannah." Jeroham shrugged.

Elkanah gave his father a hard look. "Perhaps she is simply jealous and thinks she can take what Hannah has."

But that very thought was ludicrous. Even if he thought to look for a second wife, Peninnah would not be the girl of his choosing.

This was simply not happening.

"I could never love any woman like I do

Hannah, Father, and I don't want to discuss this again." But he felt his resolve slipping the slightest as he held his father's gaze. "I can't do it, Father."

"You might never have sons with Hannah. Is that really what you want — to die childless?"

"We don't know the future."

"But it's fairly obvious that God's blessing is not on your union."

Elkanah felt as though his father had slapped him. He had waited for Hannah to grow to adulthood. He had loved her devotion to Adonai. How could God not bless a union that was centered on Him?

But was it true? He and Hannah loved and worshiped God together. They prayed together sometimes. They shared the same faith.

Yet God had withheld children. Despite their many prayers. Did that mean their marriage was cursed, as Phinehas had seemed to imply in his refusal to accept Hannah's sacrifice?

He looked at his father, but no words would come. He turned on his heel and walked off.

17

Hannah placed the bowl of stew between her and Elkanah and handed a loaf of bread to him. They had taken to eating meals alone several days a week rather than join the other family members. It had given Hannah a huge sense of relief to be free of the looks, the insinuations, the pointed suggestions, even the not-so-subtle comments that she really ought to consider Elkanah's future. But what of her future?

Elkanah broke the bread and blessed it and handed a piece to her, then motioned for her to dip hers first in the stew. She complied only because she knew he would insist, despite the fact that every other woman in his family would have served him, served all of the men, before the women and children.

She ate the morsel, watching as he did the same. "What do you think?" she asked once she had swallowed with a drink of new wine.

The pressing from the first harvest of grapes had not yet fermented, but it had the sweetest flavor, and both she and Elkanah could not resist drinking some before it turned from juice to wine.

"I think it is your best lentil stew yet." He smiled and dipped another piece of bread into the mix of lentils and vegetables. They had cheese and oil to add to their meal, but meat was saved for times when they were celebrating or sharing their food with guests. He broke another large piece of bread for her, and together they ate in silence, with only the sound of insects thrumming outside the open window.

"You stayed late with the sheep tonight," she said, wondering why he had not returned to her sooner. She had spent the day washing clothes at the river while the stew simmered over a low fire, with one of Dana's children keeping watch and stirring it now and then. She had said a prayer of thanks that the child had not allowed it to burn.

"I had a visit from my father, and I wasn't ready to come home once he left." Elkanah's brow furrowed, and she saw the strain in his eyes.

"You were not pleased with whatever he had to say." She looked at him, longed to go to him and wipe the lines of anxiety from his forehead, but she sat and waited.

He wiped his hands on a linen cloth and cradled the clay cup. "We need to talk." He held her gaze. "But let us put the food away so the mice don't eat what's left. Then we will walk together under the stars."

Hannah's stomach twisted into a tight knot. She rose and quickly took care of the leftover food, while Elkanah dumped the crumbs from the linen cloth outside, away from any scurrying animals that sometimes could sneak into cracks or spaces in the walls.

"Thank you for helping," she said, taking the linen from him and placing it once more on the low table. She brushed the wrinkles from her tunic, grabbed her robe from a peg near the door, and followed Elkanah into the cool night air.

He took her hand and they walked in silence the opposite direction of Dana's house, toward the river where she had spent most of the day. They stopped shy of the water in an open field where the stars were brightest. Hannah's heart thumped with every step, fearing, knowing, fearing again.

She could no longer stand the silence. "Why did your father come to see you?"

He stopped walking and turned to face

170

her, taking both of her hands in his. "He wants me to consider my mother's suggestion that I marry Yafa's daughter, Peninnah." The Adam's apple moved in his neck. Moonlight bathed his face, and he looked up at the heavens as though seeking answers from the stars.

She followed his gaze to gasp at the night's brilliance. Was God watching over them through the window of the heavens? Could He hear her heart sinking, feel the emotion she fought to keep in check?

"I don't want to marry her." His comment made her look at him. She swallowed hard. "I told my father I have you. You are the only one I want, Hannah."

Tears stung despite her grand effort to hold them back. She blinked, but they would not abate. He moved his thumb to catch one that hit her cheek, then pulled her into his arms. The action broke through the wall of hurt and frustration, and she wept, dampening his robe with her tears.

He stroked her back and held her until her tears were spent. "I'm sorry for the way my family has treated you, beloved. I'm sorry I have not been able to give you a son."

She held up a hand. "You and I both know that it is God who gives life. For whatever reason, one known only to Him, He has

171

decided to close my womb." She looked away from him, then studied her feet, so close to his.

"I wish it were not so," he said just above a whisper.

So he accepted the truth she had been denying for years. The fault lay with her.

"I am still glad we married. I never want to disappoint you, Hannah."

She looked into his anguished face. Compassion filled her, and she placed one hand on his bearded cheek. "You could never disappoint me."

Silence followed her words, a pause loaded with feelings she could see in his eyes. She let her hand fall away as he looked beyond her.

He turned slightly away from her, and she wanted to pull him back but for the invisible wall and the sluggishness that had overtaken her limbs.

Please, Elkanah, look at me. Talk to me. She glanced heavenward, but no prayers would come.

"Even if I took another wife?" He spoke so softly she almost missed the words. He turned and faced her once more, took her hands in his. "Even if I added a secondary wife to our home?" The repeated question hung between them as though suspended on weighty clouds.

"You mean even if you married Peninnah?" She would not let him use "wife" as though it was a thing and not a person.

Name her. Let me hear you say you want to marry her. But she did not beg him for such a thing. She could not fault him for doing what any man in his position would do. Truth be told, Peninnah's own father could have married another woman long ago — one who would have given him sons instead of only one daughter. It was the way of things, even if it wasn't the way God intended them.

And then a sudden thought occurred to her. "What if Peninnah cannot bear you a son? What if she only has daughters or dies in childbirth? Will you take another wife then too?" Her tears came again, and the helpless look in his eyes told her she was pushing too far. "I'm sorry." She brushed away the tears with her fingers. "I don't want to share you."

His expression softened. "Nor I you. And I don't want you to share me with anyone, beloved. I do not want to marry Peninnah. But I don't want to look for anyone else either. I am the one who wants to wait like Isaac did, even if it takes twenty years."

"But your mother and father are anxious

173

for you to father children, and you are tired of disappointing them?" She hated the way the words sounded so bitter, like her life.

He ran a hand through his hair and released a deep sigh. "I don't know what to do, Hannah. This is why I wanted to talk to you. I want us to be happy. But every month that you don't conceive, I know you weep in silence. Don't think me so callous that I don't see. At first I thought my mother was the problem, that living under her roof was causing you to worry too much, but even here, alone, nothing has changed. You can't give me a child."

"I know." They were repeating the same tired words again, and Hannah had no answers anymore. "We've already established that fact."

He looked at her so intensely with such love that she wanted to break down and weep again, but she stiffened her back and held his gaze, hoping he could see that she shared his love.

"I could purchase a slave woman for you like Leah and Rachel had — her child would be yours." His face lit, his idea so full of hope.

"And where do you expect to buy a slave? Would you go outside of Israel as Abraham did when they acquired Hagar? And don't forget that Laban gave those women to Rachel and Leah. We don't even know where they originally came from. Maybe they were related. Maybe they were of another culture. But we cannot say they were of Israel because there was no Israel at that time." Her words were rushed, and she did not understand why she was trying to knock down his solution. It made better sense for him to take a maid of hers to wife than to marry a woman who would have full rights as a second wife.

"So you're telling me I should marry Peninnah, that you would be equal and her children would not be your children? Is that really what you want, Hannah?" He released her hand and rubbed his neck as though trying to ward off a headache.

"No. I don't want it." She drew a deep breath and begged her racing heart to slow. "But I don't want you to have a slave wife either." She looked away. "I don't know what I want. But if you marry Peninnah, you must promise me that she will always remain second to me. She cannot claim the right of firstborn if I should ever have a child. And I will not share the same house with her." She lowered her tense shoulders and faced him again.

He stroked his beard, his look thoughtful.

"Jacob did not bless Reuben more than Joseph. Rachel's son got the double portion. But the law protects the firstborn, no matter which wife bears it."

"Then I ask too much." She looked at her feet. "You cannot break the law."

"Jacob set the precedent. If Peninnah's firstborn is not worthy, as Reuben was not . . ." He let his words trail off. "Beloved, I would give you anything. I would keep Peninnah in a house far from you. Her children would never usurp the rights of yours." He placed a hand on her shoulder.

She looked into his eyes and could not stop hers from brimming with tears again. "We need not worry about it now. Perhaps Peninnah will also be barren." Though she knew it was not a kind thing to hope for.

"Whatever happens, I will make sure Peninnah's children do not have more rights than yours," he said. "But I'm still so uncertain . . ."

"As am I, but it seems as though you have little choice if you are to honor your parents' wishes." Emotion nearly closed her throat, but she swallowed it back.

"We always have a choice, beloved. And it is you and God I want to please, not them."

"But I want you to have sons."

"There is no guarantee even Peninnah will

bear them."

"I know. And then you will have two barren women to contend with." She half smiled. "If she dies in childbirth, I will raise her child. Make sure her mother cannot reclaim him. She will be your wife, he will be your son. I will care for him if anything happens to her."

He nodded. "I will do whatever you say."

For a heady moment she almost felt a strange power over the situation. But the brief feeling didn't last as she realized power and control were illusions. She could no more stop this marriage than she could produce a child or make her mother-in-law stand up for her. She just prayed Peninnah would be agreeable and not contentious.

18

Six Months Later

Elkanah stood at the door to Hannah's house as men began to gather in the courtyard. His back to them, he faced Hannah, an exceeding sense of sorrow filling him. "Are you sure you will not come?"

Hannah crossed her arms over her chest as though warding off a chill. "I would be in the way. This is Peninnah's wedding at her mother's house. Do you really think they want your first wife among the attendants?"

He sighed, something he did often of late. "They would have no say in the matter. You belong to me, and it is my decision what becomes of this wedding." He said it to make it so, but by her skeptical look, he knew he was simply trying to convince her without good cause. Everyone knew that women handled the wedding details. Men simply acquiesced to their desires.

"You know it is the bride's day. Do you truly want to take this from her? To have her ever aware of your other wife when she is longing for her time alone with you?" She shook her head. "No, beloved. It was not an easy decision to make, but I am at peace with it." She drew in a breath and let her arms fall to her sides. "Now go, or you will be late."

He nodded, then stepped closer and gently kissed her. "You know I will be gone a week."

"I know."

He caught the hint of sorrow in her eyes and wanted in that moment to undo everything that had already been set in motion.

"Don't worry about me, Elkanah. I have Dana and her family and plenty to do here. It is time I got used to living alone . . . at least part of the time." She glanced past him. "Tahath is waiting for you."

"You will not live alone nearly as much as you think, my love. I will be here so often you will want to be rid of me." He said it to coax a smile, but her smile was sad, making him wish he could retract the words.

"I will miss you," she said softly. "Do not let her make you forget me." Her smile widened a little, and she stepped closer to touch his shoulder. "It will work out, Elkanah. You know we cannot stop it now. Perhaps this was the way God intended it."

"I would like to agree with you, but somehow I do not think so." God had never condoned polygamy, though their forefathers had practiced it.

Please, Adonai, don't let my family end up as contentious as my forefathers.

"I love you," he said, backing away from her.

"And I you." She smiled again as he moved into the courtyard and joined his brothers and the men of the town who would accompany him to Peninnah's mother's house.

They jostled him and laughed as though he were a new groom, heading down to the river and over the stone bridge they had built to more easily access Yafa's home. In the distance, he could see the lights ablaze in the courtyard and the house whitewashed and shining like freshly washed wool.

The crowd pushed him on, though his feet felt weighted and his heart along with them. The house drew nearer, and the virgins emerged carrying torches and singing songs of the bride's beauty. Elkanah's heart kicked over. He could never believe Peninnah nearly as beautiful as Hannah.

Oh Adonai, am I doing the right thing?

180

But he knew no answer would come, either to his mind or to his heart. He had made his choice, whether wise or foolish, and he would have to live with it now.

"Are you all right?" Tahath whispered, leaning close as they were nearly to the courtyard. "You look whiter than mountain snow."

Elkanah met his brother's concerned gaze. "I have never wanted anyone other than Hannah."

Tahath placed a hand on his shoulder. "You are nervous. That is all. Trust me when I say this will be better in the long term. You will have your sons and our parents will be appeased."

"While Hannah bears the brunt of all that is wrong with this situation?" His brows dipped in a disapproving scowl.

"Hannah will adjust. And you know you can choose which wife to spend the most time with. Once Peninnah conceives, your duty to her is done, so you can go and live with Hannah." Tahath shrugged as if the whole thing was simple.

"You know things are never as easy as that." He glanced at Tahath, then looked at the noisy crowd.

Tahath gave a slight nod, but before he could respond, the women noticed Elkanah

181

and shouts of the groom's arrival filled the air. He was ushered quickly into the house, knelt with his gifts at the bride's feet, and sat with her on the wedding dais as the rest of the guests presented the bride with jewels and all manner of utensils and linens. One guest even gave her a goat, which caused him to force back a chuckle. One goat alone could not produce milk unless it mated and birthed a kid. But she could mate it with one from his flock. Perhaps that was the intent. To symbolize the joining together and the hope of producing, which had gotten him into this situation in the first place.

"Welcome, my son," Yafa said once the feast was under way and she could pull away from the guests. "I trust you are enjoying the food and wine." Her smile quivered the slightest bit. "I wish my Assir had been here to witness this day." She gazed at Peninnah. "My child, may you bring much joy to this man's house and many children to rest on his knee."

"Thank you, Ima," Peninnah said, her cheeks growing pink just above the veil. She turned to glance Elkanah's way. "I hope I please you."

It was Elkanah's turn to feel heat crawl up his neck.

They had signed the ketubah at the betrothal six months before, but now the feast would last a week, and soon he would take Peninnah to the marriage tent. How would he possibly not think of Hannah while he held Peninnah in his arms?

"I am sure you will please me," he said, knowing that the only thing he truly hoped for was that the girl was pleasant to Hannah.

Peninnah seemed not to notice that he meant anything other than what was said. She took a fresh fig from the tray passed to them and broke it apart, sharing some with him. The fruit was not nearly as sweet as the date he had shared with Hannah . . .

Would he never stop the comparisons?

A sigh lifted his chest. Peninnah noticed and looked at him, her expression clearly troubled. "Does something displease you, my lord?"

He shook his head. "No. Nothing." *What a liar you are, Elkanah.*

She nodded and smiled. "I am honored to join your family," she said above the cacophony of voices coming from men and women milling about the room and throughout the house. "I hope your first wife will accept me, as I know you love her. I know you are a man of integrity, and I watch the way you treat her. I hope I can expect the same . . ."

Her voice trailed off, and her cheeks turned an even deeper shade of pink. It had cost her to say the words, but was that a challenge in her tone?

He gave her a slight nod, not certain how to respond to such a statement. How foolish of her to think that a man could love two women equally. She would have had a better chance at being loved by marrying a man who was hers alone. As it stood, he was trying desperately to tolerate this situation.

Why did he ever agree to this?

The question went unanswered even in his thoughts as drums began their distant chant from the outer court, and Peninnah looked at him, her eyes shining. It was time. There was no running away. Not with his mother watching him with a gleam of triumph and joy in her eyes.

He felt like a weight had settled in his middle, and he had to force himself to reach for Peninnah's hand. It felt clammy, so unlike Hannah's had been that first night.

"Come," he said, pulling her to her feet.

The crowd cheered as he led her through the house and into the yard, where a white bridal tent stood waiting for them. A tent that had seemed like glory when he married Hannah but now looked more like gloom this second time around.

Oh Adonai, why couldn't You have blessed Hannah with children? Why did I end up in this place?

But he knew he would never understand or receive the answers he craved, so he led Peninnah beneath the curtains and let the drums drown out the sounds of everything they said and did. He felt as though every action was perfunctory, every word prescribed.

When he emerged with the bridal sheet to give her mother, he could not help the guilt that fell over him that he had said little to Peninnah nor whispered loving words in her ear. He had not asked her questions or tried to get to know her better as he had with Hannah. He had simply done what all men did in the bridal tent. He hadn't meant to leave Peninnah in tears.

■ ■ ■ ■

PART 2

■ ■ ■ ■

Now this man used to go up year by year from his city to worship and to sacrifice to the LORD of hosts at Shiloh, where the two sons of Eli, Hophni and Phinehas, were priests of the LORD. On the day when Elkanah sacrificed, he would give portions to Peninnah his wife and to all her sons and daughters. But to Hannah he gave a double portion, because he loved her, though the LORD had closed her womb. And her rival used to provoke her grievously to irritate her, because the LORD had closed her womb. So it went on year by year. As often as she went up to the house of the LORD, she used to provoke her. Therefore Hannah wept and would not eat. And Elkanah, her husband, said to her, "Hannah, why do you weep? And why do you not eat? And why is your heart sad? Am I not more to you than ten sons?"

1 Samuel 1:3–8

19

One Year Later

Peninnah lifted her sleeping son, Eitan, from her breast and placed him in the small basket Elkanah had fashioned for him. She gazed at the basket, large enough to hold the boy until he grew a little more, but in a few months he would surely need a bigger bed. Elkanah had assured her that he would handle the matter but said little more.

She studied the child, the sense of motherly pride mixing with a hurt so deep she wondered how she could possibly continue to bear it. What misguided thinking had caused her to imagine that Elkanah could love two women equally? She had thought . . . in fact, expected him to beam with pride — if not love, at least with pride — when she announced she had conceived.

But the words had brought little more than a smile and a kiss on the cheek and the occasional question as to her welfare.

Other than that, he seemed to have disappeared to live with Hannah or stay out in the fields with the sheep.

She turned away, swiping at unwanted tears. This was not the way it was supposed to be. She loved Elkanah, had loved him from afar long before she had asked her father to give her to him. And he would have if he had lived. Her mother had taken little convincing after that. Why couldn't Elkanah see how much she loved him, how good she was for him, for his family?

She touched Eitan's cheek and turned away, crawling onto the bed, exhausted. Tears wet her pillow even as anger filled her heart. Her life was so unfair! This was not the way things were supposed to happen. Once she bore a child, Elkanah was supposed to become devoted to her, to care for her more — at least more than he had in the months before she conceived. She could tell he came to her out of obligation by his lack of communication and refusal to answer her questions.

She deserved better!

She swallowed the bitter taste of bile and forced the tears into submission. Somehow she must do something to fix things, to make him see. Surely there was a way to gain his affection.

Footsteps drew her attention and her heart skipped a beat, hoping, always hoping. But it was only her mother, who entered the room carrying fresh linens for the babe.

"I've made porridge with your favorite figs and date syrup." Her mother came closer to where she still lay crumpled on the bed. "You know you must eat."

Yafa had come to live with her when she conceived, and Elkanah had not objected. Yafa had given up her home to Elkanah's father on Galia's insistence that she would be cared for as mother to their son's wife, and since no one was likely to marry an aging woman who was long past childbearing years, Yafa had been eager to accept.

"The baby will be fine while he sleeps. Come to the table and eat, Peninnah."

Peninnah curled tighter, hating that it was her mother still giving her direction instead of the husband whose babe lay sleeping nearby. "I'm not hungry."

"You have to eat if you want to produce milk to feed him." Yafa sat beside her and stroked her hair as though she were a small child. The action was both comforting and infuriating.

She shrugged aside her mother's attempts to rouse her. "I don't care. I'll eat when I'm ready."

"You're acting like a child."

Peninnah sat up as though startled and glared at her mother. "I am a woman grown, a mother the same as you are. Don't call me a child."

Yafa stiffened and crossed stout arms over her chest. "Then don't act like one. Go out to the cooking room and eat. I will watch Eitan."

The order was given with a tone of iron, and Peninnah was suddenly too weary to argue. The fact that her stomach had been rumbling since daybreak did not help her fight. She sank back, shoulders slumping against the pillows. "I can't make him love me, Ima. I thought Eitan's birth would change things. But if anything, Elkanah stays with Hannah even more."

Yafa's expression softened, and she touched Peninnah's arm. "I am sorry, my daughter. I could speak to Galia. Perhaps his father can talk to Elkanah."

"What good would that do? They already badgered him into marrying me. They cannot follow him around and watch his every move, nor can they make him obey them. He is not a child, Ima. He does what he pleases." Admitting the truth felt like a knife piercing her heart.

Her mother looked at her for the longest

moment as though searching for the right words to say. "You know, there is a way . . . It is one that may not work . . . but if you want to change the way a man feels and seducing him has not worked, then perhaps the next step is to go after the object of his desire."

Peninnah stared at her mother. "What are you saying?"

Yafa shrugged. "Only that Elkanah loves Hannah even though she is barren. But Hannah is a kind, pleasing woman. Take away her reason for kindness . . . make her miserable . . . and she will grow bitter. Men do not like bitter women."

Peninnah turned the thought over in her mind. Was she herself bitter? The nagging truth could not be denied. "Is that why he avoids me? Am I bitter?" She searched her mother's face and found the unwanted confirmation there. "But he makes me so angry. How do I switch places with Hannah when all I want to do is complain?"

"You must change, Peninnah. You must show Elkanah a beguiling, loving woman. Dress up when he is coming. Use ochre and henna and kohl to enhance your beauty. And never complain about Hannah. Simply find constant ways to praise Elkanah. In time, he will grow to love your praises more

193

than her kindness." Yafa shifted and stood. "Now go and eat."

"But what if Hannah remains kind and loving? How do I make her miserable?" That thought had been foreign to her when she first wed Elkanah, but in the past year she had stopped longing for Hannah's acceptance. She simply wanted to replace her and thought with Eitan's birth she would.

"If Elkanah does not succumb to your praise, then turn your criticism on Hannah. But not when Elkanah can hear or see you. You must be subtle, my daughter." Yafa walked to the basket where Eitan still slept peacefully, unaware of the turmoil swirling in Peninnah's heart and the plans her mother had used to tempt her out of bed. Was her mother right? Could she win Elkanah's love by stealing it from Hannah?

Peninnah slid off the bed and walked to the door to find the porridge her mother had made. She paused at the threshold and looked back at her mother and son, wondering if she could do as Yafa suggested. She had always voiced her opinions, but she had never been mean. Had she?

"They say," her mother said softly, "that hardship either makes a person stronger or more bitter. It rarely makes them sweeter."

Peninnah read the truth in her mother's

dark eyes. Yafa had grown stronger during years of Assir's abuse, though she had never revealed the truth to anyone but Peninnah. The knowledge had been impossible to ignore when her father came home drunk and raged at her mother. Peninnah was glad he could not hurt her anymore.

But Elkanah would not be that way. Would he? If she mistreated his favorite wife, would he lash out at her as her father had done?

"Peninnah, I do not know why you are thinking about this so much. Everyone knows that Hannah wants children but cannot have them."

Peninnah said nothing.

"But you can."

"So? What am I supposed to do with this information that everyone knows?" Her stomach growled louder, and this time she stepped into the hallway.

"Just do as Hagar did to Sarah every chance you get. I will let you figure out a way."

Hannah walked with Nava, her maidservant, to the large garden behind the house, each of them carrying a basket, one for produce, one for weeds. It had taken Hannah some time to adjust to having a ten-year-old girl in the house.

"But it is just the two of us," she had objected to Elkanah when he proposed the idea.

"Consider her my gift to you." His insistence had silenced any further protest on Hannah's part, but secretly she wondered if he was giving her the maid as a possible substitute, to bear a child for her when the girl came of age. Nava was pretty, her dark, curly hair pinned back beneath a scarf, her olive complexion pink from exposure to the sun. Had no one ever taught her to cover her face when she was out tending the garden? But her unruly hair took up most of the scarf's material.

Hannah shook herself, condemning her wayward thoughts. She could not imagine having yet another wife to contend with for Elkanah's affection. She would rather remain childless. Her heart stirred at that thought, and she knew she was lying to herself.

Elkanah had also offered to give her a cook once Yafa had moved in to help Peninnah with all of the daily tasks.

"What would I do with a cook?" She had looked from him to Nava, who was still adjustment enough, and smiled. "I'm sure between the two of us, Nava and I can make some fine meals for you, don't you agree, Nava?"

Hannah glanced at the girl now, grateful that she had answered affirmatively and had turned out to be someone Hannah could trust. She stopped at the first row of leeks and sank to her knees, used a sharpened stick to loosen the soil, and then pulled the ripe stalks from the ground.

Nava took the other end of the row and began pulling weeds from between the plants. Hannah worked in silence, though she could not resist a glance toward Peninnah's house, which was thankfully out of her line of vision. Another kindness Elkanah had given her. Not only a maid, but a separate home far enough from his other wife to keep peace between them. Though peace was far from what Hannah felt in Peninnah's presence.

"Peninnah will go up to the feast and bring the baby, won't she?" Nava asked as she drew closer to the middle of the row. Had the girl noticed her looking in the direction of Peninnah's house?

Hannah nodded in answer to Nava's question. "Most likely Peninnah will go with us. She wouldn't want to risk missing the chance for time with Elkanah, and when we go to a feast, we all go together." Her jaw clenched with the admission. The last time they'd gone up to a feast, Peninnah had been heavy with child, and though Hannah had tried to make polite conversation with her, she had said little and looked away with disdain.

"Peninnah is not a nice person," Nava said, keeping her voice low.

Hannah looked at her maid. "No, she is not." Admitting it did little good, but it helped to voice her feelings.

Nava pushed a strand of that unruly hair behind her ear and yanked at another weed. "I heard at market a few days ago that my mother has returned to her father's house."

Hannah turned at the change of subject, saw Nava bite her lip and her expression grow troubled. "Tell me," Hannah said.

Nava leaned back on her heels and drew in a breath. "I don't understand why she couldn't have come for me or sent me to live with my grandparents. Why let my father sell me to that man?" She shivered, and Hannah paused in her work to touch the girl's arm.

"You are safe now, Nava."

"Thank you, mistress." She looked away. "They say my father was killed when he went to look for work from the Canaanites."

Hannah gasped. "I did not know this. Was

it recent?" The leek dangled from her fingers as she waited, seeing the sudden anguish in the girl's eyes.

"I heard it from the wife of my former master. It happened before Elkanah purchased me a few months ago." She broke eye contact and continued attacking the weeds.

Hannah turned her attention back to the garden. The girl had seen far more than she should have at such a young age. But she had been in service for five years, a mere child when she was sold.

She is still a child. Hardly fit for a maid, but perhaps Elkanah wanted to give Hannah someone to care for as much as he wanted to give Nava a place of safety. The thought brought a surge of love for him, and she wished in that moment she could tell him so.

She moved to the row of cucumbers. "I am sorry about your father," she said at last. "I wish he had come to someone in Israel for help a long time ago. I wish you didn't have to live through what you did. Elkanah might have hired him to work the fields. He could have stayed safe in Israel under a kind master."

"My father was a proud man — at least that was what my mother said of him the last time I saw her." Nava's voice was tinged with hurt. "If he had followed the law, Ima said, he wouldn't have sold his children into slavery. He would have sold himself first — or at least sought work as a hireling."

"You were five then and now you are ten. And you have not known your mother's love in those five years," she said as a statement of fact.

Nava nodded. "The woman I worked for tried to be kind — when her husband was not around."

Hannah brushed the dirt from a fat cucumber. She faced Nava. "When you come of age and your seven years of service to me are finished, I will find a husband for you."

Nava looked up. Her eyes grew wide, almost fearful. Was she afraid of freedom?

"In the meantime, I shall teach you how to manage a house. Perhaps we will find someone when you are sixteen, and by seventeen or eighteen you will be ready." Though it pained her to think of losing the girl she had begun to love, she could not withhold from her the joy of family. "I am glad Elkanah found you before your former master tried to sell you to work in the tabernacle."

Elkanah had come upon Hophni and the girl's master the last time he worked in

Shiloh. He had told Hannah that Nava's plight was one he could not ignore. Hannah shivered, though the day was warm. Would Raziela have been able to protect a child from Hophni's roving ways?

Nava touched Hannah's arm, then quickly stopped herself. Her face flushed and she swallowed. "I can never thank your husband enough, mistress. I know what would have become of me there." Tears skimmed her dark lashes. "I would bear a child for you if you asked it of me, but I am very grateful that I will not be subject to the priests' ways."

Hannah blinked at the comment. "You are too young to understand such things and much too young to be bearing children." She heard the shock in her own voice, and her gaze softened as she looked at Nava's crestfallen face. "I'm sorry, Nava. In time we can discuss these things again, but right now I want you to simply feel safe and learn the ways of caring for a home. I will teach you to weave and spin and dye thread and even take you to watch my father make pottery." She warmed to the thought, for the girl was so young Hannah felt as though she were caring for a daughter.

"That is very kind of you," Nava said. "But I would still be willing to bear a child for you if you would like me to when the time comes. When I am older."

Hannah looked at the child, on the cusp of womanhood, and smiled. "Thank you for such a kind offer, Nava. I know it is within my right to ask it of you, but . . ." She waited until the girl met her gaze. "If God sees fit to give me children, they will come from His hand, not mine. I will not give a maid to my husband for the sole purpose of bearing a child. We would be at odds with each other, and your success would not erase my hurt, nor would Peninnah stop disdaining my barrenness." She sighed. "But thank you."

"I would do anything for you, mistress." How naïve the child seemed at times, and yet so mature for her age at others. How much had she seen in her short ten years of life? The thought troubled Hannah.

They continued to garden, but Hannah's thoughts were not on the food or on Nava or even on having children. They had swirled back to Peninnah and how they would be looked upon as a complete family once they arrived in Shiloh. She and Peninnah might even be forced to share a tent with Elkanah, sleeping under the stars.

Please, Adonai, do not put me through that. Don't let my heart be torn in two in the very place where I go to find healing. How can I worship You if that woman is every moment in my presence?

She listened, hoping for some sense in her spirit that God had heard, but the only sound blotting out her ragged, heartfelt prayers was Nava's soft singing.

20

Hannah inspected the figs and raisins drying in the sun, then covered them with a cloth to keep the flies away. The harvest of fruits and plowing of fields intermingled in this seventh month of Tishri, with the Festival of Trumpets, the Sabbath assembly on the first day, and the Day of Atonement on the tenth.

The harvest of grapes and figs and pomegranates and bananas would complete their winter stores. Elkanah and his brothers hurried to finish the plowing before the early rains started and Sukkot, the Festival of Booths, began on the fifteenth day, only three days hence.

She smiled, joy washing over her. She always felt thus at this time of year, despite her trials. How blessed of Adonai they were — blessed in their crops, in their livestock, and especially in knowing that soon seven days of rejoicing were about to be upon them. Yet she had so much left to do!

She tilted her head and straightened at the sound of whistling. She would recognize Elkanah's melodic tone anywhere. She turned, saw him hurrying toward her, and ran to meet him in the courtyard.

When he reached her side, he grabbed her about the waist and swung her around. "We finished the plowing," he said, smiling. It was the job he liked the least, and his sigh of relief as he glanced at the sky made her laugh.

"It is good," she said, following his gaze, "because rain or not, we must plan to leave for Shiloh tomorrow."

He laughed with her, kissed her soundly, and set her feet on the stone court. "Yes, and there is much yet to gather." He wiped sweat from his brow. "I am hungry, though." He looked so hopeful, she chuckled and took his hand, leading him into the house.

"Then it is time to feed you."

"Oh, good. I feared you might not be ready yet, as I am earlier than usual."

She looked at him. "Even if I wasn't prepared, I would find a way to fill your belly." His smile caused her heart to sing, and she quickly kissed his cheek. "Now sit and we will eat together."

He did as she said, and she hurried into

the cooking room and gave Nava instructions to bring the stew. She returned to join him, for once glad to have someone else serve them.

He prayed over the food, thanking Adonai for their provisions, then broke the bread and handed a piece to her. He dipped his into the pot and ate before he spoke again. "Tahath and I will gather the animals for the offerings and the sacrifices, and for the sin and freewill offerings. I am hoping you and Dana can handle the food we will eat in celebration?"

"Of course — though will Peninnah gather her own food?" She realized that he was trying to figure out how to handle both women at this festival now that he had a son as well as two wives.

"Yes, Peninnah will handle her own food and fronds for booth making." He met her gaze. "Make yours big enough for both of us."

She nodded, relief flooding her.

"I am making a special offering, though I will not explain it to the priests." He seemed preoccupied with the stew in front of them. "One for us — for God to bless your womb."

She could not meet his gaze, touched by his kindness, and yet . . . was such a sacrifice worth making? They had prayed for so long, offered so much, even sacrificed their marriage to achieve what she could not give him.

He studied her above the rim of his cup, then set it down and clasped his hands in his lap. "I cannot stop trying, Hannah. I don't want you to give up hope."

I already have. "It is hard to keep hoping when it is such an unlikely thing."

He took her hand. "I love you, Hannah. You know Peninnah is only a childbearer until you can bear."

She nodded. "It is kind of you."

He cleared his throat and seemed to grow uncomfortable. "I do not plan to stay with Peninnah at the festival."

"She will not like that."

"She will not be the one to decide." He looked intently at her a moment, then released her hand to continue eating. "It will be a joyous feast."

"Yes."

"But you are not happy?" How easily he could read her expressions.

She smiled. "Only thinking about all that there is yet to do."

"And you are not concerned about Peninnah? Things will be all right between you?" He sounded so vulnerable.

She touched his arm. "If God could protect our ancestors in the wilderness for forty years, He can protect our hearts from the hurts of our families." She smiled as she twisted off another piece of the bread. "Do not fret about Peninnah or your family. Even if the whole week is one of frustration when Peninnah is near, when you come to my booth at night, I will give you plenty of reasons to laugh again."

The next day, Hannah woke before dawn and hurried to finish loading the carts already filled with branches for booth making. She and Nava led the donkey down the low hill and joined Dana's family, and as they walked, others from the town and tribes joined them. She looked for her parents in the crowd and quickly embraced her mother and sisters-in-law.

But the clans soon divided as the path narrowed, and Hannah found herself walking with Dana, helping with Dana's children, as Nava led the donkey up ahead of them. Peninnah and her mother followed behind with Galia and the rest of Elkanah's family. Galia held Peninnah's son, and Hannah could not help but hear the joyous exclamations coming from her mouth.

"I just knew you would be able to give Elkanah an heir," Galia said without any attempt at being quiet, as if she wanted Hannah to hear.

"It is my pleasure, Mother Galia. I would do anything to please your son." Hannah could hardly believe the words gushing from Peninnah's lips.

"Obviously, they are speaking loud so that I will hear them," Hannah whispered to Dana. "But Peninnah is anything but happy, if the truth were known." She met Dana's gaze.

"Shall we walk ahead a bit?" Dana asked, taking her arm.

Hannah nodded. Dana let her boys run ahead to join their father, obviously weary of continually fighting their desire.

When they were out of earshot of Peninnah and Galia and Yafa and the others, Hannah released a sigh. "Thank you." She touched the scarf at her neck, self-conscious. "You are the only one who treats me with kindness."

Dana smiled. "The others love you too, Hannah. They just fear Galia's sharp tongue and are too timid to allow her misery to be turned against them. But believe me, it was never you. Galia always wanted Elkanah to marry Yafa's daughter. It's not your fault that the man fell in love with you instead."

Hannah lifted a brow and glanced quickly behind her, making sure they were still in front of the group. "Peninnah was still a child when I married Elkanah. Surely Galia could not have wanted a match with her then?"

"Galia has been Yafa's champion for many years. You know Assir was abusive to her."

Hannah shook her head. "I was not aware."

"Well, he was. And Galia knew it. So she always hoped to help Yafa by marrying one of her sons to Peninnah once she grew up. Oh, and don't think it was just Yafa who Galia wanted to help. She tried to make many a match for all of her sons, especially Elkanah, even before Peninnah came of age. But none of her sons would listen to her."

"Until now."

Dana nodded, her expression sober.

"They are far apart in age." Hannah's mind churned with this new knowledge.

"Normally that has nothing to do with marriage. The truth is, neither does love, but Elkanah loved you anyway. You bewitched him." Dana chuckled.

"I did no such thing and you know it." But she smiled just the same. Elkanah did love her. Sometimes his love was so intense, she was not sure how to respond.

"Love is a strange thing, my sister." Dana held her gaze. "Most marriages are made for convenience or political or monetary gain. Yours is a blessed marriage, Hannah, to have the man's total affection."

"And yet I can give him nothing of worth in return." The words were out before she could stop them. "Forgive me. You are right. I am blessed to have Elkanah."

"You two are much like Jacob and Rachel, I think, and eventually Rachel had two sons." Dana smiled. "Someday you will have more than she did."

Hannah simply nodded, not wishing to mention the fact that Rachel had died in childbirth. Perhaps God was sparing her an early death by not giving her children.

She pondered the thought as they continued to walk. Women from their town joined them here and there, and brave children raced up and down the line of men and women, with mothers shouting at their sons to stay clear of the animals lest they get kicked or trampled.

Behind her, a baby cried, but Hannah refused to turn around to see if the babe was Peninnah's. She had managed to ignore taking part in Eitan's birth and most of his first few months of life. If only that separation could go on forever.

By late afternoon, when the sun was nearly set, they finally arrived at the familiar tabernacle. She followed the group to the normal spot for Kohathites and began to unload the carts. Elkanah had gone so far as to give Hannah and Peninnah separate carts and donkeys to carry the loads they would need, despite the fact that one would have sufficed. She knew it was guilt that nudged his decisions as he tried to keep her happy, lest Peninnah grow even prouder of her status as mother of his heir.

She moved to the cart and with Nava's help gathered armloads of branches. They began the work of putting the long palm fronds close together into the ground to create a wall, fastening them with flaxen cords until they had three walls. At last they placed more branches on top for a partial roof, one that would allow them shelter and a way to look up at the night sky as they rested.

Some of Hannah's sisters-in-law began fires to heat the lentil stew they had prepared ahead for the trip, while Hannah and Nava set to mixing the grain they had ground the night before to make into flatbread. Sounds of talking and laughter and a few arguments stirred the air of the camp, with the men in the center, away from the women, engaged in a heated discussion.

"I wonder what that is about," Dana said, coming to sit at Hannah's side.

"I have no idea. I wonder if it's about the priests again. Maybe they are worried that their sacrifices are not going to be accepted and end up displeasing to the Lord." After all, the priests had gained the reputation of ruining many a sacrifice, as Hannah knew too well. Was that why God had never answered her prayers? Would God hold Phinehas's sin against her?

She looked up at that moment to better see if Elkanah was among the men arguing, but it was Peninnah she caught sight of — walking purposefully toward her. Her stomach tightened. Whatever the woman wanted, Hannah was certain it could not be good.

Peninnah held Eitan close, the babe wrapped tightly in a wide swath of wool tied at the shoulder. The noise of the crowd had frightened him, and she wished not for the first time that she had not come. But to stay behind with only her mother for company . . . she couldn't bear it. Besides, she had hoped for time alone with Elkanah during these seven days of feasting and celebration.

"There, there, sweet boy," she cooed as

she walked toward Hannah's booth. Was she doing the right thing? She had thought of little else during the days since her talk with her mother, but how did one try to get in the good graces of her rival with the sole purpose of later betraying her? What evidence did she have that Hannah would even welcome her?

You are the one who bore Elkanah a son. You hold the heir. Hannah has nothing on you. You are superior to her in every way.

The thoughts came unexpectedly and sounded like her mother's voice, though Ima had never said such things. But her mother had made similar comments. And Galia had hinted.

She patted the baby's back, speaking softly to him, hoping he would calm to her voice above the noise. She drew closer to Hannah's booth, but Nava met her at the entrance, blocking her from entering.

"Is Hannah about?" She tried desperately not to clench her fists or speak through tight lips. Instead, she forced a smile.

Nava studied her as though they were equals. Tightness filled Peninnah's chest. The nerve! A child, let alone a slave, would not scrutinize her!

"I will check for you, mistress." Nava's humble reply did not match the skepticism in her gaze, but the girl turned and entered the booth. Low voices could be heard, though Peninnah could not make out the words. At last Hannah emerged, arms crossed as though she was protecting herself from an onslaught.

"Shalom, Peninnah. Welcome." She motioned to the area in front of the booth where Nava was setting cushions for both women. "Would you like some water? I'm afraid we have not yet finished unpacking all of the food and drink yet."

Peninnah shook her head. She would not be beholden to this woman despite her parched throat. "Thank you, but no." She knelt on the ground and held Eitan close. His cries had lessened and he had settled into a fitful sleep. "He is fearful of the crowd," she said for lack of something better to say. "I probably should have waited to bring him, but it is already long past the eight days for his circumcision and Elkanah wanted to make sure it was done by the high priest." She lifted her chin, looking down her nose at Hannah. She did not add that Elkanah had intended to follow the law and circumcise the child at home on the eighth day or that she had begged him to wait until the feast.

"I'm happy for you," Hannah said. "It is

215

good that Eli is willing to do the ceremony for you. He is old, but you can trust him more than you can trust his sons."

Peninnah stared at Hannah, her thoughts a mixture of jealousy and frustration. "And how do you know Eli? It is not like he has circumcised your son." The unintended barb flew from Peninnah's mouth and, by Hannah's look, hit its mark. "I'm sorry," she quickly added. "I meant no harm. Obviously God has chosen not to bless your union with Elkanah. We cannot blame you for feeling left out or forgotten. Elkanah understands."

She looked at Eitan then, but not before risking a lengthy gaze at Hannah to see her reaction. Hannah hid her feelings well — at least, she did now. Perhaps she was not as jealous of Peninnah as Peninnah was of her. She inwardly cursed her failure, for she had come here in peace, hoping to get on Hannah's good side — for a time — and she had already ruined everything.

"I know Eli because Elkanah and I served at the tabernacle several times in years past. I helped Hophni's wife with her children and met all of the priests many times. That's how I know you can trust Eli." Hannah folded her hands in her lap and smiled. No trace of bitterness or even unkindness.

"That's nice." Peninnah played with the blanket holding Eitan secure. "I must admit, I hate to put him through it. It's hard for a mother to watch her child suffer."

"I am certain he will not remember it when he is older. But I would feel the same in your place."

Nava appeared with two clay cups of water and gave one to Hannah, then offered the other to Peninnah, despite her earlier refusal.

Peninnah looked at the cup and almost declined the offer, but considering how she had already blundered her words, she thanked Nava and took a sip. She looked from Hannah to her son, weighing the option of offering to let her hold him. But her inner battle with jealousy won out. She couldn't bargain with this woman, as Leah and Rachel had done, or ask to trade the child or even time with him for time with Elkanah. No. She would win Elkanah by subtly making Hannah bitter. *Be careful with your barbs, Peninnah.* How hard it was to hold her tongue!

"If you would like to come to the circumcision, the whole family will be there." It was an olive branch. The least she could do.

Hannah did not answer for the space of many breaths. "I will speak to Elkanah of it and see what he wishes. But thank you for the kind offer. Of course, you have already chosen his name." Hannah tilted her head and leaned closer to see the boy. "Eitan is a fine name."

Peninnah hesitated, but at last she lifted the blanket and allowed Hannah to see her son's face. "It seemed foolish to wait to call him something other than 'son.' Especially with the circumcision not coming on the eighth day."

Hannah nodded, and Peninnah searched her face for some judgment, some censure, but did not find it.

"He's beautiful, Peninnah. I'm sure Elkanah is very proud."

At Hannah's soft smile, Peninnah wondered whether working to keep this woman as her rival was worth the hassle. Was her mother right? Was this really the greatest way to show Elkanah that she was the best wife for him? What if she just asked Hannah to share him more?

"Thank you for stopping by," Hannah was saying as she slowly stood, obviously dismissing Peninnah. "I'm sorry I cannot talk longer. I have a few things to finish before the evening meal."

"Of course." Peninnah stood, feeling angry and rejected on many levels. She turned to leave, but Hannah's words stopped her.

"Thank you for sharing this time with me, Peninnah, and for allowing me to meet Eitan. I hope you will come again."

Peninnah turned and offered a half smile. "I'm sure we will see each other now and then." She hurried away but felt a sense of triumph. Perhaps Hannah was going to be easier to goad than she imagined. The woman did want a child. And Peninnah had the power to remind her of all she was missing.

21

Elkanah ducked his head as he entered Hannah's booth later that evening. Food and drink had been eaten in each separate booth, and Elkanah had moved from Hannah's to Peninnah's booths and then returned to Hannah as the stars began to pop and burst in bright display in the night sky. Mothers had settled the children to sleep, and Elkanah breathed easier now that his time with Peninnah was past for this night. A sigh escaped at the memory of the look she had given him, the questions she had plied him with about the circumcision. As if they hadn't already discussed the matter at length since the babe was born.

The booth was small, not allowing him to straighten to his full height, so he crept forward and joined Hannah among the cushions. Her inviting smile sent his earlier frustrations to the wind.

"You came." She took his hand as he knelt

at her side. "Thank you."

He bent low and kissed her. "Nothing could have kept me away."

She smiled, and he lay beside her and rested on one elbow to better gaze into her eyes. The small room was lit with one clay lamp, which cast just enough light to see without stumbling.

She sifted his hair with her fingers and cupped his face. "You are tired." Her soft gaze made him long to hold her close and never release her.

"It has been an interesting day."

"I saw you among the group of men arguing earlier this afternoon. What was all the strife about?" She continued to stroke his temple, watching him.

A sigh lifted his chest, but his gaze held hers with intensity. "Many things. Issues always arise about clan troubles, but most of the men are fed up with Hophni and Phinehas and don't know what to do to stop them from stealing from the Lord." He paused. "Then I had a lecture from my father for not circumcising my son sooner, and why would I want old Eli to do so? He has a point."

"Peninnah stopped by to see me today." Her change of subject caught him up short.

"She did?" In the entire year and a half of

his marriage to Peninnah, his two wives had barely spoken.

Hannah nodded. "She invited me to the circumcision. I told her Eli was a man she could trust." She tilted her head to better look into his eyes. "But why did you not just do the job yourself when the boy was eight days old, as the law prescribes?"

He closed his eyes, remembering the arguments he had had with Peninnah. Clearly she had not been raised with boys. "She insisted we wait. I should have been firmer with her and obeyed the law. I appeased her by promising to have Eli do it. I have yet to ask him, though."

Hannah raised a brow. "Do you think he will refuse?"

Elkanah shook his head. "No. That does not trouble me. I am more concerned with Hophni and Phinehas and whether they will cause trouble at this feast." He ran a hand through his hair. "Things have gotten worse, Hannah."

She looked at him, eyes wide with a mixture of curiosity and fear. "How so?"

"You remember Lital, of course?"

"How could I forget?"

"Well, there are rumors that more women have borne children — Hophni's and Phinehas's offspring — only these women have lived through childbirth. So we have a number of illegitimate children living near the tabernacle with their mothers, who were only meant to serve here a short time. Some of the women were even betrothed, but now . . . what man could overlook such a thing? Of course, Hophni and Phinehas deny any wrongdoing and won't take the women as secondary wives or concubines. The whole priesthood is in chaos, and Eli just sits and wrings his hands as if there is nothing to be done about it." He fisted both hands, imagining they were wrapped around Phinehas's thick neck. He blinked the thought away, silently begging Adonai's forgiveness for having such thoughts.

"That's terrible." Hannah sat up, twisting the belt at her waist, clearly agitated. "Those poor women. And what will become of the children?"

"I don't know." He ran a hand through his hair. "If their fathers will allow them to return home, the children could have a place to live, but the rumors are that Raziela and Irit have had to take some of them in as servants while the women are sent home. It is shameful and heartbreaking, and I don't know what we can possibly do about it." He took her hands in his. "We must pray more, beloved. We must ask the Lord to give us a deliverer, one who can lead the people back to true worship of Adonai. One who can turn the priesthood into what it is meant to be."

Hannah nodded, and tears slowly slipped down her cheeks. How he loved her! She shared his heart for Adonai and his deep concerns for their people. Surely God would hear their prayers. Surely He could see the downward turn of morality in their land, away from all things He had commanded.

Yet, as Elkanah looked into Hannah's eyes and brushed away her tears with his thumbs, he was not so sure God was listening to them at all. Hadn't they prayed for a son for years and years? If God could not grant such a small thing, what made him think He would do something grand like fix what was broken in their entire nation, where chaos often ruled and everyone did what they thought was right in their own eyes?

Hannah patted his arm and offered him a wobbly smile. "I will continue to pray," she said softly.

He nodded his agreement. "And I too."

They sat in silence a moment.

"So Peninnah came to see you today." By her nod and the set of her jaw, he knew the visit had not been expected or necessarily wanted. "Are you going to come to the circumcision as she asked? You don't have to come, you understand. But if you want to be there, I would be happy to have you."

She exhaled slowly. "I . . . if you will pardon me, my lord, I think I would rather stay away. If you don't mind."

His whole family would be there, and he knew his mother would criticize Hannah's absence, but he did not say so. "You do whatever seems best to you."

"Thank you."

He pulled her close then, wishing they were not having this conversation and that he was not living in such a miserable time.

Hannah walked through the camp of the Kohathites with Nava, careful even here, far from the area of the priests, to never go out alone. Elkanah had warned her more than once, and she knew enough to heed his urgings.

"I can't believe we go home tomorrow," Nava said as they walked the edge of the curtained tent that separated the tabernacle from the tribal encampments. "It's been a good festival."

Hannah nodded. "It has," she said, though she could not stop the ache she felt in spite of the joy these things should bring. Used to bring.

"You don't sound so sure." Nava gave her a sideways glance. Though the girl had been with her only a year or so, Hannah found herself grateful for her presence and drawn to her easy way of reading Hannah's expressions.

"Perhaps not," she said, smiling. "I will be glad to be home again." She had come to almost dread this place, though she had to admit, Hophni and Phinehas were better behaved during this festival than in times past, and it was nice to see Raziela again. Even Elkanah's sacrifice had been accepted as though there had never been a problem between them. And Elkanah had told her how pleased Eli had been to circumcise Eitan. "But you are right. It has been a good feast." She might as well accept the good, despite Peninnah's presence in her life now, because she couldn't change anything. She couldn't make God give her a child, and she couldn't expect Elkanah to set Peninnah aside. Not now that she had borne his son.

They continued walking in silence, then stopped at the sound of voices near a small copse of trees. Hannah stilled and motioned for Nava to listen. Was that not Yafa and Galia? She strained to hear. One of them was weeping. She gave Nava a curious look,

226

but the girl just shook her head, appearing as bewildered as Hannah. Should they approach or back away? It wasn't proper to listen to another's private conversation, and yet something held Hannah's feet to the earth.

"There, there," Galia said too loudly. "It surely can't be as bad as all that."

The murmured response was impossible to hear.

"Well then, I will speak to him. He will listen to his mother. Didn't I convince him to wed Peninnah?"

Hannah's stomach tightened, and a wave of dread swept over her. Was Yafa accusing Elkanah of something that Galia thought she could correct? Which would mean Hannah was somehow to blame yet again. Could she never rid herself of the constant disapproval?

Her face grew hot and she turned to go, Nava at her side. "You cannot assume what they meant," the girl said in an obvious attempt to calm her.

"If it has to do with Peninnah and Elkanah, you can bet it is a complaint that Elkanah is not spending enough time with Peninnah because he spends his time with me." She spoke softly, darting glances before and behind. The last thing she needed was for more people, especially family members, to hear her complaints.

Oh Adonai, have I not endured enough?

"But you do not know that for sure, mistress. Perhaps Elkanah has offended Yafa in some way or not liked Peninnah's cooking." Nava smiled, the action making Hannah giggle.

"Or maybe Yafa thinks the baby is too fat and it's somehow Elkanah's fault that Peninnah feeds him too much." They both laughed at Hannah's comment, knowing the words were ridiculous but needing something humorous to relieve the tension.

"I wish I could question Yafa about it," Hannah said, suddenly growing sober. She glanced Nava's way. "I don't like the situation, nor do I like Peninnah very much." She leaned close, her voice a whisper. "But if I have done something to cause them pain —"

"What could you have possibly done? You are Elkanah's first wife. You have nothing to apologize to them for, and it is your right to expect more time with your husband." Nava pushed her hair away from her face. "Forgive me for being so bold, mistress, but whatever Yafa said to Galia is not your concern. If Galia chooses to talk to her son, then ask Elkanah what she wanted. If he refuses to tell you, then I guess it was not yours to know."

They reached Hannah's booth and entered it. Hannah sank onto one of the cushions. "For such a young woman, you are wiser than you know, Nava." She rubbed her temples, feeling the start of a headache. "But one thing I know. Whatever Yafa is up to, I don't think she is a good influence on her daughter. I think her daughter has been spoiled all of her life and given what she wants, and now she is trying to control Elkanah the way Yafa controls her."

She closed her eyes a moment, suddenly weary of the conversation, of her situation, of every troubling thing in her life. She took a long drink of the cool water Nava handed to her and tried to blot out the frustration of sharing a husband, dealing with a controlling mother-in-law, and wishing Elkanah could find a way to make Israel holy and righteous again.

If only there was something she could do to fix her life. She nearly laughed at the foolish thought. What could one woman possibly do to save her family, let alone her nation?

22

Three Years Later

The sound of a newborn's cry split the air, and even from the distance of Hannah's house, she could not help but hear. So Peninnah had given birth to a third child. And married less than five years.

"It's a boy!" Yafa's shout drowned out the baby's wail.

Another boy. A boy who would soon be carried out to the courtyard for Elkanah to bless on his knee, while Peninnah stayed in her room, attended to by her mother, mother-in-law, and sisters-in-law.

Except for Dana. Faithful Dana. And Nava, of course. One a sister-in-law, one a servant, but both the only true friends Hannah had outside of her brothers and their wives. She would lose Nava soon, though. At thirteen, the girl was nearly ready to marry, though in truth she still had four years left to serve Hannah. She glanced at the girl. If the right young man came along . . .

"A healthy, beautiful son, Elkanah." Yafa's shrill voice, loud enough to carry straight to Hannah's heart, interrupted her melancholy.

She moved to the window to see what she could of Peninnah's house, now larger than hers, just beyond the trees. But what need did Hannah have of more rooms when she had no children to fill them? The ache intensified, and despite her best efforts to fight the feeling, she turned away and went to her chamber, curling into a ball on her bed. Tears came, but she cared not. No one was here to see but Nava.

Oh Adonai, why? And now Peninnah has one more reason to lift her haughty chin and look down on me. My life is worthless.

A great sob escaped, and she covered her mouth to stifle it. Even here in her own home she could not know who might listen beneath the windows. Soon Peninnah would likely send Eitan to spy on her, something Hannah would not have thought her capable of doing but for the menacing way she looked at Hannah and the constant hint of glee in her gaze.

What good was she to Elkanah or his household? She should find a way to return to her father, ketubah protection or not. Let Peninnah have him. Wasn't that her goal in all of this? Didn't she make Elkanah's life miserable because of Hannah's presence? Now that he had a fruitful wife and sons to carry his name, he had no need of her.

The thought caused her whole body to still as one idea turned to another. She sat up and got her bearings, then moved across the room once her limbs had steadied. Nava was in the cooking rooms, and Hannah slipped past her and left the house. She walked on and on, away from the commotion coming from Peninnah's house, past Dana's home, to the river where she bathed and washed.

She passed the familiar trees and the place where they usually stopped to work. Her feet carried her ever farther until she came to that place where they had found Lital those many years ago. In the past, she'd had no desire to revisit it.

But now . . .

She sank to the dirt where the girl's body once laid. Underbrush had filled in to the point that she almost did not recognize the spot, but the bluff near the river was a landmark she clearly remembered.

She sifted the ground with her fingers as though looking for treasure stones, as she had done for her father's pottery business in those innocent days before she realized the corrupt world in which she lived. But all that remained were slugs and worms and dirt and leaves fallen from some of the oak trees.

Tears fell in drops as though she were standing in a storm, her heart burning within her. *Oh Adonai. Do You even listen to my prayers? I ask and I ask and I beg and I plead, and nothing changes. I see my sister-wife reaping blessing upon blessing while I must simply watch. She's stealing Elkanah from me, Lord.*

She tasted the salt of her tears and knelt, face to the damp ground, allowing them to fall unhindered. Did God really hear the prayers of His people? If He did, why was He always so slow to respond? She had waited years and more years and endured the displeasure of her husband's family and the taunts of the younger wife for so long.

Exhausted emotionally and physically, she slowly rose to her knees, then stood. She turned and walked to the river. If she fell in — the current was swift, the water deep and rocky here — she would not survive without help.

Right now there was no one to help Hannah. She was alone. Completely and utterly alone. And the river beckoned.

Elkanah took the boy from Yafa and looked down at the swaddled bundle into the face of his new son, seeing glimpses of Peninnah's face in the infant nose and mouth. *May you grow to be godly — and not like your mother.* That he could think such a thing at this blessed time troubled him. Was he even man enough to teach the boy Adonai's ways? The weight of fatherhood should have hit him much sooner, he knew, but somehow with three boys now looking to him for guidance, the challenge seemed greater. More daunting.

How do I help them to know You, Adonai? Sometimes I don't understand You myself.

The thought suddenly troubled him, but not for Peninnah's sake or even the child's. It was Hannah whose father was known for his devotion to Adonai. He should be blessed with grandsons from Hannah, and yet he endured Elkanah's decision to beget sons by another wife. What must the man think of him?

He studied the boy. Not much was visible except his head, but Elkanah accepted Yafa's word that he was perfect and healthy. The boy's mouth moved in a soft mewling, and he turned as though searching for his mother.

"You must bless him, my son." His mother's insistent voice grated. He knew what was expected of him. Hadn't he always done the expected thing? And yet what good had it done him, truly? For the one thing he had wanted most — to please Hannah — was the one area where he had failed.

He glanced around. Hannah never attended Peninnah's births. But the noise in the courtyard and the shouts Yafa had made coming from inside the house had surely carried to Hannah. He could not keep them so far apart that they were in separate towns.

Oh Hannah, what is this doing to you?

His mother cleared her throat, bringing his thoughts to attention. He held the boy on his knee and looked from him to the crowd of relatives and neighbors. "May you be blessed of Adonai, my son. May you prosper and always obey the Lord every day of your life."

He would say more at the circumcision, but for now, all he could think of was going to Hannah to comfort her. He handed the boy, whose name would be given in eight days, over to Yafa, who beamed with pride at this newest grandson. He was happy for her in a certain sense. At least she had purpose in helping Peninnah.

But suddenly he needed to be anywhere but here.

He abruptly stood. "I have to go," he said to his father and brothers.

"But your son is just born. We are here to celebrate," Jeroham said. He exchanged a look with Elkanah's mother.

"Your father is right, son. You must stay with your wife and newborn son. At least go in and see Peninnah and stay for the food the women have prepared." Galia gave him an accusing look.

Something inside him recoiled. He was tired of doing everything they wanted. Hannah needed him too, especially on such a difficult day.

"I have things I must do," he said, moving away from the group. "If I can, I will be back." He hurried off before his family could object, though not before his mother's shouts insistently trailed after him.

Hannah stared at the water, listening to the soothing rush of the spray as it cascaded over the rocks several steps from where she stood. Elkanah would be celebrating the birth by now, the whole family participating in a joyous feast, while Peninnah stayed in the birthing room nursing her son.

The thought brought instant pain, like that of a thorn piercing her skin, only deeper. There must be ways she could be more useful to Elkanah to keep him near. Her weaving did bring in a fair price, so at least she was adding to the family's wealth rather than simply exhausting its resources. But the sense of worthlessness lingered. Did Elkanah love her still? Did anyone truly care?

She glanced heavenward. Bright blue sky with wisps of white met her gaze.

Oh Adonai, why was I born? What purpose do You have for me? If I'm not to be a mother, then what is left?

She sank to her knees in the rough terrain, scooped up handfuls of dirt, and let it sift through her fingers into her hair. Grief, as though she had lost a loved one, filled the already blooming ache in her soul.

Why does she beget child after child and yet I am forgotten? Why won't You remember me as You did Sarah and Rebekah and Rachel?

"Hannah?" Elkanah's voice made her heart leap, and she jumped up in surprise. "Oh Hannah, what are you doing here?"

She looked down at her dirty tunic and tried to brush the earth from her hair, to no avail. She would have to go to the quieter part of the river and bathe before the day was out.

"You've been crying." He stepped closer and pulled her to him.

They stood in silence for several moments, her head pressed against his chest, feeling the pulse of his beating heart.

"It's all right, beloved," he said against her ear. "I know days like this are painful. But we must overcome them together."

"Overcome them?" She leaned back and searched his face. "Unless you stay away from her, Peninnah will continue to bear children. We cannot overcome that."

"We can overcome the hurt. You are of much value to me. Don't you know how much I love you?"

"I know." She looked at her feet. "But I am of little worth to you, Elkanah. My weaving is not reason enough to keep a wife." There, she had said it. Despite what her father had commanded be put in the ketubah, Elkanah could find a way out. She could give him one. She could offer to leave.

"I don't need a reason to keep you as my wife, Hannah." His tone had taken on a sterner edge. "I do not love you less because you have not given me children. What can a son give you that I do not? A son grows up and marries and loves a wife more than his mother. As I love you more than mine. Never forget that."

She nodded, but tears stopped her from speaking again. The sound of the river behind them reminded her again of the temptation to disappear into it. But Elkanah's arms around her now sent the reasons fleeing.

"Let's go home, beloved." Elkanah placed a hand on her back.

"I really must bathe before I return to any family gathering." She pointed to her hair, and he seemed to notice her clothes for the first time.

He clearly knew she'd been grieving, but he said nothing more of it. "Then we will gather what you need and I will go with you." He looked at her with a spark of mischief in his eyes.

Suddenly she was glad she had resisted her temptation, despite her grief. At least she had Elkanah's love. Even if she couldn't give him a child, having a husband's love was worth something.

23

Peninnah carried a basket of necessary baby things along with three-month-old Aniah as she walked toward Galia's large home. Her mother had stayed behind with Eitan and Hevel, a blessing for which Peninnah was grateful. Her mother's help was one of the few things she could count on these days — certainly not on Elkanah, and she knew Hannah was the reason.

The thought of Hannah brought the sting of envy to her heart, as it did often of late. Especially since Aniah's circumcision. Elkanah seemed to have disappeared from her life since that day, and Peninnah wanted to know why. Certainly Galia would be able to help, but as she passed Hannah's house and spotted Dana's home not far from it, she stopped. Hannah would know more than Galia would. Dana might also know, but dare she approach her? She was tired of feeling like second wife to a barren woman.

That woman was taking too much of her husband's time, and she was not going to put up with it any longer.

Decision made, she changed direction and headed up the hill to Dana's house. She would try her sister-in-law first. But as she neared the courtyard, she found Hannah and Dana both spinning and weaving, while Dana's youngest slept peacefully in a basket nearby.

She hesitated. They had noticed her. She didn't miss the way Hannah straightened, her shoulders tensing, nor the skeptical look on Dana's face. She should whirl about and go home. This was completely foolish.

"Peninnah," Hannah said, breaking the awkward silence, "have you brought Aniah?" Her voice held a cheerful quality, but one look into her eyes told Peninnah the tone was not genuine. Hannah didn't want her here, but now that she was, she would want to know the purpose for her visit.

Why could she never seem to choose the right time in her attempts to wound this woman? How was it possible that Hannah always managed to smile and treat her with kindness?

"Come, let us see him," Dana said, interrupting her irritation and convincing her to push forward.

241

She stepped through the gate into the stone courtyard and approached Dana first. She lowered Aniah and lifted the blanket from his face.

"Oh, he's beautiful. Hannah, come and see." Dana's exclamation softened the awkwardness in the air. A moment passed as Hannah stopped a line of weaving and came to peer at Peninnah's son.

"Yes, he is a fine boy," Hannah said. "He has Elkanah's chin." How she could say that when Elkanah always wore a beard in the manner of the Hebrew custom, Peninnah wondered. She gave Hannah a curious look.

"Of course you would know more about how our husband looks than I, as he spends his every free moment at your side." She flung the gibe, not caring that both Dana's and Hannah's eyes widened as though the words came as a shock.

"Elkanah works long hours in the fields with Tahath," Dana said before Hannah could reply. "Sometimes they don't even come home at night because of the needs of the sheep."

"But when he is home, he stays with *her.*" She pointed one long, accusing finger at Hannah. "What I can't understand is why he finds her company so pleasing. It's not like she's given him children to sit on his knee or chase through the yard."

Peninnah watched Hannah's expression, but the woman merely returned to the loom and picked up her weaving, not saying a word.

"I think you should leave," Dana said, standing and facing Peninnah. "Whatever reason you came for, you are finished now. You don't understand at all what you are talking about." It was Dana's turn to point a finger, but she pointed it toward the gate and indicated that Peninnah had better turn around and march through it.

"Fine. Think what you want," she said, hiding the anger brewing deep within her. "I will simply get Galia or Jeroham to remind Elkanah of his marital duties."

She held Aniah close and turned. How foolish could she be? What had possibly possessed her to be so cruel? She was never going to get Hannah to encourage Elkanah to share his time equally if she kept badgering the woman.

She stepped through the gate and headed back down the hill. Perhaps a visit with Galia would soothe her feelings. It was better than returning home so soon to her mother and two whiny sons. She released a sigh. Life was simply not fair.

■ ■ ■ ■

The walk to Galia's house took longer than she expected, and she'd had to stop to feed Aniah and change his linens along the way. The sun shone high in the sky by the time she arrived, and for a moment that same awkwardness crept over her. Why had she come? She should have stayed home and worked with her mother. What if Elkanah decided to stop by tonight and she had nothing prepared for him?

The thought caused an ache in her middle that went beyond the feeling of hunger. Her life was not supposed to be this way. By now, after she'd given him three sons, Elkanah should be fully devoted to her. But he seemed to be pulling further away instead of enjoying his sons, enjoying her. Was having her mother around causing a problem?

She approached the courtyard and heard the commotion of children coming from inside the large house. A few of her sisters-in-law were working in the courtyard, but there was no sign of Galia.

"Welcome, Peninnah," Kelila called out. "You are just in time to help us make the raisin cakes."

"She didn't come all this way with a babe

to cook," Varda said, setting her spindle aside and hurrying over to see Aniah. "He's beautiful, Peninnah. You've done well, my sister."

Peninnah smiled and lifted her chin. "If only my husband felt the same way."

Varda frowned, and Kelila moved from the entrance of the house to join them. "Elkanah is not spending time with you?"

"He stops by now and then to see the boys, but he doesn't stay. I try to get Hannah to do something about it, but she won't." A twinge of guilt accompanied the lie, but right now all she wanted was sympathy.

Batel, married to Elkanah's second-oldest brother, gave her a thoughtful look. "Hannah is Elkanah's first wife, Peninnah. You cannot expect her to willingly share him when you know even Elkanah did not wish to marry you in the first place. He had his heart set on Hannah for years. There is nothing you can do to change that." She continued to spin wool into thread as Galia burst through the door.

"I knew I heard voices! Has my newest grandson come to visit me?" Galia rushed to Peninnah's side. "Come, come, Peninnah. You must sit and rest." She glanced beyond the gate. "And you came alone? I

245

would have thought your mother would join you."

Peninnah's jaw clenched at the subtle hint that Galia would have preferred Yafa's company to her own, but she kept her feelings hidden. "Ima stayed home with the other boys. We thought it best to let them rest."

"Oh?" Galia's brow lifted. "Have they been ill?"

Peninnah sighed, debating between the truth or a lie. "They are still napping and Ima preferred to let them. I needed time away, so here I am." She spoke with a lilt on the last word, hoping her smile was convincing enough. "Besides, I have missed you." She was not sure now that she had made a wise choice. She should have walked to the fields and found Elkanah instead, as Hannah often did. Why hadn't she thought of it?

"Well, we are glad you came. Now let me see this grandbaby." Galia took a sleeping Aniah into her arms, cooing softly to him. She would wake him and Peninnah would be forced to feed him again. Irritation spiked, and she suddenly wished she had never left the house. Elkanah's family was not sympathetic to her at all! Curse them!

"So how are my other grandsons when

they are not napping?" Galia asked as Aniah lay in the crook of her arm, still sleeping.

"They are well." She paused, looked at her three sisters-in-law, and then met Galia's gaze. "Though they do miss their father."

Galia returned Peninnah's look with first acknowledgment, then a frown. "Does Elkanah not spend time with them? Surely by now Eitan goes with him to the fields. Jeroham used to carry Amminadab on his shoulders as he inspected the fields or cared for the sheep. Eitan is past three, is he not?"

Peninnah nodded. "He is not yet trained," she admitted, "so Elkanah refuses to take him until he is older."

Galia looked at her, a hint of astonishment in her dark eyes. "Not trained? Whatever is taking so long? My boys were well behaved and able to hold their water by two years of age." Disapproval weighted the air, and Peninnah longed to drag the words back.

"Some children take longer, Mother Galia," Kelila said, smiling. "Don't be too hard on the girl. At least she has given Elkanah sons."

Galia's expression softened. "Yes. Yes, she has." She beamed, her gaze taking in Peninnah. "You have done well, my girl. You have done what Hannah could not, and believe me, Jeroham and I are most grateful that our son is not without an heir."

"I just wish Elkanah felt the same way. I fear that he is unhappy with his sons because they are not Hannah's offspring." She gave a slight pout and looked at her feet.

The sound of shifting feet and hushed whispers came from the other women, but Peninnah could not make out the words. At last Galia spoke. "If my son is not pleased with his sons, I will speak to him. It is a father's duty to train them, and he cannot shirk that duty just because Hannah is not the mother."

"They are still too young," Batel said, her voice sterner than Peninnah expected. Perhaps Hannah had more supporters in this family than just Dana. "You heard Peninnah say they are not trained. Elkanah is likely waiting a little longer."

Peninnah looked up to see Batel meet Galia's darkened gaze.

"Give Elkanah time, Mother Galia. It is Peninnah's job to raise them until he can take them off to teach them the tasks they must learn." Batel glanced at Peninnah, her expression sour.

Peninnah stared again at her feet, feeling the heat of anger rise up her neck.

"Well, enough of this," Galia said, handing the baby back to Penninah. "You must be hungry after that walk. Let me get you something to eat." She hurried into the house, her absence followed by silence.

"I remember what it was like to nurse," Kelila finally said, offering Penninah a smile. "You are always hungry."

Penninah nodded. When Galia returned with a tray of dates and cheese, she accepted the food, grateful for the change of subject. "He does eat a lot."

"He's growing. Of course he eats often." Galia smiled, but even she seemed to have cooled toward Penninah. Did Batel have such power as to cause even Galia to grow unsympathetic to her plight?

She finished a date and stood. "I really should go." She moved to retrieve the basket with Aniah's linens, covered Aniah with a blanket, and held him near her heart. At least her children loved her. And her mother, when she wasn't being caustic.

"Do give your mother our greetings," Galia said as Penninah moved toward the gate. No one attempted to stop her, and she struggled to understand why. She had not said anything bitter, had she? She had merely suggested that Elkanah could spend more time with the boys, hoping that Galia might take it upon herself to intervene, as she had when Peninnah married her son.

"Thank you, I will," she said without emotion, though her thoughts were spinning wildly out of control. She walked to the road heading home, barely acknowledging the goodbyes from her sisters-in-law. Tears streamed down her cheeks as she walked, but she straightened her back and clung to her son, unwilling to let those who might still be watching see how vulnerable she felt.

No one in the family, not even her husband, cared about her or her needs. No one loved her except her boys, and they were too young to know what love was. They simply needed her. And they did need her. A wave of relief swept briefly over her. Being needed was almost as good as being wanted.

But as she passed Dana's house and approached Hannah's, she realized just how erroneous were her conclusions. Being needed didn't last.

24

Four Years Later

Elkanah kicked at dusty stones along the path to Shiloh. Tahath held the donkey's reins while a perfect lamb rested on Elkanah's shoulders — an offering he had taken to giving every time he performed his Levitical duties. Surely God would hear his prayers soon. Surely.

Memories of Hannah's request to come with him flitted through his mind. Why had he refused her? She enjoyed accompanying him and working with Raziela while he was busy performing his yearly tasks. But the truth was, he needed time alone, away from both women, the children, his household.

Even Hannah? A sigh escaped.

Tahath turned to meet his gaze. "Those thoughts must be troubling."

Elkanah quickened his pace to come alongside his brother. "Call it guilt, I guess."

"Guilt?" Tahath leaned closer. "You have

done nothing wrong, Elkanah."

"Sometimes it feels that way. I can never please Peninnah, and with each new babe, she grows increasingly bitter. She has three sons and two daughters, and just last week she told me another is on the way, yet she is never happy unless I spend every moment with her. So I flee to Hannah's house, but if I talk about the children, she grows quiet and sad. I can't please either one of them!"

Tahath smiled and nodded his condolence. He stroked his beard as if searching for the right words.

"And don't tell me it's my own fault for marrying two women." He already knew it was. He should have been stronger, should have stood up to his father and refused. Even if the law did make provision for a man with two wives, it was not so in the beginning. He knew in his heart that God intended marriage to be between only two — one man and one woman — not three or four. Or many, as the heathen kings did in their bulging harems.

"So do you want honesty or do you want me to lie to you?" Tahath's dark eyes grew serious. "You know having two wives is always a struggle. It was why you didn't want to do so in the first place, if you recall."

Elkanah shifted the lamb's weight on his

shoulders. "Am I so weak that I couldn't even make my own decisions? How could I have allowed our mother and father to convince me that this was wise?"

"It did give you sons."

"And if I had died without them, would it have really mattered? You would have all divided my inheritance and given more to your children once Hannah was cared for." Was he even glad for having had children?

"You would have eventually come to regret growing old with just Hannah and no one else to care for you in your old age." Tahath chuckled. "Admit you made a mistake and let it go, brother. You can't very well change things. If you divorced Peninnah, what would happen to her children? The law clearly states that Eitan is your firstborn and heir whether you love Peninnah or not. Even if Hannah bears a child, he can't usurp Eitan's place. And you can't send Hannah away to find peace with Peninnah because of your agreement with Hyam, so I suggest you learn to live with the situation."

Elkanah scowled at Tahath, who looked away, still chuckling. "I see no humor in this."

Tahath only laughed harder. "I'm sorry. I was just picturing your life if you *hadn't* married Peninnah. Mother would have been on your doorstep every day with a new suggestion. You know she wasn't going to quit."

Elkanah gave him a withering glance, then let himself fall back a pace. He should have brought Hannah. At least she would have taken his mind off Peninnah. She had made it a point to never complain about the woman. It was only the children who seemed to bring her pain. And though he would rather do as Jacob had done with Joseph and give the favored wife's son the double portion, he knew the law, and he couldn't in good conscience ignore Eitan's rights as firstborn. Was his distancing himself from Eitan and Peninnah's other children causing the discord he felt?

Oh Adonai, I've made such a mess of things. Please let this offering I'm coming to give You be acceptable, and in Your mercy answer the prayers of Your servant.

Would God answer? What would happen if He finally gave Hannah a son? How could Elkanah make himself favor Eitan above any child Hannah conceived? Though he knew if he didn't give Eitan his rightful place, Peninnah's bitterness would only increase. A child born to Hannah — was it even possible? — would surely make everything worse.

He closed his eyes briefly, wishing the thoughts away.

Shiloh stood as a shining city in the distance. They would be there long before nightfall. Then Elkanah would offer the sacrifice and greet the priests — and their wives for Hannah's sake — and perhaps even ask Eli to pray for Hannah. If he could summon the courage to do so.

The sacrifice went better than Elkanah expected. Even Phinehas seemed to have lost some of his arrogant edge. Perhaps Tahath's presence rather than Hannah's had made a difference in the priests' attitudes. Perhaps God had heard his silent prayers.

Weariness filled him as he made his way to the rooms where he and Tahath would sleep. Evening sacrifices had ended, and after a quick meal, Elkanah found himself longing for a place to lay his head.

He passed Levites and some of the children of the priests as he walked through the buildings adjacent to the tabernacle. He had thought to stop in to give Raziela Hannah's greetings, then decided tomorrow would be a better day. But as he looked toward the end of the row where the priests' large homes stood, he saw her walking toward him.

They met before Elkanah could turn aside to one of the sleeping rooms. "Shalom, Raziela. Hannah sends you her greetings."

The woman wore a troubled look but managed to offer him a smile. "She is not with you?"

Elkanah shook his head. "No. Not this time."

"She is not ill?"

"No." He fidgeted, not wishing to lie, but he was not about to confide in this woman. "Perhaps she will come next time."

Raziela nodded and looked beyond him, appearing distracted. "Did you see a young man pass you recently?"

Elkanah clasped his hands behind him and took a step back. "There are many men, young and old, coming and going here. Would this be someone I know? A fellow Levite, perhaps?"

"Perhaps." She looked this way and that, clearly thinking about the object of her question. "He is a servant of mine, raised in our home since he was but a babe. His mother died giving birth, so I took him in." She met Elkanah's gaze. "It was the only thing to do since Hophni said the child had no other family."

Elkanah gave her a curious look. "How old is this boy?"

"About sixteen. I sent him on an errand some time ago. I expected him to return by now."

"I'm sure he will." Elkanah studied the woman a moment, his mind whirling with past rumors. Could Raziela have taken in Lital's child, whose mother, Rinat, was now old and frail but would fairly leap for joy to know a child of her daughter's lived? "Do you want me to help you look for him?"

Raziela glanced at him, then turned slightly to head home. "No, no. Do not trouble yourself. I am sure he will return." She moved past him, her skirts flowing after her in the breeze. How much did Raziela suffer from Hophni? How much did Irit know of Phinehas's dealings?

If this boy was truly Lital's son, then Raziela was a better woman than Hophni was a priest or a man. Surely she knew. But had she heard the rumors of Lital's bereaved mother behind the walls Hophni had built to keep her in? Did Raziela know the boy's mother had died and left a widowed grandmother who could have cared for him?

Oh Adonai, why do You not act? Why do You let the evil go on and on? Why do You allow your place of worship to be continually defiled? When, Lord? When will You send us a deliverer?

Might that deliverer be him? He examined his heart as the moon shone down on his exhausted body. *I am willing, Lord.* He would do anything to bring back what Israel had lost.

But thoughts of Hannah and Peninnah flashed in his mind's eye, and he knew he could not leave them and all of his responsibilities to lead a charge against the priesthood. Could he?

Are You asking it of me?

He knew that God spoke to prophets in visions and dreams, but despite his devotion, despite his eager desire to help, to fix things, despite his prayers for a deliverer, never once had he had such a dream or vision. Never once had God told him to go and lead.

The thought pained him, and he shook it aside. Until God called him, he was in no position to bring charges against the priests or to replace them with worthy sons of Aaron, if any could be found.

He could barely manage his own household. How could he ever imagine himself capable of making a difference in anything here?

Hannah sat in the shade of the sitting room, where she had moved the loom from the heat of day. With summer upon them, she could no longer work with the sun blazing down on her. The robe for Elkanah was taking shape beneath her skilled hands, and she was anxious to finish the work before he returned at the end of the week.

How long a week could seem! She worked tan threads through the weft, her heart aching with missing him. Nava's company helped, but it was not the same. She glanced at the girl sitting opposite her, spinning freshly dyed wool into useable thread. Together they had made many garments and large lengths of cloth to sell to the merchants.

"The robe is coming along nicely," Nava said, interrupting her musings. Of late, despite Nava's company, Peninnah's taunts had put Hannah in a perpetual state of sadness — to the point that Nava had again offered herself as a replacement. Hannah always refused, more determined than ever to find the girl a husband. Surely Elkanah would agree.

But how lonely she would be then. She even stayed away from Elkanah's family except on special occasions or feast days because she knew Peninnah was the accepted one there. If not for Nava and Dana . . . but no, she could not let herself dwell on what was not.

"You agree, yes?"

She looked up at Nava's comment. "Yes, yes. It is. I hope Elkanah is pleased."

"Oh, you know he will be." Nava's voice carried a comforting lilt, and Hannah looked up from her weaving and smiled.

"That wool accepted the dye better than I expected, thanks to your extra time stirring it. I think the green will mix well with the tan and red." She spoke for something to say, but a moment later she returned to her weaving in silence. She chewed her lip against the ever-present bitterness, wondering just when she had become so obsessed with having a child. One did not go against Adonai's wishes, and He obviously had decided that she was unworthy to bear children. What more was there to be said?

Approaching footsteps and a woman calling through the open door soon broke the quiet. "Shalom, Hannah. Are you there?"

Hannah bristled at the sound of Galia's voice. She nodded to Nava to rise and greet her.

"Welcome, Galia," Nava said as she met the woman at the entrance. "Would you like some water and some sweets to refresh yourself?" She backed into the room, allowing Galia to sweep inside as if she belonged there.

"No need." Galia waved a hand at Nava in a dismissive gesture. "I only came on my way to Peninnah's to invite you" — she looked at Hannah — "to dine with us tonight. Everyone will be there, even Dana. You simply must come, my dear."

Hannah stared and swallowed against a suddenly dry throat. Galia had never once come to include her in family gatherings, not without Elkanah there. And Hannah had determined that she would never accept should such an occasion arise. If she went now, she would be subject to Peninnah and her children with no one to protect her except Dana. Would Elkanah's brothers keep the women from throwing barbs at her?

A sick feeling formed in her middle. "I don't know, Galia." She hesitated to say she was ill, for Galia would simply insist that she or someone else come and care for her. In addition, it would be lying, for she was not sick physically, only sick at heart. Sick of dealing with Peninnah and Galia and the pitying looks at market or on the road to festivals.

"Come, come, my dear. You cannot ignore your family forever. Elkanah would want you to come." Galia sank onto a thick cushion and looked at Nava. "I'll take some of that water now."

Nava disappeared outside to draw water from the standing cistern while Galia leaned closer. "You know I speak the truth, Hannah. Unless you would rather return to your father's house, you belong to our family and I insist you join us." She accepted the water from Nava's hand and took a swift gulp, then quickly rose. "I will expect you to be there." And with that, she turned and left in a whirlwind toward Peninnah's house.

Hannah's hands stilled and fell to her lap. She looked at Nava.

"Shall I set out your best clothes, mistress?" Nava's eyes mirrored the bewildered look Hannah knew must be evident in her own expression.

Hannah nodded, but her mind would not accept what had just happened. Why did Galia want her present at a meal with Elkanah not home yet? She did not trust the woman, and she most certainly did not want to be one step closer to her rival than need be. And she did not need to be there. Elkanah would understand.

But as dusk fell, Hannah carried a torch and walked with Nava and Dana and her children to the house of Elkanah's father just the same.

25

"You know," Galia said once the meal had ended and the children ran off into the back rooms to play, "I heard some of the other Levite women at the well yesterday. They said that their husbands had heard that the priests were accepting young men and women, some not much older than children, to work at the tabernacle permanently. They would have all of their needs provided for. But the boys would learn to serve at a young age rather than the accepted age of thirty. The girls would learn to help as well, I suppose, but I daresay it sounds a little too convenient for our incorrigible priests."

"I could not imagine leaving even one of my children there," Kelila said, and murmurs of agreement went around the room.

Hannah glanced at Nava, who stood near the wall waiting to serve them, eyes downcast. How grateful she was that Elkanah had rescued the girl from that place, though perhaps Raziela or Eli might have looked out for her. She shivered. If God ever saw fit to give her a child, the last place she would want to leave him would be with those priests. She would never trust Hophni or Phinehas.

"Well, Hannah will never have to worry about such a thing since she has no child to give," Peninnah said, her gaze on the food in front of her. "And Elkanah would never send one of our children to that place. He disdains those priests."

"As we all do," Galia said, glancing Hannah's way. "None of my sons would allow such a thing. I only brought it up because there was talk of others considering the priests' offer. Apparently the priests want to train their servants at a young age. Perhaps they are looking for an army of servants to counter the complaints from the men of Israel who do not like the way they handle the sacrifices."

Hannah's face remained heated despite Galia's attempts to deflect Peninnah's snide comment.

"From what Tahath has said, some of those servants are like giants and strong as oxen. When they come with that fork that is meant to be dipped in the cauldron, it looks more like a weapon in their hands. And their very presence is equally menacing." Dana quickly touched Hannah's knee, but when she looked up, Dana's gaze was focused on the other women. "It makes sense that they would take young boys and try to turn them into soldiers more than servants, but how do you tell with a young boy whether he will be strong or weak?" She glanced at her own children, her look affectionate.

"I suppose training the young men makes sense, but why accept the younger girls?" Kelila asked. "They are far too young to serve until they grow to be women. What parent would even consider giving their daughters to live near those men?"

"I don't think they harm the girls," Hannah said, surprising herself that she dared join the conversation, but one glance at Nava and she wanted to put the girl's mind at ease. "I think Raziela and Irit would care for them and put them in service in their homes. I know they don't have much sway over what their husbands do, but they have ways of exerting *some* influence."

"You mean the way you do with Elkanah?" Peninnah's barb was quiet, but the whole room fell silent at her words.

The familiar knot coiled in Hannah's middle, and she wished for the hundredth time that she had not come. None of the men were here, as most had stayed in the fields. She was easy prey in a houseful of women who disdained her.

"Peninnah," Galia said, causing Hannah to glance her way.

She caught the scowl on Yafa's face and wondered if Peninnah's mother was for or against the way her daughter acted. Perhaps she simply did not like Peninnah being so obviously vocal with her words.

"Elkanah spends plenty of time with you," Galia continued, to Hannah's utter shock. Was the woman defending her? "You would not have so many children if he did not. You cannot blame him for wanting to give Hannah his time when yours is so taken up with caring for the children."

Hannah glanced Peninnah's way, but the words did not seem to penetrate her anger.

"It is no excuse for him to spend so much time with her to the neglect of the children he supposedly wanted." Peninnah glared at Galia, then at each one of the women staring at her. She stood and tossed her linen cloth onto the cushion where she had been sitting. "Think what you want of your son, Mother Galia, but Hannah controls him, and he owes it to me and his children to listen more to me than to *her*."

She gathered up her sons and daughters

while the rest of the children murmured and the women sat in silence. At last Yafa slowly stood, her look apologetic, and helped her daughter leave.

Elkanah quickened his pace as Ephraim's hills came into view. Even a week at Shiloh seemed much too long. More than once Elkanah had intervened when Phinehas's servant demanded uncooked meat from men offering a sacrifice. But it was not enough. It was never enough.

"Anxious to see Hannah?" Tahath pulled the reins of the donkey, which trudged along behind them. Their load was much lighter than the day they had set out. "I don't blame you. I've been imagining Dana's cooking for days." He laughed at the look Elkanah gave him. "What? Don't tell me you have never wished the meals were coming from Hannah's hands rather than the Levitical cooks."

Elkanah smiled. They both knew it was more than cooking that they missed in these beloved women. And he could not wait to share his experiences with Hannah — she would understand his heart.

But how much time would he have with her before Peninnah heard of his return? What if she was waiting on the road and blocked his way to Hannah's house?

He glanced at Tahath. "I think we should take the back road and come in that way. It will allow you to be home first, and I'm sure your children are anxious to see you."

Guilt pricked him with the statement. Wouldn't his own children have missed him as well?

"You want to be sure to see Hannah first." Tahath wiggled his brows in that teasing way he had.

"You're the one who said it, not me." But Elkanah couldn't stop a genuine smile. "So are we taking the back road?"

"It's fine by me, brother. You're the one who has to figure out how to divide your time tonight."

They trudged on, Elkanah suddenly not so certain he wanted to rush this time away. Yet he missed Hannah. His pace quickened again, and he breathed a sigh at the sight of Hannah's house. There she stood in the courtyard, watching the road, waiting for him.

He bid Tahath a quick farewell and ran the rest of the way, dropped his pack, and whisked her into his arms. "Oh how I've missed you," he whispered against her ear.

She laughed as he twirled her around. "I have missed you too. Terribly so!"

Her words held a hint of sadness despite the cheeriness in her tone. Had she been sorrowful while he was away? "Tell me, how have you been?" He wasn't ready to ask about or hear a litany of complaints that he knew would come from Peninnah, but with Hannah he felt the question a safe one.

"All has been so quiet without you and Tahath. Even your brothers stayed long hours in the field with the sheep so that a meal with your family meant only the women gathered."

He set her slightly away from him, still holding her arms. "You went to a meal with my family? Alone?"

"I had Nava with me. And Dana and her children."

He searched her face. "And Peninnah was there? Yet all is well?" Incredulous. He dared not believe the strife had ended in his short week away.

Hannah glanced beyond him, seeming unwilling to meet his gaze. "Peninnah used her time well to be her normal unkind self whenever the opportunity arose. But we do not need to talk about that. It is over now."

Elkanah cupped her cheek. "I *want* to hear about it."

Hannah smiled, this time holding his gaze. "Your mother even defended me when Peninnah had her outburst. I actually thought for a moment that there might be some kindness underneath your mother's controlling layers."

Elkanah laughed. "My mother defended by you, my dear wife? I think I am witness to some kind of miracle."

Hannah laughed with him, and he felt a measure of relief that his words were not hurtful. The moment he'd said them, he thought of the one miracle God had not given them — a child. To trivialize Hannah's relationship with his mother and put it on par with a true miracle of birth . . . He shook the thought aside as she took his hand and led him into the house. They settled among the cushions on the floor while Nava brought some stew and flatbread.

"So tell me about your trip." Hannah dipped the bread in the stew and handed it to him. "How are Raziela and Irit?"

"They are well. Their husbands are still corrupt louses, but the women were friendly and accepted your greeting. You know," he said around a mouthful of food, "Raziela seemed quite concerned about a servant boy — one who grew up in her house."

"Raziela raises many children who are not her own. But there was something about this one that troubled you?" Hannah lifted a brow.

Elkanah finished eating, framing his words. "I can't prove anything, but she was looking for a sixteen-year-old boy. If Lital did bear a child, he would be about that age now." He let the words hang between them.

"Many servants in Raziela's and Irit's homes are about that age," she said. "Did you see him? Is there a reason you make this assumption?"

Elkanah set his food aside. "I didn't see him. No. But I found Raziela looking for him, and when I asked his age, it sparked the memory of Lital."

Hannah looked at him for a lengthy breath. "But there is no way to prove such a thing. The boy is likely Hophni's illegitimate child. Perhaps with Lital. Perhaps with some other poor woman. If Hophni remembers the mother, I am fairly certain he would not tell us."

Elkanah sighed and took her hand. "As I worked there, especially after I saw the concern in Raziela's eyes, I kept thinking how much we need a deliverer — and could I be that person? But I knew I could not. I don't know who can, but I know in my heart it can't be me."

Hannah nodded. "God will bring someone

271

who can do what you cannot."

He pulled her close. "Yes. Surely. Hophni and Phinehas will not get away with this forever." He rubbed her back and breathed in the scent of her, wishing he could just lie down beside her and sleep. But Peninnah waited. "I must go," he whispered against her ear. "But I will return soon. This night."

She pulled away, and her look took on that resignation she could not seem to shake, no matter their topic of conversation. He sensed defeat hidden beneath her smile, where her joy used to be.

"I will wait for you," she said as they both stood. She smiled, but it did not reach her eyes.

"It will be all right, beloved. Our family will be all right."

She nodded but said nothing, and he knew his words did not comfort.

■ ■ ■ ■

PART 3

■ ■ ■ ■

After they had eaten and drunk in Shiloh, Hannah rose. Now Eli the priest was sitting on the seat beside the doorpost of the temple of the LORD. She was deeply distressed and prayed to the LORD and wept bitterly. And she vowed a vow and said, "O LORD of hosts, if you will indeed look on the affliction of your servant and remember me and not forget your servant, but will give to your servant a son, then I will give him to the LORD all the days of his life, and no razor shall touch his head."

1 Samuel 1:9–11

26

Three Years Later

Hannah carried a basket of food and a skin of water and walked the path that would pass Peninnah's house but led to the fields where Elkanah was keeping the sheep. She thought to take a longer way around to avoid the risk of seeing her rival, but her longing to spend the day in the fields with her husband made her throw caution aside. Peninnah would be too busy with her children to be out of the house, and even if she were working in the courtyard, Hannah would simply keep her distance.

She ducked behind a large terebinth tree that stood like a sentry between her house and Peninnah's, and glanced at the courtyard. Sounds of children could be heard inside, but there was no sign of Peninnah working outside. Good.

She pulled in a breath and took a cautious step from behind the tree.

"Where are you going, Aunt Hannah?" Eitan, now ten, stood in her path, his brother Hevel not far behind him. "Can we go with you?"

Hannah stared openmouthed for a brief moment. Peninnah's two oldest sons should already be training with Elkanah to learn the tasks of a man. Was Peninnah or Elkanah the one holding them back?

"I'm sure your mother has need of you, Eitan. Perhaps another time." She attempted to hurry off, but Eitan stopped her.

"I will ask her. She will not care if I go." Eitan bounded toward the house, Hevel on his heels.

"Take me too," Hevel said, barely able to keep up with his older brother. "I wanna come too."

Hannah's heart sank. She should have gone the long way around, but never did she expect Peninnah's children to accost her. Did they suspect she had plans to spend the day with Elkanah? It wasn't that she didn't like Peninnah's children, but Peninnah had used them against her so many times that she had grown weary of their presence. It wasn't fair of her to think so, but the sight of even one of the children was like seeing their mother.

If only Peninnah were easier to deal with.

"Go with Hannah? Where is she going?" Peninnah's strident voice carried through the open windows. "How do you even know this? Hannah is shut up in her house weaving by this time of day. She doesn't want nor does she know how to take care of little boys."

Hannah should have expected the barb, be used to it by now, but she could never quite get over the sting. She had helped Dana with her children for years. She certainly did know how to care for boys.

"Please, Ima. Aunt Hannah is nice to us when we are with Savta Galia. She could watch us. She said she would take us."

Hannah bristled. Elkanah would not teach his children to lie, so had this come from Peninnah? Or were children simply born to push to get their way, even if that meant bending the truth? A sigh escaped. If she had her own children, she would not allow such a thing.

"And how do you know this?" Peninnah's voice had not lowered in tone, and Hannah could still clearly hear.

The heartache and the need to escape spurred her to keep walking. Let Eitan argue with his mother. She would not be party to a child's lies, and she didn't want her time with Elkanah interrupted by his children.

His children.

She stopped just beyond the boundaries of Peninnah's house, the realization hitting her afresh. Why did this still trouble her? A woman learned to deal with what life handed her. What God handed her. And for some reason God had found Peninnah more pleasing to bless than her.

She staggered forward, not wanting any of the children to come racing after her and find her like this. A rock formation rose before her, beckoning. A place to hide her grief. Surely the children would not wander this far. But the fear of bandits who were known to inhabit similar places made her pause.

What was she doing out here alone? Though the days of oppression from Canaanite enemies had grown minimal, a woman in a field could never be too careful. And Elkanah did not know she was coming, so if something happened to her . . . She shivered and wrapped the scarf more securely about her, glancing before and behind. If only she had thought to bring the sling Elkanah had made for her. Why did she not think to carry it?

Perhaps taking the boys would be wiser than she'd first thought. She had planned a simple meal for the two of them with some extra in case one of Elkanah's brothers was nearby. Enough for two small boys? If something did happen to her, they could run home to their mother or tell their father, and somehow someone might come to her aid.

She shook herself, wondering where the fear and ridiculous thoughts were coming from. No one was going to trouble her, with or without the children. Ephraim's hills were safe. Elkanah had said so many times. If anything was not safe, it was the very house where God was to be worshiped.

Her stomach knotted with the familiar sadness that thought evoked.

She glanced back at Peninnah's house. Perhaps one of Elkanah's sons would become the deliverer Elkanah longed for. She recoiled at the very idea of one of Peninnah's sons leading Israel. But if that was in God's plan . . .

She lifted her gaze heavenward. Clouds danced over a sea of brilliant blue, the sun shining through them like rays of pure gold. *Your will be done,* she prayed, her heart yearning to know just what that will might be. Oh to be included in God's plan to heal their nation! Oh to know her family loved and worshiped Adonai as she longed to do

— but so often failed. She knew she failed, for she could not stop the bitter hurt that Peninnah's presence had forced upon her. Sharing a husband was bad enough. But her rival, her enemy, was cruel at every turn, especially when Hannah felt most vulnerable. When everyone else's children surrounded her.

Tears stung, but she blinked them back. She would not cry. Not here. Not now. And then she saw Eitan and Hevel burst from the house into the courtyard, looking to where she had been standing. At the sight of their downcast faces, she felt a kick in her gut. She was being unfair to them. They were just children, after all. Elkanah's children.

She hurried forward and called their names.

Eitan's face brightened. "Ima said we could come!" He raced closer to her.

Peninnah stood in the doorway, watching. "Where are you taking them?" Arms crossed over her chest, she scowled.

Hannah straightened, forcing herself to stay strong. "I'm taking food to Elkanah. I think there should be enough for the boys."

Peninnah studied her, jealousy in her scowl. "Wait a moment and I'll give you more to add for them." She turned and went into the house and quickly returned with another small basket.

Hannah took it. "Thank you."

Peninnah said nothing but gave each child a stern look, whirled about, and marched back into the house.

Hannah watched the boys skip ahead of her and sighed.

At the sound of children calling his name, Elkanah looked up from pulling brambles from the wool of one of the younger lambs.

"Abba! Abba!" Eitan's high-pitched voice filled the still air.

"We're coming, Abba!" Hevel reminded Elkanah of Peninnah when she was on the verge of an outburst, though the child's cry carried far more innocence.

"What is this?" He walked toward them, catching sight of Hannah not far behind, hurrying to keep up.

Eitan raced closer and Hevel's shorter legs pumped hard to reach him. Elkanah bent low to embrace each boy and smile into his eyes.

"Aunt Hannah said we could come with her," Eitan said, glancing behind him.

Elkanah scooped Hevel into his arms and kept a hand on Eitan's back as Hannah approached. "I see I am most blessed today."

281

He glanced at the baskets she carried.

"I brought food," she said. "I wanted to spend the day with you." He caught the wistful look in her eyes. "As I passed by Peninnah's house, the boys saw me and asked to come."

"It was kind of you to let them." He searched her face.

She shrugged. "They are your children."

She said the words without animosity as though stating a fact, but her eyes betrayed her true feelings. Elkanah set Hevel on the ground and told the boys to watch the young ewe for him and to see if they could find any more brambles in her wool. They took off running to the place Elkanah pointed, while he took Hannah's hand and walked with her to the shade of a spreading oak tree.

"We can eat here," he said.

"Peninnah sent a basket for the boys." Hannah placed it on the ground next to the one she had prepared for him. Elkanah glanced at the children to be sure they were safe, then focused his attention on Hannah.

"I suspect bringing the boys was not your first intent." He traced the line of her jaw and cupped her cheek. "You are nicer to my children than their mother is to you."

Hannah looked past him in the direction

of the children. "It is nothing," she said after a lengthy pause. "But come. I imagine you are hungry, and perhaps we can have a few moments while the boys are occupied."

Elkanah rubbed a hand over his beard, guilt nudging him. "I suppose Eitan should start coming with me to learn the skills of a shepherd."

Hannah handed him some flatbread. "It seems that would be wise. I was his age, perhaps younger, when my father let me help him do little things in his pottery shop." She pulled out a goatskin of milk and some cheese and even a goatskin of qom, the tasty water left over from her cheese making, a drink he had always loved.

He smiled at her. "You spoil me."

She laughed, and he joined her. "You are my favorite person to spoil."

She was too polite to say that he was her only person to spoil. Would she treat him so well if she had the distraction of children? But he did not wish to dwell on that thought.

"I think you should know . . ." She paused, sobering. "I heard Eitan lie to Peninnah. I never invited the boys to join me, but they told her I did. I didn't want you to think I did, if Peninnah should bring it up and say something . . . different."

"Something untrue, you mean."

She nodded. "Perhaps. One can never tell what she will say."

He knew that only too well. And the regret he carried from the first week of their marriage was almost tangible.

"I will keep your words in mind. Thank you." He glanced at the boys again. "And I will speak to Eitan. I fear that he is picking up the ability to twist words from his mother. It is not a skill I admire."

She touched his arm. "One child at a time, and with your guidance they will become fine men."

"Unless their mother undoes my efforts." He sighed. "I'm sorry. I do not mean to complain about Peninnah when I have such little time with you." He broke the bread and held out a piece to her. "We will call the boys to join us after I taste that qom."

Hannah smiled, taking the bread from his hand. He bowed his head and gave thanks, a habit he had done since his youth, a habit he felt called to continue, for everyone knew that food could often be scarce and famines were never more than a few seasons of drought away. It was part of why they celebrated the First Fruits, a festival that was fast approaching — to thank God in advance for what He would provide.

He ate in silence, pondering how this next feast would be and whether Peninnah would be civil to Hannah during the celebrating. The truth was, he had come to dread the feasts since Peninnah had joined their home. What had once been a time of worship with Hannah had become a time for Peninnah to flaunt her children publicly and taunt Hannah to shame.

He should put a stop to it, but Peninnah was sneaky and Hannah rarely said a word in response. Was he living with a false hope that all would be made right somehow without his interference? That somehow the two women would become friends?

He smiled at Hannah. "I'm glad you came." He should say more. Should warn her of his worries about the upcoming feast. But Eitan's voice interrupted him, and he turned and saw the two children running toward them.

"I'm hungry," Eitan said, grasping for the basket Peninnah had sent.

Hannah stopped him. "Let me help you." She met the boy's intense gaze. "So you can help your brother."

Eitan scowled for the briefest moment, so like his mother, and Elkanah wished not for the first time that he had brought the boy with him sooner to help train him in the ways he knew were right. Ways of gratitude toward their Maker for the food and so much more.

"Is that qom? I want some." Eitan's tone turned from questioning to demanding.

"Me too!" Hevel screeched, and Elkanah nearly jolted at the sharp sound.

"It is for your father," Hannah said firmly, meeting each boy's gaze. "You may ask him politely if he would like to share, but you must not demand."

Eitan's eyes grew wide at Hannah's subtle rebuke, but he accepted her words without comment. "May we have a taste, Abba?"

Elkanah took the small bowl and sipped first, knowing he wasn't likely to get more and he did not want to disappoint Hannah, then offered it in turn to each child. The sigh of pleasure and look of thanks on the children's faces made him straighten, a feeling of pride surging through him. It was not too late to teach them. They were not yet so difficult to convince to do right.

But as they turned back to Hannah, accepting the food from the basket, he did not miss the pinched look on Eitan's face. "Ima won't like this," he said to his brother.

Hevel simply nodded, too solemn for one so young.

Elkanah glanced at Hannah and could see

by her look that she understood exactly what they meant. Eitan would complain about Hannah's rebuke to Peninnah, and Hannah would suffer for it when Elkanah was not around to protect her. All because she was kind enough to bring the boys to the field with her.

Elkanah stared at his sons, feeling helpless. Something had to change, but he had no idea how to bring that change about.

27

Hannah walked beside Dana along the familiar dusty path toward Shiloh. In her arms, she carried Dana's youngest child, asleep against her chest. She looked down at the serene face, so new and untested in the world.

"You will let me know if she grows tiring," Dana said.

Hannah looked up to meet her gaze. "I don't think that is possible." The babe was securely tied to her and held with the help of Hannah's own longing arms. She studied this sister-in-law a moment and smiled. "Thank you."

Dana brushed the words away. "You have been of great help to me, Hannah. I don't know how I would have cared for these children without you." Her eyes held warmth and confidence, and she stopped a moment and touched Hannah's arm, making her stop as well. "I do not know why

God has withheld children from you." She glanced around to be sure they were alone, despite the crowd. Peninnah was ahead of them with her mother and children, and once Dana spotted her she motioned in her direction and leaned closer. "You would make a much better mother, and Elkanah would have been happier if God had not stopped your womb. But," she said, giving Hannah's arm a gentle squeeze, "I do not believe all hope is lost. I don't know why I say this, for I do not wish to cause you pain, my dear Hannah, but I think God still has a great plan in store for you. Who knows? You may yet have a son like Isaac and bring laughter to this family. I know there is a purpose." She looked away and stepped back a pace. "Just don't lose hope."

Hannah looked ahead and began walking again. The baby squirmed a bit but then settled into sleep once more. Hannah blinked as emotion rolled through her, fighting the urge to weep, a feeling that so often came over her of late. She was so tired of Peninnah's taunts and the looks of pity from the women at the well. And the joy Peninnah's children brought to Elkanah's eyes overshadowed even Galia's attempts at kindness.

She knew Dana supported her, but until

now she had not realized how much. Dana's words swirled in her heart and, despite her desperate effort to stop them, caused a tiny bloom of hope to reside there again. Like the first bud on a new tree, the promise of a flower and fruit to come.

But she dare not trust these simple words, however comforting they were. Words could not bring life to her dead womb unless they were God's words. And Dana spoke only out of her need to bring joy to Hannah's life. It was her way, though she had never spoken quite so forcefully until now.

Why, then? She glanced at the road ahead. The men and beasts stirred the dust in front of the women and children. She should be walking closer to Elkanah, but Peninnah had hurried to the place directly behind him, and Hannah had no desire to mingle with the woman along the way.

What would life be like if God did as Dana had suggested? What if Hannah actually did have a child? Even just one, as Sarah had only Isaac?

Oh Adonai . . .

The hope burst again to a feeling of intense longing, and no more words would come. How did one make the Almighty see her need? Did God *see* Hannah as He once saw Hagar? And if He did, how could she possibly make Him hear her prayers and answer them?

The child made the suckling sounds of a nursing babe in her sleep, and the action stirred Hannah's thoughts back to her surroundings. The noise of the chattering women and the occasional sound of Peninnah's shouts at her children brought reality back with a jolt. This was her world. Her neighbors and family were all her world would ever be. Dana's kindness and Elkanah's love helped her survive the anguish, but it did not abate. How could it possibly abate? She was thirty-seven years old and had been married for eighteen years. Perhaps Sarah had waited longer, but Hannah understood now why she had given up and handed Hagar to Abraham. For the same reason Elkanah had taken Peninnah. He didn't believe Hannah would bear children, and neither did she. Better to let hope die than be heartsick over a loss she could not regain.

As the sun set upon the newly raised tents in Shiloh, a ram's horn could be heard coming from the tabernacle grounds.

"Hush now, children," Peninnah's mother said as Peninnah hurried them all to take seats on the ground, where a large mat was spread with food.

The boys seemed to listen better to her mother than to her these days, but she was with child again and in no mood for patience. At least with the meal before Passover Elkanah would join them rather than seclude himself away with Hannah. Of course, *she* would be joining them as well, which did nothing to improve Peninnah's feelings.

"There's Abba and Aunt Hannah now, Ima!" Hevel's enthusiasm for his father, but worse, for her rival, grated on already taut nerves. "Can I go to meet them?"

"No!" Peninnah winced at the crestfallen look on her young son's face, but she would not be party to giving Hannah any satisfaction of knowing that the children liked her at times better than their own mother.

She clenched her jaw as she straightened and offered a forced smile to her husband and Hannah. "Welcome," she said, pointing to Elkanah's place and to Hannah's at the far end away from him.

"Thank you, Peninnah, but Hannah will sit here." Elkanah took Hannah's hand and guided her to sit beside him, the very place Peninnah intended to sit. "And you will sit here." He pointed to his other side.

She looked at him, wanting to lash out,

but held her tongue. The upcoming Passover was not a time for arguments, especially with two more festivals of Unleavened Bread and First Fruits.

She felt her mother's hand on her arm. "It's all right, Peninnah. I will help the children." As would Nava, no doubt.

Fine then. Peninnah took the seat Elkanah had indicated and watched as he waited for Hannah to do the same. A headache began along the back of her neck, but she held her head high and tried to ignore it. How she hated this woman's presence!

"Tomorrow we celebrate the Passover and Unleavened Bread, and then I will take the barley sheaf and offer it to the Lord," Elkanah said, his gaze taking in the children. "Do you know what every Israelite man is to say to the priest when he brings the basket with the barley sheaf?"

Eitan looked at Hevel and both shook their heads.

"First, I say, 'I declare today to the Lord your God that I have come to the land the Lord swore to our ancestors to give us.' Then the priest takes the basket and sets it down in front of the altar of the Lord our God. But that is not all."

Peninnah wondered why he was trying to make the children understand something they were surely too young to remember.

"Then I declare before the Lord, 'My father was a wandering Aramean, and he went down into Egypt with a few people and lived there and became a great nation, powerful and numerous. But the Egyptians mistreated us and made us suffer, subjecting us to harsh labor. Then we cried out to the Lord, the God of our ancestors, and the Lord heard our voice and saw our misery, toil, and oppression. So the Lord brought us out of Egypt with a mighty hand and an outstretched arm, with great terror and with signs and wonders. He brought us to this place and gave us this land, a land flowing with milk and honey. And now I bring the first fruits of the soil that You, Lord, have given me.' So I will put the basket before the Lord and bow down before Him. Then we all rejoice in all the good things the Lord has given to us."

"That declaration sounds like it almost combines Passover and First Fruits," Hannah said, her voice carrying a hint of awe.

"Yes," Elkanah said, smiling at her.

Why was the woman always so agreeable?

Elkanah looked at the boys once more. "So now you know what I say when I offer God the sheaf of barley, but why do we give the first fruits to our God?"

Eitan raised his hand. "I know!"

Elkanah smiled. "All right, Eitan, tell me."

"Because He told us to?" Eitan smiled.

Peninnah scowled. "Your questions are making this too complicated for them," she said, irritated that Eitan had not given a better answer.

"I think they are old enough to learn," he said, glancing at her, then back to his children. "Yes, that's one reason. Can anyone think of the other?"

Hevel raised his hand, looking swiftly at his older brother. "Because God needs to eat?"

Peninnah caught Hannah's slight chuckle. Her headache spiked and she closed her eyes, trying desperately to stop it.

"Because God wants us to trust Him with the rest of the harvest." Elkanah's voice caused her to look his way again. "By giving God the first and best part of our harvest, we are telling Him that we trust Him to keep the rest of our harvest safe so that we will have food to eat."

"It is a good thing to trust our God," Hannah added, raising Peninnah's frustration to yet a higher level.

"A lot of good it has done you," she spat, hating the words the moment she had spoken them. "I'm sure you have trusted

God for a child, and yet He does not listen." Trying to fix her blunder was not helping. Why could she not learn to keep silent when Elkanah was present?

"Just because we trust God doesn't mean He gives us everything we ask for," Hannah said softly. "You do want your children to trust Him, do you not?"

"Of course! What kind of a mother do you think I am?" Heat filled Peninnah's cheeks.

"Enough!" Elkanah's gaze hardened, and she could not hold it. "Let us eat in peace, shall we?"

He set about to serve them portions of the food they had brought with them. Tomorrow they would feast again after the sacrifice, when meat would be in abundance. But tonight the meal was the start of celebration, a taste of things to come.

"What happens after your father offers the barley sheaf to the priests?" Yafa asked Peninnah's children as they began to eat the bread and stew offered them.

"They give a wave offering," Eitan said, sounding pleased with himself.

Though Elkanah insisted on asking the questions every year, Peninnah was never sure the boys would answer correctly. A wrong answer made her feel like a terrible mother. Besides, even she thought the ritual rather meaningless, despite Elkanah's explanations. She tuned out the responses and tried to ignore the way Elkanah spoke to Hannah and not to her.

They seemed to take great delight in this feast, and the realization left a sour taste in her mouth. What did they see in these festivities that she missed? How was God satisfied with barley sheaves and two loaves of bread?

But worse, why did she always say the wrong thing when Elkanah was around? Now it would take months once the feast ended to get Elkanah to come to her. And she would be large with child by then, keeping him away even longer. She chewed her bread slowly, casting a narrowed look Hannah's way. The sound of the woman's laughter at something Elkanah — or was it the children? — had said made the headache greater. She was so weary of this woman. Weary of her life.

Somehow she must come up with a way to make things better. She could not continue like this. Her mother's advice all those years ago to make Hannah miserable had carried no effect. The woman was as pleasing to Elkanah as she had always been.

I must be doing something wrong. Perhaps if she was nicer to Hannah . . . But the thought caused more caustic words to form on her tongue toward the woman who had the one thing she didn't. Her husband's love.

Peninnah was determined to take it from her, whatever the cost.

28

Elkanah rose early from Hannah's side before the sun crested the horizon. That she seemed to be sleeping peacefully was a relief, for he couldn't help but hear her quiet weeping in the night.

He donned his robe and slipped from the tent. The last wisp of stars had all but vanished, but the moon still clung to the side of the sky as though it feared dropping into the abyss. A sigh escaped him as he raked a hand through his hair. The camp still slept, but he wove his way past his family's tents toward the surrounding hills. Perhaps if he prayed here, prayed harder.

The tents seemed endless as he attempted to move in silence between them, until at last he reached the outskirts of the camp. He climbed the top of the hill and peered down on the sleeping Israelites. The hint of dawn caused a gray hue to lighten the horizon, and he wondered how God caused the dawn to continue on its course or the night to be so black. If not for the moon and stars they would have no light to see. No earthly lamp could illumine such deep darkness, nor could it illumine the darkness he felt filling his soul.

There is so much evil in this place, Adonai. Hophni and Phinehas make a mockery of Your sacrifice. My children will grow up thinking the priests' actions are normal. And the woman I love most on earth feels worthless because You have stopped her womb. Why must it be? Do You not hear the cries of Your people? Why are You silent?

He raised his hands heavenward, the weight of them like the heaviness in his soul. How was he supposed to go on year after year with this sameness? Nothing ever changed. Peninnah only grew angrier and treated Hannah worse with each passing year. The priests' corruption went unchecked. And he was helpless to stop either one.

What can I do? He lifted his head to gaze upon the coming dawn.

Trust Me.

Had he heard the words aloud? Surely he had conjured the thought from someplace deep within himself. And yet, he sensed in his spirit that was not true. Did not God answer prayer? Moses himself had said that God was near when people prayed to Him.

What can I do? A sense of uncompromising trust filled him. Wasn't that why they offered the sheaf of barley, the first fruits of the ground, to wave as bread before the Lord? And wasn't God Himself the bread of heaven, the One who had rained manna down on the children of Israel during their days in the wilderness? Perhaps the wave offering of two loaves of leavened bread was another way of giving acknowledgment to man's sin and God's goodness, for leaven could not sit upon God's altar even as sin could not enter His presence.

Only by the blood of a spotless lamb could the high priest enter the presence. And then only on the Day of Atonement — because of the blood and the incense, the prayers of the people.

All of it a symbol of trust.

Trust Me.

His spirit had felt the words more than heard them.

"I will trust You, Adonai Tzva'ot." He lifted his hands higher. "Praise Your holy name, for You are worthy to receive honor and glory and riches and power. All men bow to You. You are great and mighty, and You are good."

He still did not fully understand, for who could understand the Almighty One, the Lord of Hosts? But as he picked his way back down the hill with the breaking dawn, he knew he could survive even the frustration and evil around him. Because now he knew. God saw. And He would not remain silent forever.

Hannah walked with Nava past the camp to the housing for the Levites — more specifically, to Raziela's home. "We won't be long," she said, glancing at her faithful maid, who had stayed on with Hannah three years past her seven years' service.

To Hannah's frustration, Elkanah had not yet found a man who would marry a young woman who had been a slave most of her life. Surely there must be someone who could support her maid, her friend. If she were wed to another servant, they would never be able to leave a life of service, even when the Sabbath year said they should be free, for they would not have the means to support themselves. Not with the way the people had grown used to living during these corrupt times. Not unless someone could help them get started.

"Take however long you need, mistress." Nava's smile, always genuine, warmed Hannah. They turned onto the lane that led to the priest's stately home. "I hope you find what you have come for."

Hannah gave her a curious look. "I have not come looking for anything."

Nava raised a brow. "Oh, of course, I know you just want to give Raziela your greetings." She studied her feet. "It's just that . . . I sense you are seeking something more. Forgive me if I have spoken out of turn."

Hannah stopped, eyeing her servant's too-perceptive look. Nava had been at her side through almost every one of Peninnah's pregnancies, comforting her. She knew Hannah as well as Hannah would allow any woman to know her. Was she right? Was Hannah seeking Raziela for more than a greeting?

"I do not know if I seek more than mere renewed acquaintance," Hannah admitted. "I am curious about many things, but whether those questions arise in our speaking remains to be seen. I do not even know if the woman will invite us in."

Nava nodded her understanding, and the two moved closer to the priest's door. Hannah's heartbeat quickened as they climbed the grand steps leading to the home's entrance. Nerves taut at the very thought of running into either priest, she knocked on the door, glanced at Nava, and waited. A servant opened to them, a young man who looked by the length of his beard to be nearly twenty.

"We are here to see Raziela," Hannah said, looking him up and down. He looked familiar, but she could not determine why. "Have we met before?"

The young man looked at her, his expression wary. "No, mistress. I do not think we have met."

Hannah tilted her head, studying him. "I didn't see you when I visited here years ago? Of course, you would have been a child. Have you lived long in this place?" Was this the young man Elkanah had told her about?

The young man's color heightened. "As long as I can remember. My mistress tells me that my mother died in childbirth, which is why she took me in." He bent and motioned for them to sit in order for him to wash their feet.

Both women sat on an intricately carved limestone bench and allowed the young man to wash off the dust that had accumulated beneath their sandals.

"I'm sorry to hear that about your mother. Have you no idea where the rest of your family is from?"

"No, mistress. I have no other family that I know of."

Hannah pondered the thought but not for long, as Raziela strode into the room, her beautifully adorned robe flowing effortlessly as she walked.

"Hannah! How good of you to stop by to see me." She extended both hands, and Hannah took them and squeezed. The young man quickly finished drying her feet and returned her sandals to her. Hannah stood and walked with Raziela into the sitting room, while Nava stayed in the entryway.

"So tell me, how do things fare with you?" Raziela asked as they sat and accepted cups of spiced fruity water from a servant.

"I am well. We — that is, Elkanah's family has grown since he took Peninnah to wife, but I remain his alone." She refused to use the word *barren,* for it caused an ache in her soul.

"I sense that Peninnah is not an easy sister-wife to share him with." Raziela's eyes held compassion as she leaned forward to better face Hannah.

Hannah met the woman's gaze. "No. She is not. She does her best to make my life miserable." She chuckled. "I do try not to let her win."

Raziela smiled, but her gaze narrowed. "And yet she causes you great pain."

The words, said so certainly and with such kindness, brought a lump to Hannah's throat. She released a deep sigh. "Yes," she said, unable to say more.

Raziela took her hand again and held it. "If I can help in any way, please do not hesitate to ask me."

Hannah nodded. "There is nothing to be done unless you have the ear of God to pray and ask Him for a child. At least then she would only accuse me of stealing all of Elkanah's love."

"I will pray for you, dear Hannah." She looked briefly away. "Though I will admit, He seems silent to the prayers I pray as well."

Hannah's interest piqued, and she searched her friend's face. "Tell me."

Raziela smiled. "Oh, you know. It is always the same with Hophni and his brother. Irit and I are often troubled and offer secret sacrifices when Eli allows it. We want the corruption and sexual sins to cease. We want to see the women they abuse go back to their families, not die in childbirth or end up as personal mistresses of our husbands. But apparently we are not enough for them, and God is not listening."

Oh Adonai, why do You not hear?

"The young man you were talking to," Raziela interrupted her musings. "He is one of those born of a young woman who died in childbirth. We knew of no family, so I took him in. He has served me since he was old enough to know his right hand from his left." Raziela touched her temple and closed her eyes for a brief moment. "I grow weary of it all."

Hannah's mind whirled. "You have seen many women give birth here?"

"Too many. Of course, many of the mothers live and go home to their fathers in disgrace." Raziela's gaze grew distant. "Though not all of them can." She shook her head, and silence followed the remark. Hannah wondered if her friend would say more. "Some go on to serve and are not permitted by our husbands to keep their children. Some beg to leave and try to take the babies with them, but their families will not take them in. It is a sad situation."

"How many children?" Hannah rubbed her arms, but the chill would not abate.

"Perhaps thirty?" Raziela shrugged. "I've lost count. My servants raise them. I just make sure there is food enough and clothing enough to keep them warm and fed. When they grow up, some of them work in the fields and are not kept here in the house. Our husbands acquired more land than they were allotted by forcing some of the men of Shiloh to give them fields. The children, when they are old enough, work the land." Her chest lifted in a deep sigh. "I fear . . . I fear God is going to bring disaster on us for the sins of our husbands."

Hannah felt the chill grow deeper inside her. Would all of Israel feel the effects of the priests' sins? What would happen to Raziela and Irit?

"The young man you mentioned earlier," Hannah said. "He is about the age of a child born to a friend of mine whose body was found in the woods of Ephraim. It is possible he has a grandmother still living."

Raziela looked at her, eyes wide. "How can you know that? We searched for family members . . . that is, Hophni said he searched . . ."

"He has the features of one of the old women in our village," Hannah said, wondering if bringing this up was wise. "Her daughter, my friend Lital, worked here about twenty or so years ago. Elkanah's sister and I found her body. It was evident she had borne a child, and her mother later confirmed it, yet she had no husband."

Raziela's hand covered her mouth to stifle

a gasp. "And you think one of our husbands is responsible."

Hannah held her friend's gaze. "There was never any proof, except for the fact that she worked and lived here. No one ever found the body of a baby, boy or girl."

"And they searched."

"For weeks. Some even searched the river." Hannah's hands shook as she spoke, and she again questioned why this mattered to her and why she was so certain that the young servant belonged to Rinat. What if she was wrong?

"I have no way of proving you are right or wrong, Hannah." Raziela's expression held sorrow. "I do not know his mother. All I know is that one day Hophni handed me an infant and said the child had no one else, do something."

"You knew he was Hophni's child though."

Raziela gave a brief nod. "He also looks like his father. But he can never lay claim to the rights of the priesthood, for he is illegitimate and Hophni would never admit that he is his child."

"I am sorry for you," Hannah said, wishing now she had not brought up the subject. "I should greet Irit as well, but I must get back."

Raziela nodded and stood. "I understand. Thank you for telling me about the possible grandmother. Perhaps someday we can find a way for them to meet."

"Yes. Perhaps we can." Though she had no idea how that would be possible.

The two women walked to the door, where Hannah found Nava speaking with the young man in question. She looked between the two. They were of similar age, and . . . was that a sparkle in Nava's gaze?

"Thank you for your time," Hannah said as they bid the two farewell. They walked down the steps until they reached the street, where they were alone.

"Perhaps it was not just me who came looking for something," Hannah said, giving Nava a knowing smile. "What was his name?"

Nava blushed a delightful shade of rose. "Ezer. It means *help*. Rather fitting, isn't it?"

Hannah nodded. "Yes. It truly is." They walked in silence a moment. "Do you think he likes you?" A servant couldn't very well ask his mistress to let him marry, but perhaps Elkanah could approach Raziela.

Nava nodded. "I think so. He is very interesting. I would like to get to know him better."

"Perhaps you shall." Hannah hid a smile. She must speak with Elkanah soon.

"And did you find what you came for?" Nava asked.

"Yes and no." She looked heavenward and sighed. "I found that some things might never be answered unless God reveals them, and sometimes evil men marry godly wives." She looked at Nava. "I am glad that I have to share Elkanah with only one other."

29

The visit to Raziela had taken only a brief part of the morning, but Hannah slowed her step at the sight of Peninnah standing beneath her tent's awning, watching the road. Was she looking for her?

Hannah shook herself and hurried into her own tent, away from the woman's scowl and her presence, away from the worry of the woman's scorn. If only she could avoid her altogether.

"You know we can't hide from her indefinitely," Nava said, as if reading her thoughts. "She's probably wondering where we went and why we aren't already there to prepare for tonight's feast."

Hannah sank to the woven rug that doubled as a sleeping mat. On feasts like this, they did without the comforts they were used to at home and slept on the ground with little cushion between them and the hard earth.

"I'm too tired to deal with her." She met Nava's gaze. "I slept fitfully last night, and I feel as though I have aged in the two days we have been here. I'm beginning to think, by the signs my body is telling me, that my chances and my days of ever conceiving are coming to a swift end." She didn't have actual proof of that, but when she woke up aching, she felt as though her body had betrayed her yet again.

Nava came and knelt at her side. "If you but say the word, I would bear a child for you. He would be yours to raise and name. At least then you could have reason to ignore Peninnah's taunts, for you could focus on your son."

Hannah's chest felt tight with an emotion she could not name. If she truly trusted God for a child, she would be faithful and wait. She could not do as Rachel and Leah had done. What a mess they had caused each other and Jacob!

She looked at Nava, so young and comely to look upon. But she could not give her to Elkanah. "And what of Ezer?"

"Ezer is a servant who will likely never be free to live away from the priest's house. He will probably never marry." The look in Nava's eyes told Hannah that they had at least alluded to their futures in that short time away from their mistresses. Did Ezer truly believe that he would never be released? Surely Raziela could be convinced.

"Well, I think Elkanah can be persuaded to ask on your behalf." She smiled, forcing a cheerful expression. "Nava, I know you would do for me whatever you could. I love that about you. But there are reasons I cannot give you to Elkanah. I want you to be free."

Nava sat back, her long, curly hair escaping the headscarf she had worn to see Raziela. She did not meet Hannah's gaze. "But . . . there is no need, mistress. Ezer and I both realize our lot in life. We were both born to be servants."

"You were born to be like everyone else, Nava, and Ezer just happened to have the unfortunate beginning of losing his mother at birth. But no child of Israel is meant to be enslaved all of their lives. I am giving you your freedom whether you like it or not."

Nava laughed, though she sounded almost anxious as well. "I don't know how I would live on my own," she said, twisting her hands in her lap.

"That is the point. Elkanah will find a husband for you."

"Perhaps the master will find no man willing to wed a slave girl." Nava's look held a hint of sadness, though Hannah had not told her how true her words were.

"That will be for him to concern himself with. For now, I suppose we should not keep Peninnah waiting."

"You wouldn't have to go, mistress," Nava said, as though trying to make up for the good Hannah had offered her. "I could go for you. I can do enough to make up for both of us. You could rest here." She smiled. "I know the woman is hard to deal with, but with me she has no competition."

Hannah's chest lifted, and she released a sigh that felt as weighty as the sea. "I'm no competition to her, Nava. If she thinks that, she imagines foolish things."

"Nevertheless, I watch her watch you, and I think she is trying to prove something."

"She's already proven it. She can have children. I cannot."

"But you have Elkanah's love."

"She would deny me even that if she could." Hannah looked toward the tent door. Elkanah had left early with his brothers to take care of the sacrifice for the evening's meal. She could not waste the day or refuse to do her part, no matter the frustration that clung to her every step.

Hannah stood and gathered a basket of

vegetables and a sack of lentils, while Nava took a kettle and the torch that stood just outside the tent door.

"Are you sure you will not stay behind?" Nava grabbed a skin of water to fill the pot and fell into step with Hannah.

Hannah shook her head and continued walking. "I won't have Elkanah think me lacking." He wouldn't, would he? He would understand if she stayed as far from Peninnah as possible today, but Hannah just could not bear to have that woman brag throughout the meal that she had done all of the work. Not that it would stop her from bragging about her children or anything else she could think of.

"Well, there you are," Peninnah said when Hannah at last entered her tent. "I wondered if you would even bother to join us today. Where did you go this morning?"

Did this woman truly have nothing to do with her time besides check on Hannah's every move? She bristled at the thought, a caustic remark about it being none of Peninnah's concern tickling the edge of her tongue. But she drew in a breath to steady herself. What did it matter if she told her?

"I went to give Hophni's wife my greeting." She pulled vegetables from her basket and carried the sack of lentils to the door of the tent. "I will start the fire." That the fire in front of the tent was not already lit went unmentioned, for Hannah did not wish to find yet another reason to fight with this woman.

"I suppose you think me lax for not having more done, for letting the fire go out." Peninnah crossed her arms over her protruding belly, her glare like bitter frost. "Well, *you* just try taking care of five children and carrying another and see how prompt you are at keeping other things going, then you would know." She huffed, and Hannah imagined fire pouring from her lips like the dragons of the wild. "Besides," Peninnah continued, "if Elkanah's *first* wife can go visiting, there is no reason *I* should do all of the labor. I'm not a servant, you know. *I'm* the mother of his heir."

Hannah stared at her, dumbfounded. At that moment, Yafa came from behind a tent curtain holding Peninnah's youngest daughter. Hannah's heart squeezed at the sight. Was this how Raziela felt when her husband brought home a child born in illegitimacy, expecting her to care for the child that wasn't hers? But no one was asking Hannah to care for anyone's child, except Nava, who didn't deserve to be put in the position of bearing a child for Hannah. But Raziela knew the pain of sharing Hophni — far too often.

This isn't as bad, she told herself. But standing there, staring at the life that should have been hers . . . words failed her.

She turned to leave. She would not treat Peninnah as Peninnah treated her. She would not repay evil with evil.

"I know what you think of me. You think you are better than me, but you're not. Let's not forget which one God has blessed." Peninnah's tone held such disdain that Hannah again felt the tension rise within her, until she had to hurry from the tent in order to hold it back. No wonder Sarah had reacted so when Hagar flaunted her pregnancy.

You can't be like that. You can't. Oh Adonai, help me.

She knelt near the fire that Nava had started and set the sack of lentils near a sieve to make sure no stones were tossed in the pot.

"Say what you will, but I know you don't like me." Peninnah's words carried to her from the tent where she still stood.

No, Hannah didn't like her. She despised her. But she also heard hurt in the woman's tone. Was Peninnah truly jealous of Hannah? Ludicrous thought.

"She has no idea what you think," Nava

whispered as Hannah sifted the lentils and added them to the water. "She's just a miserable person."

"It doesn't matter what she thinks of me or what she believes I think of her," Hannah said, wishing the words were true. Why did she care that Peninnah berated her? The woman had her own problems.

What I wouldn't give to have Peninnah's "problems." If having children were a burden, Hannah would gladly accept it.

Footfalls sounded behind her, and Hannah braced herself when she saw Peninnah carrying a sack of barley.

Peninnah knelt to grind the grain. "If you had children, you would understand," she said, her voice mocking.

"I'm sure that I would." Hannah clenched her teeth and kept her back to Peninnah, wondering why she had even bothered to answer.

Silence followed, and Hannah prayed that the woman would just keep grinding. The grating sound was far easier on the ears than the cruel words that felt like swords piercing her heart.

Elkanah carried the boiled lamb to the fire in the middle of his family's camp. He'd stayed close to the priests' servants to make sure they burned all of the fat and that the blood was spilled on the altar, but some of the fat still remained.

The noise of children racing through the tents and the chatter of women setting the places for them to eat gave him pause. His father's household would have joined them, but with Elkanah's growing family, he wanted to share this one meal with just his wives and children. Even Yafa had gone to share the meal with his parents, something his mother found most pleasing.

He placed the meat through a whittled branch and set it over the fire to smoke the rest of the fat away. Just to be sure. Then he could transfer it to a clay platter and serve his family.

"Can I help?" Eitan ran toward him but stopped short of the fire.

Elkanah looked up and saw the eagerness in his son's eyes. The boy was growing so fast. "Of course." He handed Eitan a second branch to turn the meat and warned him not to let it burn. "You understand why we do this, don't you, Eitan?" He couldn't help but teach. It was a father's duty.

"To make sure all of the fat is burned, because the priests don't always do it right?" Eitan looked into Elkanah's face, his expression uncertain.

"That's exactly right. Normal, good priests would burn all of the fat, which belongs to God, and would spill the blood, which is the life of the animal and we are not to eat it. But our priests do not do as God has prescribed in His law. So I make sure we are obedient to Adonai." He paused, waiting for understanding to dawn in Eitan's gaze.

The boy nodded. "The priests here are not good, are they, Abba?"

Elkanah examined the meat once more. How much did one tell a child about the evils of the world? Yet he could not let his children grow up thinking that all was well, that Phinehas and Hophni were truly God's priests. "No, Eitan, Hophni and Phinehas are not good priests." He lowered his voice. "They do not obey the word of the Lord."

"Why don't we stop them then? They are just two men." Eitan's comment sounded so simple, so innocent.

"It is much more complicated than it sounds," Elkanah said, pulling the meat from the fire. "God set up the priesthood. He gave the job to the descendants of Aaron, and we can't just give it to someone else. The priests have to come from the priestly line."

"Aren't we part of that line?" Eitan asked.

"We're Kohathites." He shrugged as though that explained everything.

"We are of the tribe of Levi, the sons of Kohath, yes. And Amram, Moses's father, was also a Kohathite, but only his son Aaron and his descendants inherited the priesthood. Kind of like the firstborn gets different rights than the sons born afterward."

"I'm *your* firstborn," Eitan said, his chest puffing with pride.

Elkanah laughed, though his heart felt the sting of pain that Hannah had not been the one to bear his firstborn. "Yes, my son. Yes, you are. There now. See how the meat is browned on all sides but not blackened?"

"Yes."

"Now we take it off and put it on the plate to cut for the meal." Elkanah used a pronged fork to push the meat onto a plate.

"That smells good." Eitan rubbed his middle with one hand. "I've asked all day to taste the things Ima and Aunt Hannah have been making, but they won't let me touch anything." His pout made Elkanah laugh again.

"Well, I am sure they had good reason. You wouldn't want to spoil the feast, now would you?" At least his wives had worked together. That was a good sign, wasn't it?

Eitan glanced from side to side, then

leaned closer to Elkanah. "I wouldn't have minded a taste. But Ima is in a bad mood and I think she made Aunt Hannah cry."

"You saw Aunt Hannah cry?" What on earth did Peninnah say this time?

"Not actually cry," Eitan said, shifting from foot to foot, as if he felt guilty telling his father what his mother had done. "But I saw her blink real fast and Ima was yelling sometimes."

The yelling did not surprise him. Neither did Hannah's apparent emotion. He touched Eitan's shoulder. "Thank you for telling me. Now why don't you run and tell Aunt Hannah that I am ready to bring the meat."

Eitan tilted his head, his look curious. "Not Ima?"

Elkanah sighed, longing to give vent to the tension building within him. "Yes, you can tell them both." No doubt Eitan would tell Peninnah that he had favored Hannah yet again. The boy was obedient — to a point. But he could not trust him. He was his mother's informant, and Elkanah must be more careful with what he allowed the boy to hear.

But as he thought about what Hannah must have endured this day, he suddenly didn't feel as much like celebrating as he first had. Somehow he must make it up to her, make her feel special, even if it meant he did so in Peninnah's presence. He was tired of the foolish games Peninnah played, trying to coax him to care for her and leave Hannah behind. He was not oblivious to her ways. Perhaps it was time he remedied that.

30

The sun blazed low in an array of fiery oranges and yellows, splayed between giant fingers of wispy clouds. Hannah looked over the area where they would eat, then bent to move the bowl of cucumbers closer to the children and the plate of olive oil and spices closer to where Elkanah would sit.

"What are you doing? I had that all set."

When did Peninnah's footfalls grow so quiet? Hannah drew a breath. "I'm sorry. I did not know you had set it. I was thinking that the children might dip their sleeves in the oil —"

"What my children do is none of your concern." Peninnah squatted low and put things back the way she had them. "Worry about your own children." She laughed long and hard, the sound like metal on stone. "Your own children. That's good." She stood, face flushed.

Hannah walked away. She would not let

the woman see how she affected her. She nearly bumped into Elkanah carrying the meat toward the feast area.

"Hannah? What's wrong?" He stopped, the plate held in both hands, the scent of garlic and rosemary mixing with the sweet smell of cooked lamb.

Hannah met his gaze. How much to tell him? Should she inform him of all she had learned from Raziela that morning? Or just share the many caustic remarks his *other* wife had made to her the entire day? She bit her lip, forcing back the words and the tears.

"Tell me, beloved." He sounded so sincere. But she would only be complaining, and on a feast day of all days.

"It is nothing. It's just been a long, difficult day and I'm tired. I'm going to put on a fresh tunic and be right back." She smiled at him, though she knew he would see that her efforts were forced.

"I want you to tell me," he said, but she simply nodded as she hurried toward her tent. He would have to stay with the meat because the children could not be trusted and Peninnah did not watch them well.

Once inside the tent, Hannah went to the sack of clothing she'd brought and pulled out the fresh tunic she had saved for this occasion. She was sweaty from working and longed for a chance to bathe in the river, but there were no rivers near here or the chance to do so.

Her heart raced as she hurried to change. The shofar would blow soon now that the meat was ready, and she did not want to be accused of making everyone wait for her. But oh, she did not want to go back! If she could skip this meal, if she could eat here alone, if she could be anywhere *but* there, she would.

She used the comb to untangle the snarls she had acquired during the work and tied a clean scarf over her hair. Kohl and ochre had been left at home. She didn't care if her aging skin needed them. She knew Raziela took the time and was beautiful for her efforts, but Elkanah would have to accept Hannah as she was.

How bitter she sounded! But the hurt cut deeply, and if she allowed herself the slightest bit of anger, she could avoid tears. And she did not want to weep in front of her antagonistic rival.

Had Peninnah always been so cruel?

Pinching her cheeks to bring some color to what had to be a wan face, she took a deep, steadying breath and let it slowly out. She could do this. She could face Peninnah and Elkanah and the children and worship Adonai with them all.

Worship Adonai. That was why they were here.

She walked slowly toward the tent's entrance and glanced at the fading sun. *I want to worship You, Adonai. But I don't know how anymore. I don't know how to live with constant battering and such a deep sense of loss.*

She felt her heart soften with the admission as she made her way back to the area where she could see the candles already lit and Peninnah and Nava trying to settle the children. Elkanah looked in her direction, and when he saw her he seemed to breathe a sigh of relief.

If only she could share his feelings.

Moments after the shofar blew, calling them to begin the feast, Elkanah took his knife and carved portions of the meat for Eitan, Hevel, and Aniah, then gave smaller amounts to Peninnah's two daughters Moriah and Yemima. The youngest girl was barely old enough to chew the meat, and he noticed Peninnah take a knife and cut it finer. She looked tired, probably from the weight of the babe. How many children she had given him! He couldn't help a surge of pride rise up at the thought of so many sons and daughters and more to come.

God had blessed him. He couldn't deny it. Why Hannah could not be part of that blessing, he would never understand, but he also couldn't refute the fact that God had blessed this woman who had come into his house. Perhaps she wasn't so bad a wife, though he did wish she would not treat Hannah so poorly.

He glanced at Hannah, waiting, watching. Peninnah did not allow Hannah to help with the children at feast times, though it was obvious she could use the help. Hannah turned and said something to Nava that he could not hear, so he continued to carve the meat, giving portions to everyone seated. When he came to Hannah, he gave her double the amount he gave his eldest sons and Peninnah. Surely she would see his desire to bless her in some way.

"Oh, so you give the barren woman the bigger portion? Maybe she will grow fat and look like she is with child. Then she can pretend, though she will never know what it is really like." Peninnah glared at him, and he felt the heat of her anger settle into his belly.

"No. I give her the double portion to show her my love." If Peninnah could be cruel, then he could remind her that Hannah would always be his favored one.

"So I give you sons but I am not loved? Are you Jacob, who treated Leah so poorly she cried out to God for help?" She leaned back as though ready to raise her fists and physically fight with him. What was wrong with her?

"Leah at least turned to God. She did not lash out at Rachel." His stomach twisted, and he glanced at Hannah. He hated confrontation like this but seemed helplessly caught in it.

"So now even Leah is better than I am? We all know you love Hannah and not us, so why did you even marry me?" She was shouting now, and the girls and youngest boy began to cry.

"Peninnah, please. I never said that." He focused on cutting a piece for himself but found no desire to eat it now.

"Well, it certainly seems that way." Peninnah glanced at Hannah. "And you let that one go visiting on a day when I needed her help. Do you know she left me to do this work alone?" She moved her hand over the eating area, indicating the whole of the meal.

"That is not true, master." Nava spoke up, something she never did. "Hannah did as much work as Peninnah. More, even."

"You listen to a servant? Your wife is

330

worthless. She goes off to visit Hophni's wife and never once invited me to meet her, and then returns expecting the work to be done. But let her have five children to look after — some of whom should have gone with you!" She pointed at Elkanah. "See how much she complains then!"

"Enough!" Elkanah felt heat burn his cheeks, and the twisting in his gut turned white-hot, his anger nearly impossible to hold in check. He glanced at Hannah, whose tears streamed down her cheeks, and suddenly he could not stay angry with anyone. "Hannah?" He came to kneel at her side. "Why do you weep? And why do you not eat?" He had noticed her food untouched, though everyone else seemed to find reason to feast despite the volley of words. He touched her shoulder, but her tears fell faster. She covered her face with both hands. "Hannah, why is your heart sad? Am I not more to you than ten sons?"

Hadn't he assured her of his love over and over? Couldn't she have learned to be happy without a child as long as she had him? *Adonai, what do I say to her?*

He grasped her hand and brushed the tears with a linen cloth, then cupped her cheek. "Please, Hannah." He met her gaze. "Eat? Let us all calm down and worship

Adonai together. Can we do that?"

She gave him a slight nod, but she did not smile. When he felt certain she would not run from them back to her tent, he sat at his place again and dipped his bread in the olive oil and sopped up a portion of the lentils. His gaze shifted around the table. His sons had watched the exchange, and he could see his oldest boys' clenched jaws and frowns.

Peninnah's expression remained sour, and she spoke only to her sons and daughters, while Hannah ate very little in silence.

Elkanah took a drink of the wine Nava poured each of them and wondered how he ever thought himself blessed.

Hannah listened to the conversation and picked at the food Elkanah had put on her plate, but she had no desire to touch the wine. Not when her stomach was so knotted with anxiety and empty of nourishment. Not when she was clenching so tight to keep her emotions in check that she could barely hear the words above the roaring in her ears.

She needed to leave this meal. But one look at Elkanah watching her kept her seated and attempting to swallow a few more bites.

"If you cannot eat it all," Nava whispered,

leaning toward Hannah's ear, "when no one is looking, I will scoop most of it into a bowl and we will take it to your tent. You can eat it later when you are hungry."

Hannah half smiled at her maid's conspiratorial grin. "I shouldn't," she whispered. "It isn't right."

"It isn't wrong either," Nava countered. "It is better than sitting here pretending."

Hannah glanced at her maid and offered a brief nod. She picked up her cup but did not bring the liquid to her lips. When Elkanah and Peninnah were looking the other direction, Hannah slipped Nava her bowl. Moments later she returned to her plate and took one last bite of the bread. Elkanah looked her way, noticed what she had "eaten," and smiled. Nava excused herself to get more wine to pour for the others, a decided lump beneath her robe. But no one paid attention to a servant, and Hannah's heart surged with gratitude for the one person who seemed to understand.

If only she felt the same. But she didn't understand, couldn't fathom why God, Maker of heaven and earth, the Giver of life, would choose to forget her and bless her rival. Was it her battle with bitterness toward Peninnah? Had she been ungrateful to Galia or Elkanah or her parents or . . .

someone?

Tears came again and she could not sit a moment more. She stood. "If you will please excuse me." She looked at Elkanah, whose brows knit, but he gave a nod.

"So she gets to run off and not help clean up after I did all the work preparing?"

Peninnah's words trailed after her as she hurried away, tears now coming from a place deep within. She gulped on a great sob, unable to stop the pain.

Enough, Elkanah had said. Indeed, she had taken all she could bear. She had tried without success to be patient, to be kind when she was accused, to be forgiving even when she had to forgive over and over again.

She picked up her skirts and ran through the camp, past other tribes, until she reached the gateway to the tabernacle. The area was dark except for the menorah aflame behind the curtain where she could not go. The high priest, Eli, sat on a bench beside the doorpost of the tented enclosure that housed the holy things. He was obviously watching the courtyard, where sacrifices were made and those in service carried out various duties, and where singers offered hymns of worship, something she and Elkanah had once loved.

The thought brought more tears. She and

Elkanah had once loved Adonai above all things. They had been drawn to each other because of their mutual love of God and their longing to worship Him. But now . . . so much life had come between them. So many unmet expectations of the future they had planned. Did Elkanah still love Adonai as he once did? Did she?

She walked the length of the tent, to the side and in front where Eli sat, unable to stop herself from weeping. *I can't live like this, Lord. I feel like a little part of me dies inside every time I see Peninnah, and I feel even worse when she opens her mouth. And all I can think is . . . what have I done? Surely I have sinned against You. Surely I have withheld something, have put something in my life above You. But I cannot see what it could be.*

She wept more and fell to her knees some distance from Eli, rocking back and forth, her tears, like her words, silent. Had she withheld something from Adonai? She had given Him her trust, had done all she could to obey the commands to love Him with all of her heart and mind and strength. What more must she do?

She felt as though she had fallen into a river and was being dragged beneath the surface, the waters rushing over her, until she sat up gasping for air. But it was only the strength of her violent sobs.

Oh Adonai, do You even hear me?

She looked around at the empty court-yard, saw the brazen altar, and caught the outline of a man ushering a woman around a corner into the darkness. The sins of Hophni and Phinehas had spread to too many Levites living in Shiloh, and the mistreatment of women and children had to stop. Raziela's face surfaced in her mind's eye, and the horror of what she and those children and their mothers went through sickened her.

"We need a deliverer," Elkanah had said many times. Hadn't she agreed, even prayed for one? Elkanah claimed that deliverer could not be him, and Hannah could not imagine one of Peninnah's spoiled sons filling such a role.

But a child raised to love Adonai from his birth would be different.

The ability to breathe returned as she pondered that thought. To devote a child to Adonai meant leaving him here. If Eli raised him, he would be no better than Eli's two corrupt sons. Raziela and Irit might look after the child, but they could not keep him. That would put the boy under the direct influence of Hophni and Phinehas.

The thoughts warred within her. She had

wanted to do something to make things better, to bring the nation back to where they should be. Like Deborah of old had done. But Hannah was no Deborah, and she was not fighting a war with foreign peoples.

No. The war is within your own household, your own nation.

The realization was not new, but she saw it suddenly in a different light. How could one woman possibly help save her home, her place of worship, the land and people she loved?

I have nothing to give You, Adonai. More tears came as she stared up at the stars.

"Look up at the sky and count the stars — if indeed you can count them," Adonai had said to Abraham. *"So shall your offspring be."*

She couldn't count them and doubted her forefather could have either. But all nations would be blessed through the man who had fathered their nation because he had obeyed God, even when it meant he thought he would lose his only beloved son.

Hannah swallowed hard as thoughts churned through her. Could she obey God even at the cost of losing an only beloved child? Could she give back what God had given?

A shudder worked through her as she fought with the very idea. *I can't.* Not that she had anything to offer . . . but what if she did? To offer a child as Abraham had done — his only son . . .

She doubled over, face to the earth. *Oh Adonai Tzva'ot.*

She wept at His very name, unable to speak for a lengthy breath. Her heart warred with a promise she could make but was not sure she could bear to keep. And yet . . .

The battle raged as she rose to her knees, letting the tears fall from her cheeks to the dirt. She looked once more at the stars and clasped her hands.

O Lord of Hosts, if You will indeed look on the affliction of Your servant and remember me and not forget Your servant, but will give to Your servant a son, then I will give him to the Lord all the days of his life, and no razor shall touch his head. He will be a Nazarite all the days of his life, and I will teach him to observe all of Your commands before I give him back to You.

She glanced at Eli as she prayed, her lips moving but no sound coming out, noticing his gaze fixed on her. How ridiculous she must look to him. She wiped her wet cheeks and straightened her disheveled robe.

Eli leaned forward and called out to her, his tone stern. "How long are you going to stay drunk? Put away your wine."

"Not so, my lord," Hannah said, stepping closer and kneeling before him. "I am a woman who is deeply troubled. I have not been drinking wine or beer. I was pouring out my soul to the Lord. Do not take your servant for a wicked woman. I have been praying here out of my great anguish and grief."

Eli looked at her, his brow furrowed, then sat back as if satisfied with her response. "Go in peace, my daughter, and may the God of Israel grant you what you have asked of Him."

Hannah's heart lifted at his blessing, and lightness filled her whole being. Peace and a sense of surprising joy washed over her like refreshing rain. "May your servant find favor in your eyes," she said.

31

Hannah walked slowly back to camp, her step light, her heart lifted. She paused to gaze at the stars more than once, feeling as if God Himself stood among their far-off lights and looked down on her with kindness. Did she find favor in His eyes? Had she had His favor all along, or was it her promise that brought this feeling of rightness to her heart?

Do You see me?

Yet she knew. She knew He not only saw but He had heard.

A smile slowly filled her face, and she suddenly wanted to laugh and jump and dance and sing. Energy bubbled within her, and she quickened her pace to the camp, to Elkanah.

Elkanah. A sigh escaped as she recalled the many times they had spoken of Adonai Tzva'ot, the Lord of Hosts. The days they had pondered together the things they found difficult to understand. And other times when they had served and worshiped Him as one.

Images of Peninnah skipped through her thoughts as well, but she pushed them aside. Despite Peninnah's presence, she loved Elkanah. She had always loved him. Did he know it? Truly?

She must tell him. Must show him that he did matter more to her than ten sons. That she trusted God to give them a child, and if He did, she would return the gift, loan him back in service to the Lord. But Elkanah must agree, for her vow meant nothing if he did not support her.

Would he support her? A twinge of doubt slowed her step, but a moment later she banished it. Unless God provided the child, there would be no vow to keep. She could trust Adonai to handle Elkanah's feelings on the matter when the time came.

The familiar tents came into view and Hannah hastened her step. The lights had dimmed near Peninnah's tent, the food put away — probably something she would hear about in days to come — but the torch stood like a waiting beacon outside of her tent. She entered to find Elkanah and Nava sitting, waiting.

Elkanah jumped up and hurried to her

side. "You're back." He pulled her close. "I was worried," he whispered in her ear. "It's not safe to go off alone."

She leaned against his chest, taking in the feel, the scent of him. How she missed him! Really missed him in heart and soul, not only because she had been gone a few hours. She felt as though she had been away from their relationship for a long, long time.

Laughter rose from deep within, and she took a step back, smiling as she took Elkanah's hands in hers. "I am sorry for worrying you, my love. But I am glad that I went, for now I know that God hears and answers prayers. And I know that I can trust Him with our future."

He looked at her, his brow lifted in that skeptical gaze he had, but a moment later he smiled in return. "You are no longer sad." He must have realized that her smile reached her eyes and her laughter was not forced, for he picked her up and swung her around, laughing with her.

"No, I am not." She hoped he could read the love in her gaze. "But I am hungry!" She grinned and glanced around, noting Nava had risen and retrieved the bowl of food she had left mostly untouched.

Elkanah looked from Hannah to her maid, then back at Hannah again. "What is this?"

"I have a very sneaky maid," Hannah said, pulling him down with her to sit while she accepted the food and wine from Nava. She offered bites to Elkanah, who accepted them freely.

"And a wise one," Elkanah said, mouthing a quiet thank-you to Nava. She blushed and slipped away into the other part of the tent, leaving them alone.

"Who cleaned up the food? I suppose I will hear complaints about that tomorrow." Hannah ate a piece of the meat that no was longer warm.

"I put the older boys to work helping Nava. I gave Peninnah the night to go into her tent and rest. She took the youngest children with her and didn't look back."

"I doubt she was happy about it." Suddenly Peninnah's happiness did not matter, except where Hannah might offer her kindness. Peninnah's bitterness seemed to have lost its strength in her own newfound joy.

"She will get over it." Elkanah took her hand. "Let's not talk about her tonight. I want to know what took my favorite wife from weeping to laughter." He searched her face. "Tell me?"

Hannah set her food aside and took a sip of wine. She held the cup for a moment, then set it aside as well. "I went to the tabernacle and I prayed."

Elkanah's brows knit. "That's it?"

She nodded. "It was a long prayer with much weeping."

"But you have prayed before. We have offered sacrifices and prayed together." He scratched his beard.

"This was different. It was something I had to do alone." She paused, debating with her earlier resolve. "It involves a vow."

This time Elkanah's surprise equaled his skepticism. "What kind of vow?"

She played with the belt of her robe. He could undo the vow. He could declare it null. "It was a vow to God."

"What kind of vow?" he said again, more gently this time.

"I vowed that if God would give me a son, I would give him back to the Lord all the days of his life and no razor would touch his head." She slowly released her breath, watching him.

He stared at her for so long she wondered if he would speak.

"Well?" she said at last. "Can I keep the vow?"

"You would give your only son back to God's work after all this time, knowing you would not get to raise him or see him often?" Incredulity filled his expression.

"You have often said we need a deliverer from the evil of the tabernacle. Our son will be that person." As she said the words, certainty filled her. She would have a son. And that son would grow up to lead Israel back to Adonai. She knew it as well as she knew her own heart.

Elkanah still stared at her, and she recognized that he could not quite accept her words. He did not have the certainty she did.

"I will not nullify your vow. If Adonai sees fit to bless you with a son, you may do as you have said." He smiled, and she saw belief in his gaze. Deep down they shared the same faith. But Elkanah would need time to share her certainty and trust.

Peninnah trailed behind Elkanah and Hannah and some of her oldest sons, even avoiding Galia's company. Something had happened to change Hannah. And it was drawing Elkanah even closer to her side than he had been throughout the years.

She scowled at her mother, who had hold of Yemima's hand. "Your advice is worthless to me," she said through gritted teeth. "You tell me to make her miserable, to taunt her and goad her, and look at her now! She is singing and Elkanah is joining in, and it's all your fault."

Her mother lifted her head and looked into Peninnah's eyes. "I will not accept that from you, my daughter. Show some respect for your mother."

Peninnah's cheeks flushed hot. Anger, always so close to the surface, brought the unexpected sting of emotion. She could not speak. She would not cry.

But she had lost him as surely as she had lost her father. Was this her lot then? To be like her mother? Married but not really married? Not abused as her mother had been, but surely unloved? Never wanted and never loved?

She glanced at her daughters skipping beside her, held by the hand. Such life. Such energy. The babe squeezing inside of her had taken too much out of her this time. She was weary of fighting. Weary of children and sharing a husband.

Why couldn't Elkanah at least care for her? She had spent years giving him children and offering herself to him whenever he desired her. But those times were so few. He came to see the children, but they barely spoke unless she found something to complain to him about. He never asked her questions. Never would have cared if *she* had been the one weeping at the feast.

She slowed her step, not caring if she fell behind the others. Pain filled her middle, but she knew this was not from the babe. This pain ran deeper than something physical, and she struggled to understand. Why had her whole life been one of misery?

She sensed a presence beside her as another group caught up to her. She glanced over to see Kelila and Galia close the gap between them.

"Peninnah, why are you so downcast? Surely the feast was not that unfavorable," Galia said. She led a donkey carrying two of Kelila's younger children, while the older boys had gone off with their father.

Elkanah should take his boys with him, but that would mean they would have more contact with Hannah. *I can't bear that.*

"I am fine, Galia. It is just the heat and the weight of the babe." She smiled, knowing the lie was just one more thing to add to her growing list of sins. Surely her bitterness, her constant complaints, were not pleasing to God. Elkanah had reminded her of that often enough.

"She is just frustrated because Elkanah and Hannah are up ahead singing," her mother said, butting into the conversation.

Peninnah swiveled her head to give her mother a silent glare.

"Singing? I don't recall hearing Hannah sing in years." Galia lifted a brow and glanced at Kelila. "What on earth would make her sing?"

"She used to sing," Kelila said, "back in the early days, even before she and Elkanah wed. She loved to come to the tabernacle and sing. I think that was what Elkanah found appealing in her."

Galia nodded. "Of course. I remember now. The girl even talked about her longing to join the serving women just so she could be among the singers."

"I imagine she and Elkanah did that together when they came to work there." Kelila glanced back at her daughters on the donkey. "But she has been so sad for so long. I'm surprised she is happy."

"Surprised?" Galia said, giving Peninnah a look. "I'm astounded, considering what she has put up with all these years. And to think I thought I knew best."

Peninnah flushed hot again. So her mother and her mother-in-law had both turned against her? "Don't forget I am the one who gave your son children." She lifted her chin. "I don't need to listen to this." She stalked off ahead of the group, despite the difficulty in increasing her pace.

Why *was* Hannah happy all of a sudden?

She had been weeping at the meal, and Peninnah had felt she was so close to turning Elkanah away from her. What man wanted a weepy woman, after all? Her father never did. Her mother's tears had only made him angrier. He'd said she was just trying to get her way and he wouldn't stand for it.

When Elkanah had left her in tears on their wedding night, Peninnah had vowed to never cry in front of him again. Why then had Hannah's tears made him want her more? Why had her tears turned to joy?

The thought nagged her, ate at her, and she could not fathom what the woman could possibly have to be happy about or grateful for. She was still barren. She still carried that disgrace. God still had not answered her prayers.

She had to be pretending just to get back at Peninnah and keep Elkanah away from her. That was surely it. Hannah had found a way to override her attempts to steal Elkanah away — again.

She bit her lip, turning that thought over in her mind. Well, it couldn't last. Peninnah had plenty of barbs to bring back the sorrow and weeping, and one of these days they were going to work.

And Hannah would lose Elkanah for good.

32

Three Months Later

Hannah sipped mint water and watched Nava spin Elkanah's newly shorn wool into thread. Her stomach slowly settled with ginger and mint, but she did not mind the discomfort in the slightest. She touched her middle, the knowledge too wonderful to believe, but the town midwife had confirmed her suspicions and Dana had assured her several times that she had all the signs of pregnancy.

Thank You, Adonai.

The words of praise never ceased. She awoke each morning with a song in her heart and laughed when she heard Elkanah whistle his greeting. God had heard! What had seemed completely impossible *was* possible! God had answered her prayer when she had lost all hope.

How good You are, Adonai.

She sipped again, feeling stronger at last,

and slowly stood to retrieve her own spindle and distaff. "We will have many clothes to make if we are to have a baby *and* build you a suitable dowry for you to take when you leave us." She met Nava's gaze.

"We don't know for sure that I will be leaving yet." But Nava's hope could not be extinguished any more than Hannah's joy could be lost.

"Oh, you will." Elkanah had already spoken to Raziela, who assured him that Ezer was free to marry. Though he was Hophni's son, Hophni would not acknowledge him, so Raziela was free to keep him or sell him or free him. She intended to free him and to send him off with enough to get him and Nava started in their own home. Hannah smiled. This answer to her prayer was just one more wonderful blessing God had given since her visit to the tabernacle that day.

"But it doesn't seem possible," Nava said, doubt in her tone. "How can she just release him? Won't Hophni hear of it and grow angry?"

"Hophni pays no attention to the servants except the ones who serve him at the tabernacle and do his despicable work of stealing sacrifices." She hadn't thought it possible, but Elkanah had told her it was true. When he had approached Raziela on Nava's behalf, he had found Raziela eager to make the arrangements for Ezer.

"How soon?" Nava asked, the light shining in her eyes once more.

"Raziela should release him before I give birth to this little one. We shall celebrate the wedding after my days of purification are past. But we will hold the betrothal within the month. Elkanah said he is looking for a place where Ezer can build a home to take you there."

"You both have done far too much for me. I am very grateful." Nava brushed a wisp of hair away from her face.

"Nonsense. You never should have been sold into service in the first place. And your grandparents and mother should have reclaimed you when they could." The thought that Nava's family seemed incapable of caring for their grandchildren troubled Hannah from time to time. But she had always been grateful that Elkanah had rescued the child, and how glad she now was for their friendship. "I do hope Elkanah finds somewhere close where you can still come to visit. I am going to miss you terribly."

"And I want to be here to watch the baby grow. I can't go all these years praying for you and, now that God has finally answered, miss the joy of the child!" Nava's words brought tears to Hannah's eyes.

"You prayed for me?" A warm tingling moved through her, her heart full. *Adonai, did You have Your people praying for me all this time?* And yet the answer took so long in coming! *I don't know that I will ever understand Your ways, Adonai, but I am thankful that You saw fit to finally bless me too.*

"Every day, mistress."

Hannah stared at her. "Please, call me Hannah. You are no longer my servant. You are my friend, and soon I will give you to Ezer as though you were my daughter."

Nava's eyes misted. "I love you like a mother."

They looked at each other, both emotional, spinning the thread without thought.

"And I love you as well. You are the daughter I never had," Hannah managed at last. "We have much planning to do. You will need sheets and new garments and a robe for Ezer, and we will trade some of the cloth for cooking utensils at market. My brother can make us some clay urns for water, and cups and plates. My father cannot keep up with the work anymore, but I am glad he still lives to hold this child on his knee."

The realization of the child still humbled her. She had begged and pleaded and demeaned herself, receiving only God's silence, and all along He had a plan she just could not see. She was part of something bigger than herself. Part of something she wasn't ready for in those early days. But now . . .

Now she knew it would be hard to part with this child she could not yet feel — excruciatingly so, because she already loved him. But she also knew that the God who made him would give her the strength to carry out her vow. She would give the boy back to God because he belonged to God. Because she had promised. Because none of them were really their own. God, Maker of all things, was the One who gave and took away, and she had been given a great gift. Too soon she would give that gift back, because God had need of this child. Just how, she did not know, but somehow, someway, her son would do God's will and bring Him glory.

Who will you be, little one? What will you be like?

"Do you think we can get so much made in time, along with all of the baby's things?" Nava asked, interrupting her thoughts.

"We will enlist Dana's help and Galia's. I am sure all of the women in Elkanah's household will be happy to give us aid." Except Peninnah. The woman had spoken not a word to her since Elkanah had announced their good news.

"Will you invite Peninnah to help us?" Nava's question startled her, causing a moment of discord in her spinning.

She stared into the distance toward Peninnah's house, where a new infant son had brought the number of her children to six. "I am sure she is much too busy with her own children."

Nava nodded. "She would probably just be unkind to us anyway."

Hannah pondered the thought. "I suppose it might be an offer of peace, so she does not feel left out. All she has is her mother and her children. Even Galia does not treat her as well as she once did."

"None of your sisters-in-law do either, from what I have seen."

"Peninnah has brought a lot of her friendlessness on herself." It was true. She had extended her cruelty to gossip about all of Elkanah's sisters-in-law and even his sister, whom they rarely saw.

"I suppose I could be kind to her," Hannah said, realizing by the shocked look on

Nava's face that she had spoken aloud.

"You're serious?"

"I'm willing to consider it."

Nava sighed. "Consider it. That's fine. Just don't make too hasty a decision."

Hannah agreed. Peninnah was not one she cared to be close to, and even offering her an olive branch of peace was not something she was sure she wanted to do. After years of verbal barbs and angry retorts, Hannah had rather enjoyed these three months of silence.

"*Maybe* consider it," she amended, the more she thought on it. "There is plenty of time to do so."

Nava laughed. "Right up until my wedding." When they wouldn't need Peninnah's help at all.

Hannah smiled. It wasn't the kindest thought, but she was not so sure she was ready to be kind to her cruel rival.

Peninnah slammed the door to the stone house Elkanah had built for her and marched through the courtyard toward the hills. Never mind the screaming baby and noisy children clamoring for her attention. She needed to get away. Needed peace. Let her mother handle them. She seemed to think she knew the best way to deal with them. Let her nurse the boy who would not stop feeding.

She inwardly scoffed at that and nearly laughed out loud. The child never stopped. He would not sleep or let her sleep. He wanted constant feedings. And all she could think about was the fact that *she* had borne Elkanah a fourth son — six children, and yet he was elated over his favorite wife's *first* pregnancy.

Ungrateful, wretched man! The hurt of her own thoughts cut deep, and she felt as though she was bleeding from a place deep within. Why did he ignore her so? Why was everyone against her? Would her children turn against her too once they were grown?

She would be left.

Alone.

With no one.

Even her mother would not live forever, and she was the only friend Peninnah had. The thought brought the sting of tears, which she quashed quickly with fierce anger. She deserved better.

You could learn to be kinder.

She turned the thought over in her mind.

I don't know how to be kind.

She walked to an outcropping of rocks some distance from the house, where the sounds of her children could be blotted out, and sat, staring at the fields of wheat waving their brown stalks like greetings on the breeze.

When had her life grown so bitter? Why couldn't things be like they had been when she was small? When Abba gave her everything she wanted, before he had turned cruel against her mother. Had he been trying to buy her affection the way she had tried to win Elkanah's love?

Tears stung again at the way she had begged him to give her to Elkanah, but he had died before that could happen. Her mother had agreed with nary an objection, for what else was she to do? Peninnah had been certain she could make Elkanah love her like he did Hannah.

How foolish she'd been to think a man could divide his love. Why didn't her mother tell her that men were incapable of sharing their affections? They either loved the one and hated the other or despised the one and cared more for the other. Elkanah was definitely a man designed to have one wife, and someone should have told her that. She should have seen it.

You wouldn't have listened.

Was she truly that naïve and self-centered?

The realization felt like a kick to her gut, and she nearly stumbled with the force of it. It wasn't true. She was not like that. She had loved Elkanah longer than Hannah had, even when she was a child.

Not with that kind of love.

Stop it! She wanted to scream her thoughts from existence. She could not go on like this. This questioning of her past, of her motives, of her whole life's choices, had to stop. She could not have been that wrong. Hadn't she given Elkanah his heir?

Hannah's child could usurp that heir.

No! He couldn't. The law said so.

She straightened, crossing both arms over her chest as a new thought hit her. Would Elkanah break the law to give the double portion to the son of his first wife? Jacob had done it with Rachel's son. What was to stop Elkanah, especially if he outlived her?

She fisted her hands around her belt, her mind whirling. Somehow she must ensure that Elkanah did not think Hannah's child would have any part with her son's inheritance. He must not. Eitan must be trained in the ways of a Kohathite and learn to shepherd and plant and harvest and follow the law to be everything his father would want him to be. She would make sure. She had to make sure.

She moved forward on shaky limbs, anger and fear rushing through her like a mighty wind. She must speak to Elkanah of this. Soon. If she could get him away from Hannah long enough to do so.

Six Months Later

Elkanah walked beside Tahath, the sickle slung over his shoulder, his body feeling the aches of a long day's work. "I'm getting too old for this," he said, glancing at his older brother, who seemed to feel no effect from the cutting and bundling of the wheat.

"You are simply worn down by the pressures of two families." Tahath patted his back. "Do not fear, brother. Things will improve once Hannah gives birth."

Would they? "Her time is close now." She had missed the Feast of Weeks, for she was too far along to travel, but still the babe had not come. Would she have a safe delivery?

"Yes, I've heard. Dana tells me that Ima fairly hovers over Hannah and is there with Hannah's mother, both watching her like swirling hawks at a killing field." He looked at Elkanah. "Sorry — that was probably not the best comparison."

Elkanah laughed. "No, but I could picture Ima and Hannah's mother hovering like such birds. I don't know how Hannah remains so gracious, but I know she is glad that her mother traveled to be closer when the time comes. And Nava's wedding is soon after, so all of the women have descended on my house and there is barely room to sit!" He rubbed the back of his neck, fighting off the start of a headache such thoughts evoked.

"You can always stay with Peninnah. Dana tells me that she will have nothing to do with the goings-on at Hannah's house." Tahath gave Elkanah a sly smile. "You could avoid so much commotion that way."

"Your sarcasm is beneath you, brother." Elkanah smirked and looked away. The truth was, Peninnah's house was worse than the commotion at Hannah's, for ever since Peninnah had accosted him several months ago about Eitan remaining his firstborn with all the rights of the firstborn, he had been in turmoil.

"Just trying to help," Tahath said.

"Well, it's not helping."

Tahath stopped and faced him. "Tell me what's troubling you. You've been acting out of sorts for months now. I figured it was just because you were worried about Hannah giving birth, but now . . . is that all it is?"

Elkanah kicked a stone and looked toward Hannah's house. A deep sigh escaped him. "I couldn't say anything with Eitan here."

The boy had been working with him for weeks, but he had sent him home early when it was obvious that the binding of the sheaves was beyond his ability. "A few months back Peninnah made it very clear that she expects Eitan to keep his rights as firstborn."

"And she would be within her rights to say so," Tahath said, brow furrowed in concern. "The law supports her, after all."

"Yes, I know. And I assured her she had nothing to worry about." He glanced into Tahath's square face. "But there is a part of me that would do as Jacob did and give the blessing to Hannah's son regardless."

Tahath rubbed the back of his neck, his look thoughtful. "You are not so different than anyone else, brother. In your position, I might feel the same, but I know you. Jacob's actions came before the law, and you are too honest to go against what God gave to Moses, despite how you feel." He patted Elkanah's back. "Don't be so hard on yourself." He began walking again and Elkanah fell into step with him.

They walked in silence for several moments, Elkanah's thoughts moving from Eitan to Hannah's promise to God. How would he ever bear it after all this time of waiting?

"Hannah made a vow," he blurted as they drew near to Hannah's courtyard.

Tahath stopped, his head tilted as if to better meet Elkanah's gaze.

"She vowed to give our son back to God," he said, wondering why he felt now was the right time to share what he had kept from his family for months. "The child will grow up under Eli at the tabernacle when he is old enough to go there."

The news was met with wide-eyed silence. At last Tahath spoke. "You let her keep the vow."

"Yes. It was a promise if God would give her a son."

"Maybe she will have a daughter."

"You know that is not likely."

Tahath looked beyond him for a brief moment, then met his gaze. "I know. Then I guess your worries of firstborn rights don't really exist, do they? Hannah's son will belong to God, not to you. So Eitan keeps his place. As he should."

"Yes. As he should." The thought should not grate as it did. He loved Eitan, after all, and the boy showed signs of becoming a good worker. Perhaps with the right encouragement, he would care for both his mother and Hannah if the day came when Elkanah was no longer there for them.

He nodded to Tahath. "You are right as usual, brother."

"The vow will not be easily accepted by our parents," Tahath said.

"I am very aware of that. Why else do you think I have said nothing until now?" He raked a hand over his beard.

Tahath rested a hand on his shoulder. "I do not envy you." His eyes held sympathy, but a moment later he simply smiled and moved on toward his home.

33

Hannah woke with a start. The pains that had been a dull ache for the past few days suddenly caused her whole middle to cramp. She cried out, unable to stop herself, and was relieved when Nava rushed into the room.

"Is it time?" Nava's sleep-mussed hair was the only evidence that she had not been awake the entire night, for her eyes were wide with fright now.

"I think so," Hannah managed through clenched teeth. "Yes."

"I'll get your mother." Nava hurried from the room before she could respond. Elkanah had stayed away from her bed for weeks, ever since the days for giving birth had drawn near. But now, oh how she wished he were here! To grasp his strong hands against the strangling pain.

She stifled a cry as another contraction overtook her, and she breathed slowly, then panted until she could sit up in bed. Her mother rushed into the room and Galia soon followed. Lamps were lit, and the room glowed like daylight as the women helped her walk about until at last, hours later, it came time to sit upon the birthing stool.

"I see his head, Hannah," her mother said, her voice soothing. "A few more good pushes."

"That's right, my dear. He's almost here. You can do this." Galia had never sounded more excited or encouraging to Hannah until this moment.

But she did not dwell on the thought as every part of her energy focused on bearing down to deliver the child. Another contraction. Then another. At last a scream escaped her lips, along with a gush of blood and water — and her son.

"Oh Hannah, he's here! He's beautiful!" Her mother's exuberance caused Hannah to exhale a long-held sigh of relief. She knew he would be fine, but she wasn't as young as she once was, and though she had faith, doubt had crept in now and then.

"Let me hold him," she said a moment later.

"I should clean him up first," her mother said, though her tone held hesitance.

"I want to hold him now." She didn't care that he was covered in the messiness of birth. She held out her arms and her mother handed him to her. She opened her robe and placed his tiny body against her skin, letting him feel the beat of her heart. "I want you to always remember me, little one," she whispered against his ear. "Always remember that I love you with all of my heart. No one will ever love you more than I do."

The room grew silent and Hannah knew they had heard, but she did not care. The boy's mouth moved, and she directed him to her breast and nearly laughed at the contented sound he made.

"Now can I take him?" her mother asked after she had held him not nearly long enough. "Elkanah will want to bless him, and he should be clean for that."

"And don't forget to salt and bind his limbs," Galia said, bustling about the room.

Dana helped Nava clean her up, while the mothers attended to the sheets and clothing and dressing the babe.

How empty Hannah's arms felt in those few moments that her mother had taken her son to clean him and swaddle him. *Oh Adonai, how will I ever let him go?*

"I'll bring him right back to you," her

mother said as she and Galia left the room to bring the boy to Elkanah. She paused a moment at the threshold. "What will you name him, my daughter?"

Hannah looked at her son, now swaddled and hard to see but for his head. "Samuel," she said without hesitation. "Because I asked the Lord for him."

Her mother nodded and smiled, and the two women hurried to the waiting men in the courtyard. As Hannah watched her son being carried away, she knew her vow was going to cost her far more than she could have ever imagined.

Elkanah held Samuel on his knee, his heart surging with love for this child. *Oh Adonai, thank You!* How was it possible he had ever doubted? If only he had waited for God's timing. If only he had not listened to the voices of those who thought another wife was the only way.

"Are you going to bless him, Abba?" Eitan stood near him, trying to peer into the child's bundled face.

Elkanah looked at his oldest son, recalling the moment the boy had sat in this very place on his lap, near his heart. "Yes, my son. As I also blessed you."

The boy smiled, and Elkanah stood as the

crowd of family and friends looked on. "In eight days we will circumcise this child according to the covenant God made with Abraham, and he will then officially be called Samuel, 'asked of God.' But right now I lift him up to Adonai" — he held the boy aloft — "and bless him in God's holy name. May Adonai Tzva'ot make His name great through this child all the days of his life, and no razor shall ever touch his head, for this child is dedicated to the Lord."

Elkanah sat again and held Samuel close.

"He is a Nazarite then," Jeroham said, his brows knit in concern. "That is a weighty vow to put on a child, my son."

"It is a vow Hannah and I made before he was conceived, Father." Elkanah avoided meeting his father's gaze. The Nazarite part of the vow did not trouble him, though in time Samuel's hair would grow well past that of a man's normal length. No, it was the other part — of leaving him at the tabernacle with Eli and his corrupt sons. Was this God's answer to his constant prayer for a deliverer? But why choose one so young? Why did Hannah vow such a thing, to give the boy back at such a young age?

Suddenly he had the urge to hold his son close and never release him. But pulling him closer caused the boy to fuss, and Elkanah knew from experience the mewling sounds meant Samuel wanted Hannah. No doubt he would always want Hannah, but one day too soon he would have to live apart from her.

Oh God! How can I bear it? How can she? Emotion clogged his throat, and he swallowed back the bitter taste of bile.

"Are you all right, Abba?" Eitan still stood at his side, apparently watching him closely. No doubt to have something to report to his mother, who conveniently stayed away.

Can you blame her? Hannah did the same at every one of her births.

"I'm all right, my son," he said, rising and handing Samuel back to Hannah's mother. "The blessing is past until the circumcision, so if you wish, you may go home and tell your mother."

Eitan's thin brows drew together. "I don't want to go home, Abba. Ima is always crabby when I'm there. I want to stay with you." He gave Elkanah a toothy grin.

Elkanah smiled. "Then you may come with me to check on the sheep. But first I am going to step into the house for a moment to see your Aunt Hannah."

Eitan nodded. "I'll wait here."

Elkanah looked at him, surprised at his

insight, realizing that his children were growing up like olive plants around him, faster than he could keep up and faster than he would like. What would happen when Peninnah could no longer bear children? What if Hannah could and Peninnah could not? Would God turn things around on them like that?

He stepped over the threshold and walked to Hannah's room. He wouldn't go in, but he would thank her from the doorway and gaze on his wife and son.

Peninnah stood in the courtyard, rocking her newest son's basket with one foot, trying to keep him calm. She was weary. So weary. And the sounds of joy coming from Hannah's home did not help.

She glanced around at her cluttered house, listening to the younger children chase each other in the adjoining field. Her mother had chosen to lie down in one of the sleeping rooms with Yemima, who had grown impatient and fussier ever since Nadav's birth.

She blew out a frustrated breath. Yemima was spoiled. Everyone coddled her and gave her what she wanted because she had been so tiny at birth. And even though she was the youngest of five at the time, she had grown into a small tyrant by the time Na-

371

dav was born.

She sank onto a bench but still rocked the basket, glancing at the child. No wonder her children had run off and Yemima was always cranky. Nadav was the worst of her children, never happy, always fussing. And her mother was getting too old for this. She needed a maid, like Hannah had in Nava.

Nava was leaving to marry soon. But Hannah had only one child to care for, and by the sound of it she would have plenty of help from Elkanah's family. The realization stung. Not once had Galia offered to come and help with Nadav. Or take Yemima or Moriah to stay overnight with their grandparents. And Eitan and Hevel and Aniah kept running off with Elkanah, so they were no help to her whatsoever.

She crossed her arms over her chest, tasting the salt of tears. She brushed them away, but they would not stop coming. What was wrong with her? She was not one to weep like Hannah. She was strong. Capable. She did not cry.

She sniffed and quickly gathered herself at the sound of someone approaching. One glance up and her heart fluttered for the briefest moment, then grew hard as Elkanah and Eitan came into view.

"We are going to check on the sheep,

Ima," Eitan announced. "We just came to get Hevel. He'll want to come too."

Peninnah nodded. "That's good. He is out in the field with Aniah and Moriah." She glanced up at Elkanah. "So the child is born."

Elkanah shifted from foot to foot as though he could not wait to be away from her presence. "Yes. A boy." He met her gaze. "He will be Samuel, 'asked of God,' and a Nazarite all the days of his life."

Peninnah lifted a brow. "A Nazarite? That seems rather extreme to place on an infant."

"It is part of a vow we made."

We. He and Hannah, of course. "I see."

"Will you visit her?" He asked it as though he expected her to say yes.

"Hannah did not visit me, if you recall."

"Eventually she did." Was he pleading with her? But no. He was simply asking.

"Did Hannah ask after me?" She searched his face for any hint of a lie.

He held her gaze but then shook his head. "She was too tired and caught up in the birth." He paused. "You have not spoken to her since my announcement of her pregnancy. I simply wondered if we could get past that. You are never around my family, and it seems like at some point my two wives ought to be able to be kind to one another."

Was he kidding? "What you are really saying is that you think it's time *I* be kind to Hannah and the rest of your family, but when have they been kind to me? When have they invited me to spin with them or offered to watch my children? You won't even purchase a maid for me, when I am the one who has needed the help, not Hannah!"

He stared at her, and she knew her outburst was foolish and futile. Nadav must have agreed, as the rocking no longer soothed him. Loud wails came from his basket, and Peninnah bent to lift him out, silently cursing herself for not keeping her voice lower. She put him to her breast, not caring what Elkanah thought of her.

She looked up just as Eitan and Hevel came racing into the courtyard. "We're ready, Abba!" Hevel said.

"Hush!" Peninnah whisper-shouted.

"Go wait for me by the rock at the edge of the field, where I can see you," Elkanah said, pointing in that direction.

The boys looked from one parent to the other and ran off. Peninnah released a deep sigh as the tears started again. What was wrong with her? She must not weep in front of him!

"I will seek a maid to help you," Elkanah said softly. "I did not realize that you needed help beyond your mother."

"My mother does not admit that she is getting older, and the care of children is not easy."

"No, I imagine it is not." He raked a hand along the back of his neck. "And I can see that it is wearing you down. When is the last time you slept?"

She shrugged. "I never sleep like I used to. Nadav wakes to eat nearly every hour."

His look grew thoughtful. "Do you want me to find someone to nurse him for you?"

"Like who? Hannah?"

"No. I would not put you through more struggles with her. Someone from town, perhaps."

Peninnah felt the tug of Nadav's little mouth and the sweet pull of her milk letting down. It was the one thing about infancy that she loved, though not quite as often as this child wanted it.

"No," she said at last. "I will manage."

"Then just a maid to help with the others, to clean and cook or whatever you need."

"That would be helpful, yes."

He released a deep sigh. "Well then, I better be off. I will bring the boys home soon." He paused as if he wanted to say more but wasn't sure how. "If you do not think it a bother, I will dine here with you and the children tonight."

She looked at him, her heart softening ever so slightly. "And shall I set a bed for you as well?" He couldn't sleep with Hannah, but everyone knew he'd been sleeping in the sitting room there.

"Yes, you can set a bed for me. Perhaps I can help you with Nadav."

His offer brought tears again, and she could not speak. He did not come to her as he had to Hannah at the feast the year before and offer his sympathies. Instead her tears seemed to make him uncomfortable.

He hurried off and left her alone as always.

34

Six Months Later

Hannah bundled a wiggly Samuel into a small tunic and undergarments and lifted him to her shoulder. "What a fine boy you are growing to be," she whispered in his ear. "Are you ready to go visit Aunt Nava?"

The boy made some happy gurgling sounds and squealed with delight, but Hannah wondered if he understood a word she'd said. He did seem to enjoy Nava's company.

Hannah had been thrilled the day Elkanah came home and announced that he had found a merchant in town who was willing to sell some of his land to Ezer and Nava in exchange for help working his fields. Elkanah's brothers had helped Ezer build a small house, and two months after Samuel's circumcision, Ezer had come for Nava in a beautiful wedding ceremony.

The memory of that day, the joy in Nava's

gaze, and the tears neither of them could contain lingered in Hannah's heart. She missed her friend, for she had thought of her as such soon after she had reached womanhood. And now with Samuel to care for, she missed the adult companionship — someone to talk to who could do more than squeal with delight or cry when he had a need.

"Well, little man," she said, shaking the thoughts aside, "I think we have everything, so why don't we go ahead and take a walk?" She wrapped him in her scarf and tied him securely to her chest to help lighten the load of carrying him. How fast he was growing!

How she wished she could slow the time.

She checked the basket with extra clothes and some food she planned to take to Nava — a round of cheese and a flask of new wine — and headed to the door, then stopped cold. Peninnah was coming toward her with Nadav in her arms. What could she possibly want? They hadn't spoken since before Samuel's birth, and Hannah did not want to start now. Not when she had plans for a pleasant day. But she forced herself to step out of the house into the courtyard to meet Peninnah before she could cross the threshold.

"Peninnah. This is a surprise." Hannah

took the woman's measure, looking her up and down. "What can I do for you?"

Peninnah seemed to cling tighter to Nadav, until the child fussed in an obvious attempt to be free to toddle about the yard. Was the woman nervous? By the way she would not meet Hannah's gaze, she wondered.

"Has something happened?" The hair on the back of Hannah's neck stood up. "Is Elkanah hurt?"

"I left the children with my maid and sent Aniah to get Elkanah," Peninnah said, looking at her feet, her voice catching. "I found Ima . . ." She looked at Hannah, tears in her eyes. "I found my mother dead on the floor next to her bed shortly after we broke the fast this morning." She drew in a breath as though straining for composure.

"Oh Peninnah, I'm sorry!" Hannah dropped her basket and simply held Samuel close. "What can I do?"

Peninnah swallowed, and her expression seemed to change between hurt and anger, as though she could not decide which way to turn. "I don't even know why I am here. I should have sent my maid."

"You need help and I want to help you." Hannah was not sure in that moment that she spoke truth, but Elkanah would want his wives to pull together at such a time as this. "I can go and get Galia and our sisters-in-law to help. They will call the women to come and mourn, and the men will get busy building a bier. Do you have food? Perhaps we can send the children to stay with Galia?" She slowed, trying to read Peninnah's expression. "Tell me what I can do."

Peninnah looked beyond Hannah a moment, her eyes misting with unshed tears. "I've lost them both now. I have no one else."

Hannah studied this woman, this usurper of her time alone with Elkanah, and could not stop the many questions from surging through her thoughts. Why had she come here instead of going straight to Galia's? What made her so cruel at times and so normal, even friendly, now? What would Galia do without Yafa?

Yafa gone? The thought pained her, for Yafa seemed to be Peninnah's only friend and confidante. What would Peninnah do without her mother, when she had caused so much strife with every other woman she knew?

"I'm sorry for your loss," Hannah said at last, once it became obvious that Peninnah seemed unable to move or do anything but stand in her courtyard and cling to her youngest son. "Come. Let me take you home while I go to Dana's house and send one of her children to get the others."

Peninnah rallied at that. "Can I go with you?" It was as if she suddenly could not handle the thought of returning to her own house, where her mother's body lay.

"Of course. Do you want some water first?"

"No. I am not thirsty."

Hannah nodded and led the way to Dana's house, not far from hers. She entered the courtyard and called Dana's name as she opened the door without knocking, something they had grown used to doing.

Dana hurried to the court, her arms filled with a basket of clean linens. "What is it? I thought you were going to see Nava today." She stopped short at the sight of Peninnah and gave Hannah a curious look.

"Peninnah found Yafa dead in her room a short time ago." Hannah looked at Peninnah, who seemed dazed, and exchanged glances with Dana.

"Oh my!" Dana put a hand to her mouth. "I'm sorry to hear it, Peninnah."

Peninnah simply nodded, and Hannah led her to a bench, fearing the woman would collapse from the shock. She turned to Dana. "I thought if you could send one of your children to get Galia and the others, we could get started on preparing Yafa for burial. Peninnah said she sent one of her children to get Elkanah, and her maid is staying with the youngest ones."

Dana nodded. "Yes, of course. I'll send word to Tahath to get his brothers. They can build the bier and get the entrance to the cave opened. She will have to be buried by nightfall."

"And I will somehow try to get word to Nava so she does not think I forgot about her. She will want to help." Hannah's mind whirled as she spoke, but her gaze was on Peninnah, who didn't seem to be seeing clearly even now.

"Do you have some wine?" She looked at Dana. "I think she needs something to help revive her."

"Mint water might do a better job. Let me run to get the girls and send our young messengers on their way." Dana turned to enter the house, and Hannah stood in indecision whether to follow and help make the water or to stay with Peninnah for fear she would faint. "I'll hurry," Dana said over her shoulder. "You stay here and watch her."

Hannah sighed. It wasn't what she wanted to do, but she sat on the bench near Peninnah just the same.

Peninnah's house was buzzing with the chatter of women as Elkanah approached with Eitan and Hevel racing ahead of him. Tahath had found him on the way, and they had left Tahath's oldest son in charge of the flock.

"This is so unexpected," Elkanah said. "She seemed perfectly fine when I saw her a few days ago."

"Death is no respecter of people or age, brother. Yafa did seem wearier the last time I saw her, but that was at the last feast. It's not like I saw her as often as you did." Tahath offered him an empathetic smile. "Do you have what you need to build the bier?"

Elkanah shook his head. "We're going to have to cut some tree limbs. Hopefully the women have some linens already made."

"Dana tells me that such linens are a staple in every home. No one could possibly weave enough cloth for a bier in a day, so it is something the women do to make sure at least one is ready — in case." Tahath rubbed a hand along his jaw. "We are actually fortunate that none have been needed, even with so many children born, until now."

Elkanah glanced at his brother, then quickened his step. They were blessed not to have lost any women in childbirth or a child to some disease or accident. God had shown them great kindness. Kindness he was certain they did not deserve. But to lose Yafa . . .

"There is the tree near the house that should have a straight limb," he said, pointing to a tall oak. "We will cut it to fit the length of her body and wrap the linen around the ends." He was talking just to feel alive, for the silence was not something he could abide at this moment.

"Let's get your tools and start then. Where are they?" Tahath moved ahead of him toward the house. He knew what his brother was trying to do — keep him from having to see Peninnah in whatever state she was in at this moment. But he knew he could not ignore this wife indefinitely. Especially now.

"I will pick the limb," he called. "The tools are just inside the door to the left in a goatskin sack on a tall shelf."

Tahath ducked into the doorway, and Elkanah noticed his other brothers coming up the road toward the house. In no time they would have the bier built and the cave opened, and Yafa would rest beside Assir in her final place on earth.

Tahath returned moments later and greeted his brothers. "Hannah is asking for you," he said, leaning close to Elkanah's ear. "I think you should leave this to us."

Elkanah's stomach knotted with the very thought of entering the house, but the fact that it was Hannah asking for him caused him to nod and walk through the courtyard.

Hannah placed a sleeping Samuel in a basket and greeted Elkanah at the door of Peninnah's home. He kissed her cheek, his look one of curiosity and dread. "Peninnah needs you," she whispered.

He leaned down. "I did not expect to see you here."

Hannah met his gaze. "This is one of those times when we do what we must, yes?" A soft sigh escaped. "She came to my door this morning and told me. She looks so lost. She nurses Nadav and weeps, but will not look at anyone or talk to anyone — not since she spoke to me this morning. I think you should go to her."

He glanced about the room, noting that at least this part of the house was quiet. Samuel lay so peacefully in his basket that Elka-

385

nah's heart hurt for the joy of seeing the boy, his boy, here, alive.

Hannah touched his arm, gently pushing him toward the inner rooms of the house. "Go, beloved."

"What do I say to her?" He gave Hannah an imploring look.

"You take her in your arms and hold her. You don't even need to speak." She smiled at him as though what she had just said did not bother her at all, but he knew how much being here was costing her. Being kind to her enemy was not a normal thing to do.

"You amaze me," he whispered, cupping her cheek. "Most women in your place would not do this."

"Well, you need not be amazed. I am only doing what I would want others to do for me." She pushed him on again, and he did not resist her nudge.

The hall to the sleeping chambers grew noisier at his approach. He passed his mother weeping, rushing from Yafa's room to . . . somewhere. She didn't even see him. Mourners arrived, their loud wailing coming from the courtyard, and the children grew quiet, clinging to their mothers.

Elkanah glanced back, saw Hannah nod for him to continue. Why was this so hard? He forced one foot in front of the other and approached the room he sometimes shared with Peninnah. The shutters were closed, the room dark, but as his eyes adjusted to the darkness, he saw her lying on the bed, curled around Nadav's small body.

"Peninnah?" He stepped closer and knelt beside her. "I'm so sorry, my love." Had he ever called her that? By the look on her face and the wide, weepy eyes, he didn't think so. He couldn't recall bringing himself to a place where love came between them. Only procreation. Never love.

Had he said the wrong thing? But it was too late to retract the words.

Peninnah stared at him in silence for the longest moment, then looked beyond him. "I didn't even get to say goodbye to her," she said at last. "I had finished with the morning meal, and she said she wasn't hungry and wanted to go lie down. But then she never came out of her room, and when I looked —" A sob escaped, and she held Nadav as though she would never release him.

"Hush now," he said, feeling completely awkward. He sat beside her and stroked her hair, her face, her arm. "Why don't you let me take Nadav and put him to bed so you can get ready." He coaxed her to look at him. "I'm very sorry for Yafa's loss, Peninnah. She was a great asset to us both and a good mother to you. I can't imagine what you are feeling right now, but my brothers will have the bier ready soon, and we have to walk to the cave and put her there before nightfall." He gently loosed her grip on Nadav and placed the boy in a basket near the bed, then took hold of Peninnah's hands.

She lifted her gaze to his, and he brushed a stray tear with his thumb. "Oh Peninnah, I do wish this had not happened." He pulled her close to his chest until she relaxed and wet his robe with her tears.

"Do you love me?" she asked when her tears were spent.

The question caught him off guard, but after his unfortunate comment, he knew he could not simply ignore her now.

"I care for you," he said slowly. "Of course I love you." He did in a sort of second-wife way, didn't he? But a nagging feeling that he was lying to appease her pricked his conscience.

"But not like you do Hannah." It was a statement said without feeling.

He looked at her, uncertain. "I've known Hannah much longer and have loved her for many years. It's different than it is with you, but it doesn't mean I do not care. What kind of a man would I be if I treated you unfairly or unkindly?"

"Then I should expect more time with you." Her look, despite her tears, held challenge.

A sigh escaped, and he could not speak for many breaths. "I give you what I can, Peninnah. If you were kinder to Hannah, it would make things better between us."

Her brows drew down. Why was she growing angry when her mother was about to be buried in a cave? "So it's my fault? Everything is up to me to fix the relationship with Hannah, and then you will love me equally?"

He relaxed his hold on her arms and took a step back. "Please, can we talk about this another time? I have to get out to help my brothers, and you need to get ready to lead the procession with me. You and our children."

It was the best he could do, and before she could say more, he hurried from the room. He wasn't sure what good his presence there had done or why Hannah thought it so important. All he had done was blunder his words and make her angry. Peninnah was always angry.

He stomped out of the house, gave Hannah a frustrated shrug, and went to help his brothers.

35

One Year Later

The Feast of First Fruits approached, but Hannah could not bear to go to Shiloh. Not yet. Not when she knew the day would come when she would have to leave Samuel in Eli's care. She held the boy to her breast, comfortably nursing in the shade of the overhanging awning of the courtyard, catching the early summer breeze. How fast he had grown in the past eighteen months!

Oh Adonai, I don't know if I can bear to let him go. She sensed that God knew her feelings. Hadn't He given them to all mothers? Wasn't it better to be honest with Him?

It's just so hard. She stroked Samuel's ruddy cheek, and the boy opened his eyes and smiled at her. Something stirred within her that made her ache for the mingled joy and pain of motherhood. She had given birth and her shame had left her, but what would people say when she went to the feast and Samuel didn't come home? Peninnah would love that. And the taunts would surely begin again.

Footsteps caused her to look up and swipe an errant tear away. Elkanah trudged into the courtyard and sank onto a bench beside hers.

"He's growing fast." Elkanah touched the boy's soft hair.

"Too fast." She swallowed to avoid the emotion churning within her.

Elkanah nodded and clutched one of her hands. "The plans for the feast are almost done. Are you sure you don't want to join us?" He searched her face. "I hate leaving you alone."

"I'm sure," she said, keeping her tone confident. "I don't want to take him there until he is weaned and I can fulfill my vow."

He nodded. "Do what seems best to you. Stay here until you have weaned him."

"Thank you. And besides, Nava is nearby and not going because her child is due soon, so I won't be the only person left in the city."

"I'm not afraid of that," he said, touching her cheek. "A few of my sisters-in-law are staying behind as well, so if you need anything . . ."

"I will know exactly where to find them."

He stood. "If you're sure."

He seemed so hesitant to leave her, yet he had to go to the feast not only as a Kohathite but to keep the law. She studied him a moment. "Are you afraid of sharing the feast with just Peninnah and your children?"

His brow quirked, and he lifted one shoulder in a shrug. "I'm sure Peninnah will be quite happy." She didn't miss the sarcasm in his tone. "She has not been easier to deal with since Yafa's passing. I had hoped it would change her."

"Only God can change a person's heart, beloved. You and I both know that."

He nodded. "I know. Perhaps I need to pray for her."

"And I will do the same. Perhaps it will cause her to understand kindness if we ask God to help us show it to her."

Elkanah bent down to kiss her cheek. "I love you, you know."

Hannah smiled. "I know." She met his gaze just as Samuel stopped nursing.

The boy sat up and lifted his arms to his father. "Abba . . . up."

Elkanah laughed and took Samuel from her arms. How good it felt to be a whole family. She would not think about the day when they would go back to being two instead of three.

■ ■ ■ ■

Four Years Later
Elkanah held Samuel's hand and walked beside Hannah on the way to his parents' home for the Sabbath meal. It was the week before the Feast of First Fruits, the last moment when they would be together as a complete family before he had to present Samuel to God in Shiloh. Every memory of the vow Hannah had made pained him now.

He glanced at her walking beside him, carrying a clay dish of food she had prepared to help feed the many family members. Even his sister, Meira, and her husband and Hannah's entire family planned to join them, a rare occurrence.

"All of my cousins are going to be there?" Samuel asked, skipping along beside Elkanah.

"All of your cousins and your brothers and sisters and your aunts and uncles and grandparents," Elkanah said, hoping his voice sounded lighter than his heart felt.

"A big celebration!" Samuel's enthusiasm did little to lift Elkanah's spirits.

Why, Adonai? Why did it take a vow to give us this child? I don't want to give him to live at the tabernacle. Hophni and Phinehas are as corrupt as ever. He had seen it only a few months ago on his regular trip to work there. Nothing had changed, at least not for the better. How could he put his only son by his favorite wife in such a position?

"Yes, my son," Hannah said, keeping in step with the boy. "This is a big celebration. Do you remember why?"

Samuel stopped suddenly just as his grandfather's house came into view. Elkanah looked at him, saw his son's gaze move between mother and father. "It's the last time I will be eating with all of you, because I'm going to live where Abba goes to work sometimes."

A knot formed in Elkanah's throat and he couldn't speak.

"That's right. And why are you going to live there?" Hannah had surely already asked the child these questions, but Elkanah knew she was simply trying to reinforce his understanding. At five, Samuel was a bright boy, but still a young boy. Could he possibly understand separation?

"Because you promised God that if He would give me to you, you would let God have me back to do His work." He gave Hannah a toothy grin, minus the few teeth that hadn't yet come in.

"And God has some great work for you to

do there, my son. He hasn't told us yet what it is, but in a few years He will show you, and Eli the priest will teach you more than Abba and I can." Hannah knelt to meet Samuel at eye level. "But you know that Abba and I will visit as often as we can. I will still make you new robes and tunics, and Abba will see you every time he comes to work there. And the priests' wives will look after you too."

Samuel nodded, his expression suddenly serious. "I won't see you every day." He frowned.

"No," Hannah said softly. "No, my love, you won't." She opened her arms and he came close and hugged her hard. "We've talked about this for a long time, but it's different now that it is so close, isn't it?"

Samuel nodded against her chest, and Elkanah felt completely helpless. In the five years since Samuel's birth, Hannah had not borne another child. She was giving God all she had.

He swallowed hard against that thought. He still had sons to raise, and daughters too, but Hannah would be left with nothing but him. How was she able to speak to Samuel so peacefully? *Oh God, this is so hard.*

"But you will come to see me," Samuel said.

"As much as I can. At every feast and maybe even when Abba works in Shiloh. We can count on those as our special visits, and in the in-between times we will do the things God has for us. Okay?" She kissed his forehead and held him at arm's length.

Samuel nodded slowly, but a moment later his face was wreathed in a grin. "I will be the only one to have two homes. One with you and Abba and one with God." He turned and skipped ahead, then stopped to look back. "Can I go see my cousins?"

Hannah nodded and Samuel ran off. Elkanah looked at her as she picked up the dish she'd set aside and began walking again toward his parents' home.

"You are truly all right with this?" He put his hand on her shoulder.

She nodded, but he didn't miss the tears in her eyes. "It will not be easy," she said, slowing her step as they neared the entrance to the courtyard and heard the rumblings of men and women and squealing children racing about the yard or talking inside the house. For a brief moment the court was empty. "But it is the right thing to do. And God will take care of him."

Elkanah held her gaze. "I wish I had your faith."

"You do. You're just grieving."

"I wish we didn't have to leave him."

"Me too."

They stared at each other in silence a moment. "May the Lord make good His word," Elkanah said.

Hannah smiled. "He will, beloved. If He could give us Samuel, He can be trusted to do the rest of what we entrust to Him."

Elkanah nodded, marveling at this woman. He didn't deserve such a woman of faith. Not when his own faith seemed so fragile at this moment. But as they entered the house with the entire family gathered, he knew he would have to announce their intentions. Pray God he would have the words to answer their questions.

Hannah stood over an exhausted, sleeping Samuel, her heart pounding. She knew she should lie down beside him and rest, but her mind would not settle from all of the questions thrown at her and Elkanah after the announcement to their families. Should they have told them all sooner?

"How could anyone do such a thing?" Peninnah had been the first to throw out a barb. Though she might have meant it as sarcastic, the gleam in her eyes had given away her delight in Hannah's loss.

"Hannah, how can you bear to do this to

us?" Galia's comment had been no better, and Jeroham had supported his wife, for he had come to dote on the boy. "We love Samuel. You know how long you waited and prayed."

"Yes, I do," she said, looking to Elkanah for support, but even his composure seemed to be hanging by a thread. "You all know that I was barren for years." The word had lost its sting, even though every female head nodded in solemn agreement. "And that God granted my petition after I prayed and vowed to give my son back to Him. So please, do not fret or think this a bad thing. God has brought about this moment for a purpose. I believe He wanted me to be willing to give Him everything because He has a greater purpose for Samuel."

The room had grown quiet after that, until everyone started to ask questions about how they could help or how she could bear it and how Samuel was taking the idea of not living with his parents. Even now she could not stop their words from creating a hint of doubt in her heart.

Oh Adonai, I know I am doing the right thing, for to break my vow to You is not possible. But please give me strength to carry it out, because living without Samuel's voice in this house or holding him close each day is going to be impossible without Your help.

Soft footfalls sounded behind her, and she turned to see Elkanah enter the room. He came to her and wrapped her in his arms, the two of them looking down at their innocent son.

"It will be all right," he whispered into her ear.

She leaned against him, felt his heart beating steadily as he himself was always steady, always there for her.

"I know. It will be hard, though." She looked at him. "But God has given me peace."

Elkanah nodded. "Strangely enough, even through the chaos tonight, I felt His peace as well. I don't know what God has in store for our son, but I feel certain that he is chosen to bring change to Israel. Good change."

She smiled and rose up on her toes to kiss his bearded cheek. "I am sure of it too."

He kissed her, a kiss full of promise, of a future to come. "We have a week left with him."

"Until the next feast."

"Yes. Which reminds me that we need to gather what we will sacrifice on his behalf."

"I have already chosen a three-year-old bull."

"And I have an ephah of flour and a skin of wine waiting."

"Then we will enjoy this last week until that day."

He kissed her again as though he needed her, suddenly more than she had realized. Until that last day she would enjoy her son. But right now she pulled Elkanah aside and showed him she needed him too.

36

One Week Later

The walk to Shiloh felt wrapped in mystery and solemnity. Except for the noisy children running ahead and back again to their watching mothers, Elkanah's family had grown quiet, even the women.

Hannah walked with Elkanah and Samuel separate from the rest of the clan. The three-year-old bull was tied to the back of the cart that held the flour and wine and food for the feast and the other supplies they would need while they were there.

Even Samuel seemed to realize the gravity of the moment, for he stayed between his parents and did not run after his cousins. As Shiloh grew closer, his eyes widened and he looked at Hannah.

"Shiloh is big." How astute he seemed for one so young.

"Yes, my son, it has to be. The Levites have housing near the tabernacle so they can care for the house of the Lord, and the priests live here along with many servants. Most of the city is made up of those who work to keep the tabernacle and the sacrifices going the way God intended."

"But I will stay with Eli."

"Yes," Hannah said, her heart constricting with the sudden thought that Eli might be too old, might refuse her. He would not do that, would he?

They walked down the familiar slope of the hill to the area where the Kohathites set up camp. Elkanah stepped away from her for a moment to give Peninnah instructions and direct her sons to set up Hannah's tent, then made sure Tahath would oversee the boys, who he'd admitted to Hannah could not always be trusted.

"We will present him to the Lord tonight," Hannah said once Elkanah returned. "After the sacrifice."

Elkanah's expression changed from worry to acceptance in one brief moment. "I'll be back with the bull." He walked off again to untie the bull from the cart.

Hannah took Samuel's hand. "It is time for you to meet Eli." She looked into his innocent eyes and noted how long his hair had already grown past his shoulders. But a Nazarite did not cut his hair, so by the time

402

he was old he would have it growing to his knees unless the Lord kept it from growing as fast as it was now.

"It's all right, Ima." The boy's words startled her. "I know you would not leave me here if Eli was not good."

Hannah sighed, and Elkanah came into sight with the bull ambling behind him. "Only God is good, my son. Eli will treat you well, but you must remember that only God is good."

Samuel nodded, though Hannah wondered how much a five-year-old could possibly understand. She herself had trouble understanding how God could be good sometimes, especially when so much evil happened around her.

But she tucked the thought away as the three of them made their way to the altar. Elkanah placed Samuel's small hands on the head of the bull before Hophni slit the animal's throat and Phinehas caught the blood. She watched as they put the blood on the altar and burned the bull as the law commanded, surprising her. Perhaps God was keeping them from ruining this sacrifice as they had done to the one she offered so many years ago. Was this His way of encouraging her vow?

"Is it time now, Ima?" Samuel's eagerness

surprised her. She exchanged a look with Elkanah and felt that sense of peace creep over her as they led the boy to where Eli sat by the doorpost of the tabernacle.

"Pardon me, my lord," Hannah said as they approached.

Eli roused from a lazy stupor. He rubbed his white beard and studied them for a long moment. "Yes? What is it?"

Hannah cleared her throat. No doubt he didn't remember her, but she would trust God that he at least would not reject her now. "My lord, forgive me for interrupting you, but we are here to present to you our child, Samuel." She searched his face, which had alighted on her son, looking him up and down.

"As surely as you live," she continued, "I am the woman who stood here beside you praying to the Lord. I prayed for this child, and the Lord has granted me what I asked of Him. So now I give him to the Lord. For his whole life he will be given over to the Lord."

Eli looked from Samuel to Hannah. "You are leaving him here to serve the Lord?"

"Under your guidance, yes."

"You are the woman I thought was drinking too much wine." He rubbed the corners of his beard. "I remember you."

"Yes, my lord. I am that same woman."

"And you prayed for this child."

"Yes, my lord. And God has graciously granted my request. But I made a vow that day to give my son back to the Lord, so we are here to present him to you, to serve you here at the tabernacle." She watched him, trying to assess his thoughts.

"He is very young."

"He is weaned and he is a quick learner."

Eli looked at Elkanah. "And you approved this vow?"

Elkanah nodded. "Yes, my lord. We believe God has destined Samuel to serve Him and this is the best place for our son to learn how to do that."

Eli straightened. "Come here, child."

Samuel stepped close to Eli.

"How old are you?" Eli blinked as if he was trying to make sense of their offering.

"Five years." Samuel held Eli's gaze. "I am here to help you and to let you teach me. That's what Ima says. So where do I stay?"

Eli chuckled and a twinkle filled his eyes. "An eager one you have here."

"He is a gift from the Lord," Hannah said, smiling through a mist of tears.

Eli nodded, seeming to realize their difficulty in leaving him. He slowly stood.

"Well then, we must not keep our gift from God waiting. This boy wants to see the tabernacle, so we must show him." He looked from Elkanah to Hannah. "Would you like to come?"

Eli showed them the grounds where Samuel would learn, places Hannah and Elkanah knew well but now seemed new through their son's eyes. Of course, the actual tabernacle was off-limits to them. At the end of the visit, they held Samuel tight one last time, then made their way back to the camp.

Myriad emotions moved through Hannah as thoughts of missing her son mingled with the joy of knowing that Samuel was happy and she had fulfilled the vow she had made to God. To obey Him, even when it was so hard, filled her whole body with a sense of such joy, she almost could not contain it. Was this what it meant to trust? To give everything to the Creator and trust Him with the outcome? Was this what God had intended for her to learn all along?

Oh Adonai, I didn't think I could bear it. But now she realized she could. Despite the corruption, there were good people here to help Eli. Raziela and Irit had loved Samuel the moment they met him, and Hannah's heart was full, knowing how far her friendship with both women had come, especially Raziela. How blessed she was to have earned her trust, and now to trust her with keeping an eye on Samuel in return. God had not abandoned her son to grow up under an old priest who may or may not do all He required. He had provided support, just as He had given her Elkanah and Dana and Nava all these years to support her in her times of trial. How could she not thank Him?

As they approached the camp and joined the family for the feast, Hannah stood. "Before we partake," she said, looking to Elkanah for approval and quickly receiving it, "I want to offer Adonai a prayer."

Galia gave her a curious look, but Dana nodded, smiling.

Hannah did not even look Peninnah's way. She stepped away from the group and lifted her hands heavenward. "My heart rejoices in the Lord," she said. "In the Lord my horn is lifted high. My mouth boasts over my enemies, for I delight in Your deliverance." She closed her eyes, lest Peninnah think the words were aimed at her. But were they?

She shook the thought aside, focusing her heart on Adonai. "There is no one holy like the Lord. There is no one besides You. There is no Rock like our God." She smiled at the heavens and turned in a circle, dancing for the Lord.

"Do not keep talking so proudly or let your mouth speak such arrogance, for the Lord is a God who knows, and by Him deeds are weighed. The bows of the warriors are broken, but those who stumbled are armed with strength. Those who were full hire themselves out for food, but those who were hungry are hungry no more." She opened her eyes and glanced at the group, her heart full of love for them, and for a brief moment she even gave Peninnah a smile.

"She who was barren has borne seven children," she continued. Of course, she had only borne one. Still, it felt as though God *could* give her seven. "But she who has had many sons pines away. The Lord brings death and makes alive. He brings down to the grave and raises up. The Lord sends poverty and wealth. He humbles and He exalts. He raises the poor from the dust and lifts the needy from the ash heap. He seats them with princes and has them inherit a throne of honor. For the foundations of the earth are the Lord's — on them He has set the world."

She paused a moment and knelt at Elkanah's side, looking into his eyes. "He will guard the feet of His faithful servants, but the wicked will be silenced in the place of darkness. It is not by strength that one prevails. Those who oppose the Lord will be broken. The Most High will thunder from heaven. The Lord will judge the ends of the earth. He will give strength to His king and exalt the horn of His anointed."

She stopped, realizing that the prayer had turned into a song near the end. "I hadn't expected . . . The words just came to me."

Elkanah took her hand. "God gave you the words, beloved. Since we have no king, you could not have made the song without God's help."

"It is a beautiful prayer, Hannah," Dana said. "Thank you for sharing it with us."

Galia wiped tears from her eyes. "After such a difficult day, my daughter, I am amazed that you can pray with joy. You are an inspiration to us."

Hannah's eyes filmed. Never had Galia spoken so kindly. "Thank you, Mother."

Galia stood and came over to hug Hannah, and every sister-in-law did the same, until at last the children started to squirm and ask when they could eat.

The only person still sitting in her seat throughout the hugs and tears, unable or unwilling to show comfort and kindness to Hannah, was Peninnah.

37

Three Months Later

Hannah sat at the loom, working the warp and the weft. How big should she make the next robe and tunic? Dana had given her a few of her sons' worn childhood garments to give her an idea of what size to make the clothing, but Samuel had grown faster than Dana's children. She did not wish to make the wrong size.

But next month Elkanah would take her to work at the tabernacle. She could take Samuel's measure then and add some extra length for growth. She would bring the robe to the Feast of Passover and First Fruits nine months hence.

She glanced up at the empty courtyard. How quiet it was. How much she missed her son! And Nava's company had always been a balm during her most trying times.

It would have helped if upon their return from Shiloh she had conceived again, but three months later she still showed no signs of pregnancy. A sigh escaped. *Is this it then, Lord? Only one?*

She did not want to appear ungrateful, for Samuel was certainly worth her vow, but oh how her arms ached to hold another child, to raise a houseful of children. Even Dana's children did not need her now, as they had grown into young men and women, and her daughters were nearly ready for marriage.

Though Peninnah's older sons had grown, she still had her youngest son and daughters and, from the rumors Hannah had heard, was expecting another child. In a strange sense Hannah was happy for her, especially since the loss of Yafa. Peninnah needed someone to love.

Don't you as well?

She rolled that thought around in her mind, wishing it were not true. She did have Elkanah's love, and Samuel loved her from afar. What more did she really need?

But it was the wanting that hurt more than the need. The longings unfulfilled. The vow that had cost her closeness with the little boy who had changed her. If only she could go back and relive those first few years.

She looked at the weaving again, blinking away the sting of tears. A few moments later she heard her name called from the road. *Ima?*

She stopped the shuttle and stood, meeting her mother at the gate to her courtyard. "Ima! What brings you to see me?"

"Does a mother need a reason to visit her only daughter?" Adva set a basket she'd been carrying on the ground and pulled Hannah into her arms. The warm embrace was nearly Hannah's undoing. Had she truly needed her mother that much? Did Samuel need her the way she needed him?

"I thought that after three months without him you might be feeling the loss more acutely." Her mother picked up the basket with one hand and guided Hannah into the house with the other. "I've brought things to make your favorite pomegranate milk." She moved to the cooking area where Hannah kept a large board and knife for chopping vegetables.

Hannah sat on a stool, watching. Her mother never allowed her to help in times like this, so she simply waited.

"I won't need the knife, as I already spent the morning removing the seeds from the pomegranate. We just need to heat the milk and add the fruit." She smiled, glancing up at Hannah, who could not stop the sudden tears.

"Is it so bad, my daughter?" Her mother came to hug her again.

Hannah shook her head. "No. Yes. At times. I am just overwhelmed with thinking that right when I was praying in self-pity, the Lord sent you to cheer me up. How often He finds ways to bring joy where there had been only pain." She smiled as she wiped the stray tears from her cheeks.

Her mother returned to working on the milk while Hannah sat again. "Tell me," Adva said, "how have you been, truly?"

Hannah glanced about the house, so often empty, and sighed. "It is quiet, Ima. I miss Samuel's laughter and the way he would chase one of his cousins or brothers in the yard — when Peninnah allowed them to play together. I miss Nava's presence, though I would not wish her back from the happy life she finally has for anything in the world. And I wish . . ." She looked away, unable to meet her mother's gaze.

"You wish God would give you more children."

Hannah nodded. "You know Peninnah is pregnant again."

Adva made a disgusted sound. "Elkanah ought to stay away from her bed. The woman breeds like sheep."

Hannah laughed but quickly sobered.

"She is fertile, I will admit that. Sometimes I wish Elkanah would stay away, but they are his children. And when he cannot be with me, he goes to her. She is his wife, after all."

"And as always you give him your blessing." Her mother shook her head. "You are too kind to him, my daughter. It wouldn't hurt you to tell the man how you feel and ask him to keep his distance from her."

Hannah's shoulders slumped, defeat settling over her. "Ima, I can't do that. We can't take back what is done. He can't divorce her, and his children need him. He always comes to me at least once in the day, and next month he is taking me to Shiloh, where we will be away from Peninnah for an entire week." She realized in that moment how much she longed for the day to arrive quickly.

Adva nodded. "That's good. I am happy that you are at peace with this, Hannah. When you told us about your vow . . . well, I must admit I did not want to believe it. Samuel is such a sweet child —" She stopped, choking on the words. She looked at Hannah, her smile sad. "I miss him."

Hannah felt the tears creeping up again, suddenly wondering if her mother's visit was as helpful to her as she'd expected it would be. But a moment later she found herself clinging to the woman who had given her life, grateful that someone else understood her struggle.

"Would you like to help me with the weaving?" she asked once the emotion had passed. "I'm making a new robe to take to Samuel during the next feast, and I am not quite sure which size to make it. Dana's samples from her own children are helpful, but I could use your opinion."

Her mother nodded, handing Hannah the cup of warmed fruity milk, and the two walked back to the courtyard. The time was sweeter than Hannah expected, for as they worked it struck her that her mother was aging more quickly than she had realized. How much time would they still have with each other, especially when these visits were so rare?

She looked at her mother and smiled. "Thank you for coming, Ima. You are just what I needed." If only life could stay this way and everyone she loved never had to walk through the door and leave her.

Peninnah doubled over from the sharp pain to her middle, unable to keep a cry from escaping. Her new maid, Dalit, hurried to her side.

"What is it, mistress? Are you ill? Is it the babe?" The girl flitted about the room like a mother hen, straightening cushions on the couch and leading Peninnah to sit.

"I can't sit," she said through gritted teeth. She pressed both hands to her middle and groaned. In six pregnancies she had never experienced such a thing. "I don't know what is wrong." She looked at Dalit, wishing not for the first time that it was her mother who stood by willing to help. She would have known what to do. But God had taken her mother to Sheol, and all Peninnah had left was an incompetent young woman hardly older than her own sons.

"Let me run to get help then." Dalit's tone was clearly agitated, and Peninnah realized she would be of no use to her just standing there. She was too young to understand the details of childbirth, and it was clearly too soon for this child to be born.

"Go to Hannah's house," Peninnah said at last, regretting the words the moment she had spoken them. "She is the closest and she will know what to do." At least she could send for Galia or Dana or someone. Surely they would come to her aid as they had when her mother passed. "And find Moriah." Stubborn girl was probably off with her sister in the fields picking wildflowers instead of weeding the garden as Peninnah had instructed her to do that morning.

"Yes, mistress." Dalit rushed toward the door, then paused and turned back. "Should I take Nadav with me?" At little more than six years old, the boy was always getting into mischief, and his older brothers were off in the fields with Elkanah.

Elkanah. He was the one she wanted the most. She winced as another pain grabbed her, nearly making her stumble.

"Mistress?" Dalit hurried closer. "I don't want to leave you like this."

How comforting. At least the girl knew a few words of kindness.

"Well, you have little choice. Now go! Nadav will be fine. Wherever he is." She shooed the girl out the door and stumbled to the couch she had earlier refused. She needed to make it to her bed. She should have had Dalit help her there.

She tried to stand, but the pains would not abate. She sank to her knees and crawled toward the hall where her room was but reached her mother's old room first. How fitting. Perhaps she would die in the same place her mother had passed.

The thought brought a wave of sudden, overwhelming fear. *Oh God, I don't want to die.* Women died in childbirth. She knew

418

that. And women lost babies before their time and lived. And sometimes both were lost.

She crawled onto the bed in the room that they had planned to use for Nadav and the new baby. Tears slid down her cheeks as the pain increased. *There isn't going to be a new baby, is there?* It was a prayer, as best as she had ever prayed, but she expected no answer. Why should God respond to her when all of her life she'd been angry with Him? Hated the way her circumstances had turned out? Hated everyone she came into contact with, even Elkanah? Yes, she even hated him for not being the husband she expected.

Bitterness tasted like bile as another pain rocked her. Would Hannah come? Would she send for help or let her die here alone? *Please don't let my children find me as I found Ima.* They still needed her. She was too young to die.

Tears wet the pillow beneath her head as she lay there begging God to have mercy.

"Mistress Hannah, Mistress Hannah!"

Hannah looked up at the sound of Dalit's voice calling from the road as the girl raced toward the courtyard. Adva exchanged a worried look with Hannah, who stood and hurried to meet Peninnah's maid.

"What's wrong, Dalit? Tell me quickly." For a blinding second she feared, as she did on occasion, that something had happened to Elkanah, then quickly realized that Dalit would not be near Elkanah at this hour.

"It's Mistress Peninnah. She doubled over in pain and said she needs help. I fear it's the baby, Mistress Hannah. She asked me to get you." Dalit's words were rushed, her breath coming fast.

Hannah touched the girl's arm. "Calm down, Dalit. It will be okay." Would it? "I will gather linens and bring the water I drew from the river this morning." She looked at her mother, who now stood beside her. "I will need your help."

Adva nodded, then met Dalit's worried gaze. "Run next door to get Dana, and either have her send for Galia or go get her yourself. We will help Peninnah."

Dalit raced off without needing to be told twice. Hannah hurried into the house to gather linens, her mind whirling. It sounded like Peninnah was going to lose the baby, but would she live through the ordeal? *Oh Lord, is she dying?* There were so many risks with childbirth. Peninnah had been blessed with six children and never had a problem, but she was older now. Was that the reason?

Hannah was five years Peninnah's senior, and Samuel's birth had been easy. But there had been no children since, she reminded herself. There did come a time when birthing children became impossible.

She snatched everything she could think to take and met her mother in the courtyard, handing her the cloths while she lifted the heavy jug of water. The two made their way quickly down the path.

"Peninnah would surely have water," her mother said.

"But if she is losing the baby, we will need more than we normally draw. And if it takes hours, her family will need to be fed, and that means water to make bread."

They would put some of the girls to work grinding so the men would not go hungry. Surely Dana would bring her daughters, and Peninnah's daughters were capable — if they would listen to her. Suddenly Hannah wasn't so sure. Peninnah had done nothing to make her children obey or even listen to Hannah over the years. There was no reason to think they would obey her now.

A sigh escaped. "I wonder why she called for me." Hannah glanced sidelong at her mother.

"You were the closest." Adva shrugged. "She must be truly hurting to do so or she would have bypassed you for Dana or Galia."

"True." Hannah hurried up the incline and entered the courtyard. She set the clay urn in a niche in the ground, and the two women rushed into the house.

"Peninnah?" Hannah called, half running down the hall. She stopped short at the room Yafa once occupied. The groans coming from her rival wife were disconcerting, and for a moment Hannah stood speechless. This was much worse than when Peninnah was simply grieving her mother's loss.

She stepped into the room and knelt at the woman's side. "Where does it hurt, Peninnah?"

Peninnah groaned and clutched her middle. Hannah heard the heavy breathing, saw the tears tracing down her cheeks. She moved to the end of the bed and noticed blood staining the sheets. She looked at her mother, whose grim expression brought a hard knot to Hannah's middle.

"It's going to be all right, Peninnah," Hannah said, bending close to the woman. "I need some cool cloths," she said to her mother.

Her mother retrieved them and Hannah placed them on Peninnah's forehead. She slowly coaxed Peninnah onto her back so her mother could examine her. She did so, looked up, and shook her head.

"We will need the birthing stool," Adva said, "and pray Galia or Dana gets here soon."

"Someone needs to send for Elkanah," Hannah said, having no idea who to send. "Where is Nadav?" The child should be in the house or napping. Dalit should have kept him with her. Thoughts of Samuel surfaced, and she realized that if she could trust her son to God and Eli, she would have to trust that God would take care of Peninnah and her children.

Adva rummaged through the house until she found the stool Peninnah had used to birth six children. But Peninnah seemed unable to move to help herself. She simply groaned and slipped in and out of fitful sleep.

Hannah looked on, feeling completely helpless. Where was Galia? Or Dana? They had given birth far more often than Hannah. She looked at her mother and motioned to the hallway.

"What are we going to do? I can't lift her, and she hasn't any strength to push."

"The babe will come of its own accord. It's the way of things in a miscarriage. The babes are so small — she won't need to push. There will just be pain and blood." Her mother's gaze held a faraway look. "At least that's how it was for me with the daughter I lost before you were born."

Hannah stared at her. "I didn't know."

"There was no need to tell you."

"Were you as listless as she is?"

Adva shook her head. "No."

Hannah glanced back at Peninnah. "I'm scared, Ima. I've never watched anyone die, and I don't want to lose her. Her children need her."

"We will do our best to save her."

At that moment Dana and her older daughters burst into the house. They met Hannah in the sitting room. "Galia is coming," Dana said, breathless. "What happened? How is she?"

"She is losing the child and she is in and out of consciousness. I don't even know if she can hear me." Hannah clutched her hands to her chest, trying to still the fear.

Dana's eyes widened, and she immediately looked at her daughters. "Go now and gather Peninnah's children," she said to the oldest. "And you two run to the fields and find Elkanah and your father."

They rushed off to do as Dana had said.

"I didn't want them to hear this, but if Peninnah is dying, we need to get busy.

Perhaps we can yet save her."

Hannah nodded and followed Dana numbly into the room, her mother at her heels.

"We must try to help her up and hold her over the stool," Dana said. "Once the child is born, we can mix herbs and try to ease her pain and hope and pray that sleep will heal the rest."

"There is so much blood." Hannah's stomach recoiled at the sight. No matter how often she had seen blood spilled in a sacrifice, she never got used to it, especially the lifeblood of a human being. "It is worse than it was a few moments ago."

Her mother grabbed some cloths to sop up the flow while Hannah and Dana tried to lift Peninnah to the stool.

"Perhaps if we can just keep her propped up," Dana said after their efforts proved unsuccessful. "She's too much weight without her helping us."

"Peninnah, can you hear us?" Hannah knelt close to her ear. "Dearest, you are going to give birth, but we need you to help us." She replaced the cloth on her forehead. "Please, Peninnah. I know we don't get along, but think of your children. They need you. Elkanah needs you." She paused, not willing to lie but desperate to get through to the woman. How frail she looked compared to all of the times she had been so cruel.

"I need you, Peninnah." Hannah realized she meant the words. She could not take Peninnah's place as mother to her children, even if she wanted children to raise. They needed their mother.

Please, Adonai, have mercy. She needs time to get to know You. I don't think she has ever given herself a chance to trust You.

But the prayers did little good as the baby, too small to survive, came forth, and Peninnah lay still in an unwakeable sleep.

38

Elkanah half ran, half walked ahead of Tahath, following Dana's girls to Peninnah's house. Something was terribly wrong, but Dana had obviously kept the full truth from her unmarried daughters. Was it the babe? That Peninnah was pregnant with her seventh child had surprised them both, but Elkanah had thought it a good distraction because of Peninnah's listlessness since the loss of Yafa.

Had something happened so soon into the pregnancy? He had heard of such things, but Peninnah had always been so strong — despite her bitter outlook on life.

What would he do if he lost her?

The thought brought a sick feeling to his gut. It wasn't that he loved her. Not like he did Hannah. But how would he handle her children — the younger ones . . . the girls?

He ran faster and only slowed when the house came into view. His mother greeted him in the courtyard, where she was standing over a fire stirring linens in boiling water.

"How is she?" he asked, afraid of the answer.

His mother shook her head. "The babe is lost."

A weight as heavy as a millstone settled in his middle. "And Peninnah?"

Galia shook her head again. "It is too soon to tell. She was not conscious when she lost the babe, and we cannot wake her even with the strongest herbs. I do not know if she will recover."

Elkanah turned away and kicked a small rock from the court into the yard, just missing Tahath. "Sorry," he said. He rubbed a hand over his face.

Tahath put a hand on his shoulder. "Not to worry, brother, but try not to kill me."

Elkanah found himself wrapped in his brother's arms. "What will I do if I lose her?" he rasped. "Who will care for the children?"

"Hannah would help you. You know that." Tahath held him at arm's length. "And we are family. We will all take turns caring for the young ones."

Elkanah stared at the ground. "I should go to her."

Tahath patted his back and nodded agreement.

Elkanah shuffled forward, past his mother, barely able to make his feet move. A lump had formed in his throat and he fought the threat of tears.

Hannah met him in the sitting room and came to him.

"How is she?" Though he had already asked his mother, he wanted to see the truth in Hannah's eyes.

"Not good." She searched his face. "We are doing all we can. If you know of a physician we can send for . . . We have always relied on each other for our knowledge of herbs, but, well . . . I don't know what else to do."

The look in her eyes scared him in a place he did not want her to see, lest she think his heart was bound to Peninnah. But the woman was the mother of his children, and he could not deny that to lose her was not something he wanted to bear. "The elders may know of a physician." He looked toward the hall where Peninnah lay.

"I will send Tahath to ask them," Hannah said, sounding relieved.

Elkanah nodded. "Good. Good. In the meantime, take me to her. And pray, beloved. God alone is the One who heals."

Hannah led the way down the hall. She pointed to the dim room where Kelila sat near Peninnah. Hannah waited behind as he entered the room and came to kneel at Peninnah's side. He couldn't blame Hannah for not joining him, though a part of him wanted her near.

"Peninnah?" He spoke close to her ear as Kelila stood and walked away from the bed. "Can you hear me, beloved?" So few times he had called her that.

No response. He touched her forehead, then replaced the cloth with a cooler one. She felt warm to his touch, which increased his anxiety. "Peninnah, please don't leave me. I need you," he whispered.

She did not move or speak despite his pleas.

He took her hand and stroked the back of it. He waited, hoping, praying for some change, but after nearly an hour had passed, he kissed her cheek and left the room. Pray God she would be better by morning.

Hannah watched Elkanah's lined face as they sat over a simple meal a few days later. Peninnah had improved only a little, but at least she was awake now, and Elkanah seemed relieved by the news.

"Do you think she will make a full recovery?" he asked, breaking the bread.

"I think there is a chance she will heal. But I don't know if her heart will heal." Hannah searched his gaze. "She has lost much — first her mother, then her place as the only mother of your children, and now the babe. Only God knows whether she will recover from the grief. Some never do."

"You mean like Rinat after she lost her husband and daughter."

She nodded, surprised he remembered the old woman. "Yes. In a way." All hopes that Ezer was Rinat's long-lost grandson had been impossible to prove, and Rinat had died shortly after Samuel's birth, leaving no more chances for Ezer to claim her as family. "Though Peninnah still has you and her children."

"True." Elkanah ate a few bites, focused on the meal. "And the young ones should give her a good reason to revive."

"If she lets herself care again." Hannah watched the changing emotions on his face and wished she had some way to comfort him. But now that the immediate danger had passed, she had work to do on Samuel's coat and things to gather for their trip to Shiloh.

"Do you think . . . that is . . ." He paused, and a sick feeling settled in her middle. "I was thinking that perhaps now is not a good time to go to Shiloh."

"But —"

He held up a hand. "I know we both want to see Samuel, but with Peninnah so ill . . . what if something happens to her while we are gone?"

Hannah told her roiling emotions to calm. Elkanah was just being practical, as he always was. But the words she wanted to say would not come. A part of her wanted to lash out at the very idea. She had given up her son! She wanted to see him, not have to give up her visit because Elkanah's other wife was grieving.

Oh Adonai, forgive me. I know I am being selfish. Sometimes she found herself frustrated that Elkanah had any feelings for Peninnah at all. Especially after she had made Hannah's life so miserable.

"You are thinking something, beloved. Please share it with me." He set aside his cup and took her hands, but she pulled them back and stood.

"This is not something I can discuss easily, Elkanah. I think Peninnah could grieve or remain listless or face whatever ails her for months, and with your mother here, what can we possibly do? They would send for us if something serious happened. But

432

to deny me time with my only child . . ." Her voice caught and she could not finish. She walked to the window and looked out at the deepening dusk.

She heard Elkanah rise and felt him at her back. He placed both hands on her shoulders. "Then we will make the journey. It would be hard for me to switch at such a late date, and you are right, Peninnah is well cared for."

She turned to face him. "You truly do not mind? She is your wife, after all."

"As are you. And I want to see Samuel as much as you do." He kissed her forehead. "I will check on Peninnah before we leave for Shiloh to confirm how she is doing, but if nothing has changed for the worse, then we will go."

"Thank you, my lord." She lowered her gaze, feeling as though she had shamed him into the decision yet not wanting to retract her words.

He kissed her then, fully this time, and she knew that his answer was what he had wanted to do all along.

Nine Months Later

Passover and the Feast of First Fruits came again, and Hannah counted the days, even as she put little finishing touches on the items she had made for Samuel. The robe and tunic had been ready for months, but she had decided to add other garments and even made him a small ephod as Eli had said she should.

At last the day came when the family gathered. The sacrificial lamb was tied behind the cart pulled by the donkey, and the sheaves of barley and food they would need were piled in the cart. Hannah walked with Dana, her heart light, anxious to hold her boy close again.

"I have not seen you quite so happy since your last visit here nine months ago," Dana said, laughing. "No one would ever accuse you of not being a doting mother, even if you gave your son back to God." She touched Hannah's arm. "You are a good mother, even from a distance."

Hannah's face flushed. "I doubt that. But thank you." She walked on, forcing herself not to run the whole way to Shiloh.

"I'm surprised Peninnah did not join us," Dana said, interrupting her thoughts of seeing Samuel again. "She seemed better."

Hannah sighed. "She only acts that way around Elkanah, who probably told Tahath, but when I've stopped in or Galia has come by after a visit there, we agree that Peninnah is still listless and seems to be pining for the child she lost. It's as though she doesn't even see the six children who still need her." The thought troubled her, and she did not want to feel such emotion on this day. She had suffered too long to have these few days of joy taken away, and yet . . . was she being unfair? Peninnah had suffered loss and seemed unable to pull herself out of the grief. Even her bitter barbs had ended, for she spoke little, as though she was pulling inside herself.

"It can be hard to lose a child, though," Dana said, surprising Hannah by defending the woman. "I mean, I never lost a child, but I lost my mother and that's not easy. Especially when Peninnah had no one else she allowed close to her. I think she is incredibly sad."

Hannah nodded, the thought sobering. Was there anything she could do to help the situation? Nothing came to mind.

"It's almost as if your song last year was a prophecy from the Lord," Dana said.

"My song?"

"The prayer you offered after you gave Samuel to Eli. You said, 'She who has had many sons pines away.' That seems to be what Peninnah is doing, doesn't it?"

Hannah felt a shiver rush through her. She was no prophet, and she certainly had not aimed those words at Peninnah. She'd had a general sense of the barren woman finally feeling gratified, especially over everyone who made her feel she was "less than" because God had chosen not to give her children for so long.

If only He would see fit to give me more. The longing had begun since their last visit and since Peninnah's children did not seem to need her.

"She does seem that way, but my prayer was no prophecy, Dana. I was simply offering praise to Adonai." Or was it a prophecy?

"Well, it seemed like such to all of us there. I just never expected Peninnah to mimic the words so truly."

Hannah nodded, feeling a sense of guilt for having uttered words that had hurt her rival. For whatever trouble Peninnah had shown her over the years, she did not wish harm on the woman. And yet she had stayed home and daily sat in her room pining away as though life had no use or meaning to her anymore.

Oh Adonai, please help her. It was the only prayer Hannah could utter and mean, for she was at a loss as to how anyone else could reach Peninnah.

The next day as they arrived in Shiloh, Hannah and Elkanah set up camp and took the lamb to the altar for sacrifice. *Forgive me for any wrong thoughts or deeds, Adonai,* Hannah prayed as the lamb took her place on God's altar, appeasing His wrath over all sin. Though this was not the Day of Atonement but a happier Passover and Feast of First Fruits, Hannah still prayed whenever an animal gave its life for hers. Guilt offering or not, she knew none of them were ever truly free of guilt or sin. The blood covered their sin in God's eyes and allowed Him to forgive. And someday God would make a way to deal with sin permanently, but for now, Hannah was grateful for temporary forgiveness.

The deed completed, Hannah took Elkanah's hand and pulled him toward Eli, where Samuel stood at his side.

Elkanah laughed. "A little anxious, my love?"

She smiled at him. Nothing on earth made her quite as happy as her son, though she would not tell Elkanah such a thing. She loved her husband, heart and soul, but the bond with Samuel was different. One she would never outlive.

They reached the place where Eli sat and greeted him. Hannah bent to give Samuel a fierce hug and held him for a few moments.

She heard Eli and Elkanah talking but paid no heed until Eli's tone changed. He cleared his throat and she turned to look at him, her arm still around Samuel.

"May the Lord give you children by this woman to take the place of the one she prayed for and gave to the Lord," Eli said to Elkanah. "Your son is a great blessing to me, and I pray often that God will bless your wife with more sons like him, to be a blessing to both of you."

"Thank you, my lord," Elkanah said, then turned to hug his son.

Hannah stared at Eli a moment, her heart stirring within her. Eli had prayed for her and blessed her.

Dana was right. There would be more children. She knew it as well as she had known she would give birth after her vow to the Lord. Not immediately, of course, but in time. She would raise a family to love Adonai and guide them to keep His ways. But for now, she would love Samuel in the few days they had with him.

And as they spent time together, she could not keep her heart from singing.

39

Eleven Years Later

Hannah rubbed her protruding middle, grateful for the kick of the child beneath her hand. Would the child be born healthy as the others had been? A sense of fear often accompanied the thought. She was so much older now than when Samuel was born. Seventeen years. How was it possible that so much time had passed since that glorious day? Her son was such a fine man now, still serving with Eli in Shiloh. Though from all that she had heard, things there were worse than they had ever been.

"May I join you?" Elkanah's voice startled her from her thoughts. She looked up at him and smiled.

"I fear you catch me at a lazy time, beloved. I should be spinning or weaving, but the air is so fresh and the babe so active. I needed to sit for a while." She searched his face, now lined, the hair on his head and in his beard streaked with gray. "How did we get to this place?" The question was one she had long pondered, but suddenly seeing Elkanah looking older and feeling the aches of age herself, she wondered if she would live long enough to raise these children God had given.

Elkanah sat beside her and cupped a hand over her middle, smiling at the baby's kick. "We got to this place by trusting the Lord," he said, his gaze thoughtful. "I never would have imagined He would give us so many children at this stage in our lives."

She smiled for the joy of his presence, for the ability to do so with peace in knowing all was well. At least she hoped so. *Please, Adonai, let all remain well.*

"Chayim and Doron and Maor seem to love caring for the sheep, though I think Doron is going to be our farmer, as he loves to watch the plants and help with placing the seeds. He always tells me when he prays for rain or sees too many insects eating the crops." Elkanah rubbed a hand along his neck. "Eitan doesn't seem to mind them tagging along, though I think at first he resented them. He likes to do things his way, that boy."

"He is a boy no longer, my love. Peninnah's sons are grown men with wives, remember."

The realization only added to the knowledge that life had come to her in such a backward way. Her sons should be the ones grown by now, but here she was at fifty-four years old and about to bear a sixth child while her youngest, Tehila, was barely three. She had nursed two children at once for nearly ten years and weaned Tehila earlier than she'd planned when she discovered she was yet again carrying a child. That she could beget while she nursed was a mystery, as it was not the normal pattern of things for most women, though Peninnah seemed to also be an exception. And God had been more than gracious in His answer to Eli's blessing.

"Sometimes it is hard to believe that you are the one with the young children," Elkanah said, accepting a drink from Hannah's new maid, Rona. "So much has happened in these passing years." He sipped, then gave a deep sigh.

"Is there news from Shiloh?" Elkanah had gone faithfully for Samuel's sake even when she was confined at home. It was her one regret that she saw so little now of her oldest son.

Elkanah rubbed the back of his neck. "Samuel speaks of judgment coming," he said, his gaze fixed on hers. "Of course, we know that God now speaks to him, but Samuel believes the prophecy against Eli's house will soon be fulfilled."

"Hophni and Phinehas will die soon then." She shivered at the very thought, as she often did when she recalled what Samuel had told his father, that God would kill both priests for their corruption on the same day.

"Yes."

"I fear for Raziela and Irit. If Irit is indeed pregnant again, and she as old as I am, things may not go well for her." She took his hand and squeezed. "I wish we could help them."

"I fear that is not our problem to fix, beloved." He kissed her fingers and then intertwined their hands.

"I wonder how Eli will take it when it happens." The man was so old, in his late nineties, and could barely see.

"Probably as well as you or I would if something devastating were to happen to one of us." Elkanah's expression grew thoughtful. "Samuel is already assuming the priestly duties, and God is raising him up to lead."

Hannah nodded. "Yes." She sighed. "I can't say I am sorry for my vow, but I do miss him."

"I know you do. You would not be a loving mother if you did not."

She looked at him more closely, saw the strain in his eyes. "Tell me, my husband, why are you here with me in the middle of the day? You are feeling well, yes?"

He looked beyond her, and her heart felt a kick that wasn't the babe.

"Elkanah?"

He shook himself. "Do not fret, beloved. I am well. I just grow a little more tired of late. And I wanted to spend some time with you before this next little one takes you away from me." Though his smile reached his eyes, she was not sure she believed he was truly all right.

"I wonder," he said a moment later, before she could fret over him, "whether you would consider something."

"That depends on what I am to consider." She gave him a wary look.

"Eitan tells me that his mother is not well." He paused. "Even his wife and his brothers' wives cannot seem to rouse her from the feelings of sadness she has carried these many years. I had thought when the girls began to beget children that it would give her purpose again as it did my mother — Adonai's rest be upon her — and as it did Yafa. Yet Peninnah does little but sit most of the day. The girls do most of the work, she has no friends, and she seems so lost."

"Peninnah has pushed most people away, my love. You know this."

Elkanah sighed, the sound defeated. "I know. And I have tried, truly I have. I fear it is my fault because I could never give her the one thing she asked for."

"Your love."

He nodded. "I guess I was just not made to love two women. You have always been my only love, Hannah."

She smiled and squeezed his hand again. "And you mine."

They stared at each other in amiable silence a moment. Hannah felt the babe kick, and she sensed this child, likely her last, might have a gifted purpose much like Samuel's, only in a more personal way. But what? She could not imagine. She only wanted the child to be safely born.

"So what am I to consider?" Despite his lengthy explanation, she was not sure what he was asking her.

"I guess I was wondering if there will ever be peace between the two of you. If there was something you might say to her, might do . . ."

"You mean like offering to let her have all the time she wants with you? That is the only thing I can think that might appease her, beloved. She wants you, not me. I daresay she probably wishes I would disappear from her life. Then she could have you uncontested, as Leah finally had Jacob." The thought brought another tick of worry to her heart. Would she survive this birth? Would God bless Peninnah in the end by taking Hannah to be with Him?

Oh Adonai, I love You, but I do not want Peninnah raising my children.

"No, no. I do not want to give in to her demands. I want you. You've always known that." He sipped from the cup again and glanced heavenward. "I wish life had been easier for us."

"Life is never easy," she said, sobering. Too many losses had accompanied the joy of the past ten years. The loss of both sets of parents. Samuel's absence and her inability to visit him as often as she once did. Dealing with Peninnah's spoiled girls because their mother seemed incapable of training them.

"But there is good too," she added, not wanting to feel sad as Peninnah always did. Especially during Elkanah's surprise visit. "Nava has had three sons, and your older boys have made you a grandfather."

Elkanah smiled. "Yes, those are good things. And I am sorry to have brought up Peninnah. I just grow weary of trying to figure out what to do with her. I wish —"

"Do not regret the past, beloved. You cannot go back and change what is. She gave you six wonderful children, and you are about to have your twelfth child. There is much to rejoice in."

He smiled. "We are back to the place where we were when I first met you. You always remind me of the joy, and that makes me want to worship Adonai for His goodness."

"He has been good to us."

"Especially since He gave us Samuel to be the leader Hophni and Phinehas are not." The comment brought a telltale frown to his face. "I do not envy Samuel having to deal with the fallout once the prophecy against Eli's house comes true. I may have to go to Shiloh to help him."

"As I would expect you to."

"I don't want to miss this little one's birth," he said.

"You must do what is best for the country, Elkanah. You can bless our child when you return."

He nodded. "Tahath and I are planning to

go to Shiloh tomorrow."

"And you didn't tell me this at the first?" It wasn't like him to skirt around a problem. "Tell me what is really wrong, Elkanah."

"There are rumors of war with the Philistines. I fear that the war could be part of the prophecy, and I want to be there for Samuel." He cupped her cheek. "You understand, don't you?"

"Of course. I would want you there for our son." The sudden fear in her heart was not for herself but for him. "Tell me you will not go to battle against the Philistines no matter what happens."

"I will not go to battle against the Philistines." He stood and helped her up. "But I do not know how bad things will get. Samuel is still young, and Eli is too old to guide him any longer."

"Of course you must go. Samuel needs his father. And do not worry about me. I have Dana to help me deliver. And your other sisters-in-law if I need them."

He kissed her and she returned the kiss. "Just promise me that you will be safe." He held her close. "By God's grace, I will do all that I can to stay safe as well. And while I am gone, be extra cautious of strangers. I've asked Eitan to watch over your house and keep the boys with you until I return."

447

She didn't tell him that his words added to her fear. No. She had learned long ago to trust the Lord, hadn't she? She could not return to faithless doubt now.

He turned to go. "I have to speak to Tahath, but if you could pack me a bag, we will leave at first light."

She nodded. In her condition, she would have Rona help her, but she would decide what would go in the sack. "Dinner will be ready on time," she called as he stepped through the gate. But she had a foreboding feeling that something was about to change, and she was not sure she was ready to face it.

40

As Elkanah and Tahath approached Shiloh, the shining city did not carry the light it usually did. Elkanah glanced at his brother. "The crowds are large and it is not feast time."

"The war drum is coming from Philistine territory. With so many years of quiet from them, why now? It makes no sense." Tahath held the reins of the lone donkey that carried their belongings. His brother showed even greater signs of aging than he did, and Elkanah wondered what had possibly crossed his mind to think that two grandfathers could help in a time of such upheaval. Did they think they would talk the tribes of Israel out of going to war? Did they think they could somehow talk sense into Hophni and Phinehas at this late hour? Did he doubt Samuel's words about the prophecy?

"It is the Lord," Elkanah said at last, realizing that there was no other explanation. "Samuel warned me that something was coming, something that God would do to punish the house of Eli. Perhaps He is going to use the Philistines to accomplish it."

Tahath shook his head. "I do not like it. It is not that I doubt Samuel. Obviously God is with him. But war . . ." He shook his head again. "War is never a good thing, brother."

Elkanah could only nod his agreement. "There is nothing to do but go and see if we can help Samuel. And fulfill our Levitical duties."

They made their way down the hill and hurried past the crowds toward the housing where they would normally stay, then sought out Samuel.

"Father!" Samuel ran to Elkanah and held him close. "I'm glad you came." They kissed each other's cheeks and held each other at arm's length.

"How tall you have grown, my son." Elkanah straightened to better look up at this son whose hair came to the middle of his back and whose beard was beginning to fill in.

Samuel smiled and greeted his uncle. "Yes, Father, I have grown, but I am not as glad of that as I am of your presence now. I sense the prophecy is going to come true in the next few days. Hophni and Phinehas are belligerent and leading the people to take the ark into battle with the Philistines. Eli is distraught about the ark but too weak to stop them, and they do not listen to me." He glanced about, though the place they stood was quiet in comparison to the rest of the city. "Hophni and Phinehas are even now with the men of Shiloh and the other tribes that have gathered. The Philistines are just over the ridge, and war will surely start within the next day or two."

"I did not realize it was so imminent," Tahath said. "We would have come sooner."

"There was nothing you could have done to stop it, Uncle. Things happened so quickly even I could not have gotten word to you in time. I am pleased that God sent you to me." Samuel faced his father. "Ima is well?"

Elkanah nodded. "She is due to give birth in a week or so. But do not fear. She has many of your aunts to help her."

Samuel smiled. "I shall be pleased to come visit soon and see all of my brothers and sisters."

"Only one sister so far, my son."

"This one is also a girl," he said, his tone more confident than Elkanah had ever heard.

"I am glad to know it," Elkanah said, amazed at the gift God had given his son. This son whom God had taken so long to give them. This son whom Hannah had directly prayed to have.

"I am glad you are here, though, for Eli will not take it well when he hears the news. Phinehas's wife is about to bear a son, and I do not know how I will restore order once things begin to fall apart here." Samuel's look showed his earlier lack of confidence, and Elkanah realized that though God was with this young man, he still needed his father. The thought brought a sense of joy to Elkanah's heart. This son whom he had agreed to loan back to God still wanted an earthly father.

Suddenly he felt new purpose and his feelings of aging slipped away. How good it was to be needed in the very place he had always loved and prayed would become an honorable house of worship. And now it was at last coming to pass.

"God will show you how to restore things, my son," he said, wrapping one arm around Samuel. "But in the meantime, your uncle and I will do all we can to support you to make things right in God's sight once more."

Samuel smiled, and the three of them

moved off to find a place to pray for all that was about to happen in Israel.

Hannah sat with her spinning, one eye on Tehila while Rona turned the grindstone. The boys were happily playing in the field in front of the courtyard where Hannah could see them. Good to his word, Eitan had come each day to check on them. Hannah never would have expected him capable of such caring in his younger days. Elkanah's firstborn had truly grown into a man of whom Elkanah could be proud.

But with each passing day, it was not Eitan's presence that comforted her. She longed for Elkanah's safe return, to know how things fared in Shiloh, in Israel, with Samuel and the whole priesthood.

She moved the spindle and distaff with practiced ease, feeling the pressure of the babe, knowing the time was soon. Chayim and Doron were already asking her daily if it was time to get Aunt Dana. But each dawn and midday and evening before she put them to bed, she assured them the time was not yet.

The afternoon breeze was cooler today, as winter rains would soon be upon them. She looked at the sky, but only white clouds dotted the horizon. In the distance, she heard a call and turned her head to listen.

"Aunt Hannah!" The voice was Eitan's, a surprise to hear in the middle of the day.

Hannah straightened and slowly stood, her heart shifting inside of her. Had something happened to Elkanah? Had Eitan heard something she had not?

She met him at the courtyard gate. "What is it?"

He drew in a breath as if trying to speak.

"Did you run the whole way?" Where had he come from?

"I ran from my mother's house," he said, looking at her with a cautious expression as though afraid of what she might say. "Aunt Hannah, we can't find her."

Hannah let the spindle stop and set it on top of the stone wall. "Why don't you sit a moment and start at the beginning." She motioned him inside the court and to a bench not far from where they stood.

He sat on the edge while she leaned against the house, reading the fear in his eyes. "I left for the fields this morning, and my wife said that at that time all was well. My mother was sitting in her usual spot, doing nothing unless asked to help. It is often this way. If not for our wives, there would be no food cooked or clothes made for my brothers and me. Ima has been list-

454

less for so long . . . well, we are used to it."

Hannah nodded. She knew this from Elkanah.

"But today when Chaya returned from helping Yemima with something in the cooking room, Ima was not in her seat. So she looked for her throughout the house. Then all of the women searched the house, the yard. At last Yemima came to find me, and we have combed the fields and anywhere Ima used to go, even the river where she used to wash the clothes, but there is no sign of her." He raked a hand over his beard. "I don't know what to do."

Hannah stared at this man who used to annoy her, the one she always thought would turn out to be like his mother but who had proven her wrong. Concern etched itself across his dark brows. Peninnah had been a burden to her children and to Elkanah for years, but this . . . Where would she go?

"Obviously she is somewhere, and more importantly, I don't think she wants to be found right now." But a sense of fear in her middle told her that finding Peninnah was exactly what they needed to do. "What she wants, though, is not what she needs. She needs us to find her. Have you checked Elkanah's father's house?" Amminadab had inherited the house and property — the firstborn's double portion — when his father passed into Sheol, but everyone still referred to it as belonging to Jeroham.

"I sent Hevel there. We even went to Ima's old home before she married but found nothing. I'm growing worried." He stood and paced as though he could no longer contain his energy.

Hannah watched him, her mind racing. Peninnah would not recall the place near the river where Lital's body had been found all those years ago. The place where Hannah had gone in her despair upon the birth of Peninnah's third child. So there was no reason to check it now.

"You are sure you looked up and down the river?" she asked just the same.

Eitan looked at her with an odd expression. "What are you saying?"

Hannah sighed. She had never told anyone her true thoughts that day at the river, though she knew Elkanah had suspected. But Peninnah had been so sorrowful since Samuel's birth. Even before that, with the loss of her mother, and then with her last son. Her bitterness had kept everyone at arm's length, and even as her sons married, she could not seem to pull herself back to the light. Was it possible that she had come to the last of her hope?

"A long time ago I felt as your mother feels now, as though my life held no worth. I went to the river." She stopped and held his gaze until he seemed to grasp her meaning.

"But the river is long and wide and we could search for days." Despair tinged his tone.

"Let me take you to where I went. Perhaps she knows more than I think she does." Had Elkanah told Peninnah the full tale of Lital? Had she somehow discovered the place where Hannah and Meira had found their friend's body? Peninnah had been a child then but had known enough to want to see. She was just demanding enough that it could have happened.

"Is it wise for you to walk too far from home?" Eitan's gaze held skepticism. "If you just tell me where to go, I will take one of my brothers."

Hannah shook her head. "No. I want to go with you. And when we get there — *if* she is there — I want you to let me talk to her alone. Agreed?"

Eitan nodded. "If you promise me not to have this baby along the way."

Hannah laughed, and it coaxed a smile from him despite the dire circumstances. "I promise." She had no pains to indicate the birth was that close. "Let's go." She gave instructions to Rona to watch the children, then led Eitan to the place where she and Meira had once found Lital's body and the river that had beckoned.

Peninnah stood at the incline above the water's edge, staring at the black depths. Was she in the right place? Nothing looked the same as it did when Elkanah had shown her the forest years ago. So many years had passed. He hadn't come because he wanted to. He had come only because she had badgered and begged him. Like she had done with so many things in her life. She only got her way by pushing for it.

She was so tired of pushing. Nothing brought pleasure anymore. She had lived with this weight of bitterness like a millstone about her neck for so long that she longed to be free of it. She wearied of trying to pretend life brought joy. There was no joy. There was nothing close to the joy Hannah sang about since Samuel's birth. Nothing had been the same since Hannah had gotten *her* way.

A feeling of heaviness settled over her. Even her bitterness could not give her the motive to keep striving, keep working at

458

gaining what she'd always wanted most. El-kanah's love. She should have set her sights on a different man, one without a wife, instead of thinking she had some power to win him away from Hannah.

Hannah. Perfect Hannah. And in the end even God had blessed the woman. Every-thing Peninnah had ever longed for or loved had been lost to her. She was worse than a burden to her children. She was a useless life.

The waters rippled past her as she continued to stare into their depths. Up ahead was an outcropping of rocks that made the waters rougher, and even farther down was a dip large enough to take a body far, far away. Where they would not find her. Where she could finally be free of this awful weight of grief she could not shake.

She stepped forward, making her way slowly down the bank. One sandaled foot touched the surface and pulled back. So cold. But that was good, wasn't it? Soon she too would be cold, unfeeling. And the pain in her heart would finally cease.

Hannah hurried as quickly as her bulging body would allow. The woods were beyond Dana's house, past the place where Yafa and Assir used to live. If she was wrong, then

459

this exercise was going to bring on this baby sooner than she expected. But she had to try. For Elkanah's sake.

"Is it much farther?" Eitan asked, his tone worried. Was he worried for her? No. Probably only for his mother. "I should have brought Aniah with me."

"We are almost there." Hannah puffed for breath. She should slow down. She must slow down. But something told her — perhaps Adonai? — that there was so little time.

They rounded a bend and continued on a little way until they came to the place Hannah remembered. She stopped, trying to catch her breath, her eyes searching the area. Eitan began calling, "Ima? Ima?" and walked up and down the edge of the river. But he'd gone too far to the right.

Hannah drew in a breath and went left and closer to the embankment, heart pounding. *Please, Adonai, don't let her be like Lital.* What would she do if they found her body without its soul? A shiver worked through her.

"Peninnah?" she called as she neared the edge, fearful of getting too close lest she lose her balance and fall. "Peninnah?"

She leaned forward as far as her belly would allow and caught sight of a woman sitting at the river's edge, head bent, unmoving.

"Eitan!" Hannah shouted.

He was at her side in a heartbeat. "Did you find her?"

Hannah nodded and pointed.

Eitan crept down the incline. "Ima?"

Hannah breathed a relieved sigh when the woman turned her head.

Eitan scooped her into his arms, carried her up the incline, and set her among the grasses a safe distance from the water. Hannah waddled closer and exchanged a look with Eitan. He came to help Hannah kneel beside his mother and then backed away.

"Peninnah, will you please look at me?" Hannah said.

Peninnah did not move for the longest time, and Hannah's knees felt as though they would cramp. But at last Peninnah looked up and held Hannah's gaze.

"I never should have married him," she said, her voice lifeless. "It was always you he loved."

Hannah took one of Peninnah's hands, surprised when she didn't pull away. "I will admit, I never wanted to share Elkanah with anyone, not even a slave wife. I also did not want to claim a child that wasn't mine just to say I had children. So when he married you, hard as it was, you gave him children, and that was a good thing. You have fine sons and daughters who love you and daughters-in-law who love you and a full house, Peninnah. They have all been frantic to find you."

"I am just a burden to them. You don't understand. You have never been a burden."

Hannah silently prayed for words to break through the woman's pain. At last she drew a breath and squeezed Peninnah's hand. "We can all feel as though our lives have become a burden to others, especially when they seem to have no purpose. When I was barren, I felt that way nearly every day." She paused, waiting for Peninnah to fully meet her gaze. "When you birthed a third son, I could not bear my life a moment more. So I stood at this very spot." She waved a hand toward the water's edge. "And I expect we shared the same thoughts." Hannah glimpsed a slight show of interest in Peninnah's dark eyes. "I almost went through with it too. What good was I to El-kanah if I could not have children? What woman in Israel doesn't want sons?"

"For years I wished you were gone," Peninnah said softly. The admission didn't surprise Hannah, but she was amazed the words did not sting as they once would have.

"I know you did."

They stared at each other for the longest moment, until Hannah winced at a sudden cramp in her middle. "Oh!"

Peninnah pulled her hand from Hannah's as she looked Hannah up and down. "You are nearly due."

Hannah nodded but could not speak.

"And yet you came all this way. For me?"

She nodded again as Peninnah pushed to her feet and called Eitan to help Hannah stand.

"Are you in labor?" Peninnah's words seemed to hold genuine concern.

Hannah shook her head. "It is the first pain. Perhaps I simply knelt too long." She rubbed her middle. "Though I think we should go home."

They started walking, Eitan holding his mother's arm and Peninnah linking hers through Hannah's. Suddenly the woman came alive with concern over the child. "When we get you home, you must rest. My girls can watch the children if you want them to, and is Dana going to deliver? We must send for her right away."

Peninnah prattled on, more animated than Hannah had ever seen her, more concerned and caring than Hannah had experienced in all the years she had known her. Had her brush with ending it all changed her so completely? Had she met Adonai in that dark place?

Another pain came with the thought, and the closer they came to home, the more intense the pains grew. Apparently she wasn't so far off in thinking that hurrying to help Peninnah was going to bring this baby sooner than she expected.

She couldn't get home fast enough.

EPILOGUE

Three Months Later

Hannah held her newest daughter in her arms — Shiri, meaning "my song." For indeed this child had brought a new song to her heart. Like the prayer and song she had known since Samuel's birth, this female child had brought a different kind of music. The song of new beginnings — of a new relationship with someone who had been her fiercest rival.

She marveled at the thought even as she looked at her beautiful sleeping daughter, whose face was wreathed in a mysterious smile, as if she knew something no one else could possibly understand. Perhaps that was the secret of infancy — that "knowing," yet never being able to recall later in life whatever knowledge was held in those early infant moments.

"And how are my beautiful daughter and wonderful wife today?" Elkanah poked his head into the sleeping chamber and came to sit at her side.

Hannah gave him a mischievous look. "I see how it is — that I'm now taking second place to this girl. Always the wife first, then the child," she chided, laughing softly as she spoke. "But I forgive you for it just this once."

Elkanah chuckled, his smile wide. "Well, thank you for that. It is just such a relief to be home, to find you and Peninnah are actually speaking, and that my daughter is safely here. I am a man more blessed than I deserve."

She looked at him intensely. "None of us deserve blessing, but I am so glad God gives it anyway."

He nodded, sobering. "On that you are right, my love. After what we just went through in Shiloh, with the ark taken and Eli and Hophni and Phinehas and Irit all gone the same day . . . It was hard on Samuel."

He had told her the details when he got home, how the war with the Philistines had gone terribly wrong and many Israelites had died. The priests had taken the ark into battle, the Philistines had captured it, and then the priests died in the same battle on the same day. The news had been too much for Eli, who had fallen over in a faint and broken his neck. And then poor Irit had gone into labor with the news of losing so much and had died in childbirth. A horrible day in Israel, and all happening while she was nursing Shiri, oblivious to it all.

"But things are better now? With Samuel, I mean?" she asked. Elkanah had stayed a month, helping their son set things in order so that the Levitical practices could continue and his role overseeing the priesthood could go on unhindered.

"He is settled and God is with him, but once the rightful heir of Aaron's son Eleazer is found, Samuel will likely become judge and prophet and leave the priesthood in its rightful hands. He said he intends to come see you soon."

Hannah smiled. "I count the days. How I long to see his face again."

"And you will. His biggest regret is that the ark is gone, and that is a tragedy. We can't go after it lest Israel lose more men fighting, and we have no direction from God to do so."

"God can take care of His ark. The covenants are still ours. We have nothing to fear." Hannah kissed Shiri's forehead and then handed her to her father, who cradled her in his experienced arms.

"God will send the ark back to us one day. Samuel is sure of it," Elkanah said.

"Hopefully soon."

"Yes."

Silence followed the remark, peaceful, poignant.

"So Peninnah actually helped you deliver and still comes to visit you each week?"

Hannah nodded, a slow smile settling on her face and in her heart. "She does." She would never have expected to be glad of such a thing. "God does amazing things when we trust Him. And Peninnah and I had something in common besides you." She winked at him and he laughed softly. "We both knew grief and what it feels like to think no one wants us or needs us. To feel useless is a terrible thing."

"And neither one of you feels that way any longer?" His tone sounded so cautious yet hopeful.

She laughed. "Not anymore. I think we both see that God used us in different ways to accomplish His will. Though our situation was never ideal, we are finally old enough to understand how to make the best of it. Actually, I think I finally like her."

He stared at her, and she couldn't help the joy bubbling inside of her at the realization that she had given him an incredible gift — and had given herself permission to be free of the past pain. She really could make the best of the worst because of Adonai's grace. What He had given to her she could give to others, whether they deserved it or not. And though Peninnah had never deserved her kindness from a human perspective, Hannah knew that God did not look on the outward person but on the inner workings of the heart.

And that made all the difference.

NOTE TO THE READER

Hannah's story is one I have wanted to write for many years, but the timing wasn't good until now. And in truth, I think every writer has her own growing to do as a person to make her ready for certain stories. My early attempts at this novel looked nothing like what ended up on these pages. And that's a good thing!

Hannah's life was much harder to experience than I first imagined. Scripture only gives us a small glimpse of her story. We know she was married and that she shared her husband with a second wife. We know she was barren and that her fruitful rival wife taunted her continuously. And we know that she asked God for a child in sheer desperation when the pain of her rival's malicious words grew too great to bear.

We also know from a little research that Elkanah was a descendant of Kohath, a son of Levi, which would have put him in line for Levitical duties to carry out at the tabernacle in Shiloh. There he would have come into contact with Hophni and Phinehas, the corrupt priests.

Hannah lived during the period of the judges, a time when "everyone did what was right in his own eyes" (Judg. 21:25). It is my opinion that this particular period in Israel was especially dark because evil practices were going on in the one place where the people came to worship God. The men who were supposed to set the highest example of virtue and obedience to Adonai were the most corrupt.

So I did my best to show what it might have been like for true worshipers to survive in a culture of dishonesty and perversion. While there did not seem to be threats from outside nations during the early years of Hannah's life, she was not free of the threat of corruption from within her own society.

I find it fascinating that God shows us through this period of the judges that sin comes at us from a variety of sources. But none of us are immune to its pull or its consequences. In every era, across every culture, we have had need of a deliverer. The judges and kings merely saved Israel for a time. The real Deliverer was yet to come. And when He came, His mother, like

Hannah, rejoiced in a song of praise. May we all learn despite hardship to be as gracious and joyful as Hannah.

In His Grace,
Jill Eileen Smith

ACKNOWLEDGMENTS

If you had told me in early 2007 that I would have the privilege of working with the fine people at Revell for all of these years, I would not have believed you. And yet Hannah stands as a testament — my tenth book to date (not counting the four ebook novellas or the final King Solomon novel set to release in 2019, or the two nonfiction books about Old Testament women yet — and two more novels — to come).

My gratitude to each one of you with whom I've worked is profound.

My wonderful editors: Lonnie Hull Dupont, who actually saw my very first attempt at Hannah at least twenty-five years ago — right before biblical fiction was about to go out of vogue. And yet here we are! You're the best! And Jessica English — please don't ever stop editing for me! I'm not sure I will ever get the commas in the right places or the grammar correct without you!

Michele Misiak — your marketing is way above par! Thanks so much for help with the launch teams and putting up with my endless questions.

Karen Steele — you amaze me with so many interview opportunities. Thank you!

Cheryl Van Andel — another astounding cover. I honestly feel so blessed, and perhaps a little spoiled, by your amazing work.

Wendy Lawton — I know I call you agent, but it is a privilege to also call you friend. I truly appreciate you! (But I don't think our cats would get along — Tiger is too picky for playful kittens.)

Jill Stengl — thank you for the brainstorming help. As always, your friendship and suggestions make me a better writer — though I think we have more fun just talking than actually brainstorming!

To my family and friends — longtime forever friends and new-acquaintance friends — you make my life richer.

Randy — I think my pen would dry up without you. You're by far my best friend. I'm so glad we get to do life together.

Jeff, Chris, Ryan — the sons for whom I prayed. Love has new meaning because of you.

Molly and Carissa — you add meaning to

476

our lives, and it's nice not being the only girl anymore!

Keaton — precious granddaughter who changes everything.

I love each one of you.

Thank you, Adonai Tzva'ot, for being mighty and able and giving me strength when I have needed it most.

ABOUT THE AUTHOR

Jill Eileen Smith is the bestselling, award-winning author of the Wives of King David, the Wives of the Patriarchs, the Loves of King Solomon, and the Daughters of the Promised Land series. Her research has taken her from the Bible to Israel, and she particularly enjoys learning how women lived in Old Testament times.

When she isn't writing, she loves to spend time with her family and friends, read stories that take her away, ride her bike to the park, snag date nights with her hubby, try out new restaurants, or play with her lovable, "helpful" cat Tiger. Jill lives with her family in southeast Michigan.

Contact Jill through email (jill@jilleileen smith.com), her website (http://www.jill eileenmith.com), Facebook (https://www .facebook.com/jilleileensmith), or Twitter (https://twitter.com/JillEileenSmith).

The employees of Thorndike Press hope you have enjoyed this Large Print book. All our Thorndike, Wheeler, and Kennebec Large Print titles are designed for easy reading, and all our books are made to last. Other Thorndike Press Large Print books are available at your library, through selected bookstores, or directly from us.

For information about titles, please call:
(800) 223-1244

or visit our website at:
gale.com/thorndike

To share your comments, please write:
Publisher
Thorndike Press
10 Water St., Suite 310
Waterville, ME 04901